The Wolves of Fireborn Pack

FOREVER MATED

USA TODAY BESTSELLING AUTHOR

GENEVIEVE JACK

Forever Mated: The Wolves of Fireborn Pack Book 3
Copyright © 2024 Carpe Luna Publishing
Published by Carpe Luna, Ltd., Bloomington, IL 61704

FIRST EDITION: Feb. 2024

eISBN: 978-1-962757-01-0
ISBN: 978-1-962757-07-2

Cover art by Deranged Doctor Designs

V1.7

ABOUT THIS BOOK

An alpha always puts his pack first.

Alpha Silas Flynn wants revenge. Since the day Alex Bloodright murdered his parents, Silas has made it his mission to bring the rogue werewolf to justice. After months of hunting his nemesis, he's closer than ever to neutralizing Alex for good. But when he's unexpectedly assigned a new partner, Meredith, his wolf takes an unusual interest in her. Now is not the time for the goddess to grant him a fated mate.

Fox shifter Meredith has her own reasons for wanting revenge on Alex. Her werewolf father's pack was slaughtered by him. But convincing Silas to let her help while dodging the feelings she has for him leaves her struggling to keep her eye on the target.

As the two close in on Alex, it becomes apparent that someone on the inside is helping him. Stopping the rogue will force Silas to question everything, including his ability to be the alpha fate has demanded him to be and exactly how far he's willing to go for the woman he loves.

ONE

For Silas, the difference between a good day working as a detective and a barely tolerable one often hinged on the quality of the coffee. Today, it seemed, was tipping toward barely tolerable. He twisted his lips, his cheeks puckering at the semi-tepid bean water trickling down his throat. He managed a swallow only to have a long, cinnamon-tainted finish burn on the way down.

Humans.

He could always tell when one of the non-supernaturals working with him in the Carlton City Police Department made the coffee. The shit was weak, barely discernible from tea, and weirdly flavored. He swirled the concoction in his cup. Thin. Translucent. He could see the crack at the bottom of his favorite mug—the one with a dachshund on the side that said DON'T BE A WEINER—right through it. The crack, which probably harbored all sorts of nasty bacteria, reminded him he should have replaced the thing months ago, a fact he could have ignored one more day if the coffee had been brewed correctly.

He looked both ways before dumping the pot down the little sink in the break room. In the CCPD, supernaturals and humans worked side by side, although the latter were unaware that their coworkers sprouted tails or cast spells during their time off. Human detectives were assigned to human cases; Silas, as the only supernatural detective in the department, was assigned to the supernatural ones. Humans outnumbered supers in the PD in the same proportion as they did in the city's population. And with the local demigoddess witch, aka a Hecate, Grateful Knight, also policing the supernatural community in the area (at least when it came to supernatural involvement with humans), he usually had no problem keeping up with his caseload.

Silas liked humans for the most part. His best friend, Logan, used to be human. But he was glad his captain was fae. Made it easier on everyone when he needed accommodations for his condition, namely three days off a month to shift into a werewolf.

"What the hell? I thought Wendy said she brewed a new pot. Someone drank it all already?" A woman Silas had never seen before stood in the doorway to the break room looking peeved, an obscenely large mug dangling from her fingers. The thing was practically a soup bowl with a handle. His werewolf nose twitched as his supernatural olfactory senses sorted out her scent. Coffee grounds, coconut hair conditioner, generic dryer sheets, a crumb of orange-vanilla scone that clung to her shirt, and an undercurrent of something gamey and wild.

His inner wolf roused, and Silas drew a deeper breath. He had the strongest urge to bury his nose in her hair. Tall, with an athletic physique, the stranger sported blue jeans, low-heeled boots, and a white cotton blouse that looked freshly ironed. She was square-jawed and solid-boned, but it was her deep red hair that fascinated his wolf, the unusual color catching the light and toying with his senses.

Silas cleared his throat, both embarrassed and shocked to catch himself staring, his fingers twitching to touch her. "Did Wendy send you back here? This is the employee break area. There's a separate coffee station up front for the public." He pointed out the door. "Although, if you hang out for a minute, I can fill you up." *Fill you up? Yeah, he'd like to fill her up.*

She folded her arms across her chest, one side of her mouth lifting. "He didn't tell you."

"He who? Didn't tell me what?"

"Captain Manahan... Patrick. I'm new. Meredith Turner." She extended her hand. "Nice to meet you."

Her voice rang low for a woman, although not at all masculine, with a gritty quality like she'd been a smoker at some point in her life. After shaking her hand tentatively, he gave his palm a good sniff under the guise of scratching his whiskers. A gamey scent was evident. Not human but not wolf either. For the life of him, he couldn't quite place what she was, although usually he excelled at discerning supernaturals. His wolf, however, wasn't concerned at all with her species. His inner beast practically leaped inside his torso, his wild side urging him to grab her and grind himself against her. Weird. It wasn't even the full moon. He shoved the instinct down.

"Is this the part where you try to smell my butt?" she asked. "I heard you werewolves were into that."

Shocked speechless, Silas did a double take. His jaw popped open. The lupine side of him was, in fact, extremely interested in her ass at the moment.

He was relieved when Meredith laughed. "No offense. Just breaking the ice. Let me put your curiosity to rest. I'm bispecies. Dad's a werewolf. Mom's a skinwalker."

Half wolf. Hmm. "Do you shift?" His voice came out abnormally low and gritty and he cleared his throat. It was a personal question, but since she'd been forthcoming with her heritage, he couldn't help but ask.

"Whenever I get the urge, and only into a fox." She smiled again, this time flashing a few beautifully symmetrical teeth. "I don't participate in the compulsory three-day wolf fest your kind does."

"Interesting." Silas turned to the sink and began filling the pot. He'd heard they might need another supernatural officer, although he was surprised she was in plain clothes. Maybe a secretary? Goddess, he hoped she was a secretary. No one would say a word if he dated a secretary. "So what exactly will you be doing here at the CCPD?"

She worried her bottom lip. "Maybe Patrick is the right person to tell you."

Silas snorted. "Why? What's the big deal? Is it some supersecret new role I'm not supposed to know about?"

"No..."

"Well, then just tell me."

"I'm a transfer from Merrimack... where I was a detective."

Silas paused, the spoon he'd used to shovel coffee grounds hanging over the paper filter. "Detective? What will you be doing here?" He snapped the lid closed and stabbed the Brew button with his finger before pinning her with a questioning stare.

With a shrug and a resolved sigh, she announced, "I'm your new partner."

MEREDITH TURNER HADN'T EXPECTED TO BE THE ONE TO BREAK it to Silas that he was getting a new partner. She definitely hadn't expected his presence to be so... overwhelming. Sure, she'd known he was Alpha of Fireborn Pack, and with that role came certain self-aggrandizing tendencies. But his physical effect on her, considering she wasn't a member of his pack, was nothing short of surprising.

He was big with a deep voice that made her knees turn to water when he spoke. It was all she could do to stand her ground. And she must stand her ground. Because Silas Flynn was not going to like taking on a partner, especially, she guessed, a female one. All these alphas were misogynistic assholes. The hell if she would let him ruin this assignment for her though. She was here for a reason, and she wasn't going to let him shove her around.

Pushing past her, Silas stomped across the department and barged into Patrick Manahan's office without an ounce of respect for the uniformed officer already sitting in the chair across the desk from the captain. Silas practically vibrated with annoyance.

Meredith rolled her eyes and murmured, "Here we go" before following him.

"Patrick, will you tell this woman there's been a terrible, unfortunate mistake? She seems to be laboring under the misguided notion that she works here as a detective." Silas pointed a hand at her, his lip curling into an incredulous half smile.

"Silas…" The captain scratched his balding head, the heel of his hand brushing the point of his ears. That particular feature wasn't visible to humans, but Meredith found it a good reminder not to mess with the captain, whose powerful fae side dwelled just below the surface. "Let's talk about this."

All humor drained from Silas's expression as he realized there was no mistake. Meredith folded her arms against the tension rising in the room. The werewolf was not going to accept this without a fight. *Oh shit, here it comes.*

"Talk? What? Who the hell is she, and why does she think she's my new partner?" The words came out along with a background growl that rumbled straight from his chest.

Meredith braced herself against the alpha vibes rolling off the man. God, it reminded her of when she was a teenager and her father would get angry and puff up like a blowfish. Well, she was not a teenager anymore, and she wouldn't let an arrogant, spoiled brat of a man intimidate her.

"I tried to break the news gently," Meredith said, not bothering to keep the smugness or the grin from her voice. She shrugged one shoulder as if she found Silas's tirade amusing.

"Not your fault," Manahan offered, then turned his attention to the uniformed officer who was still sitting in one of the two chairs across from his desk. The guy's ears were red and he was glaring at Silas. It seemed Meredith was not the only member of the CCPD who thought the man needed to be taken down a notch. "Officer Brighton, would you give us a minute?"

"Yeah," Brighton gritted out. The young man rose, bumping shoulders with Silas on his way out the door. It didn't look like an accident.

Meredith took the liberty to close the door behind him, drawing a fortifying breath. Silas's alpha tendencies and hair trigger weren't exactly a secret, but she didn't love experiencing a werewolf tantrum in person. Part of her enjoyed watching him be put in his place, but a bigger part didn't relish what it was going to take to win him to her side. And the truth was, she probably needed his help to do what she'd come to do. Probably. If he didn't fall in line, she'd find a way to catch Alex on her own.

"Explain," Silas demanded, getting in Patrick's face. He braced his hands on the desk, leaning forward so that his wide shoulders cast a shadow over the captain's bulky form.

Way too aggressive. Meredith silently chuckled to herself. Patrick was not going to go for that.

Manahan glared at Silas, his normally warm blue eyes turning icy. "Sit down. Both of you."

Cracking her neck, Meredith slid into one of the molded plastic chairs, but Silas stayed right where he was. "Uh-oh," she murmured from behind a smile she fought to keep from taking shape. The wolf was about to get his furry ass handed to him, and she was here for it.

"I said, *sit*!" Captain Manahan's voice reverberated in the tiny room, his fae side coming to the surface. As an aerial fae, the captain's voice was a literal weapon. The sound rumbled deep within Meredith, sending a flare of heartburn into her throat. She shifted in her seat.

Silas was not immune to the captain's power and had been on the receiving end of most of it. He coughed into his hand and promptly sat. This time she couldn't fully suppress her chuckle. *Yeah, sit the fuck down, Alpha.*

"Better," Manahan barked. "Now we can have a civilized conversation." The captain spread his hands, eyes darting between them.

Meredith smirked as a vein in Silas's temple popped and his cheeks took on a ruddy hue. This was getting good.

The captain pointed one meaty finger at Silas. "You need a partner."

"I don't."

"You do. This Alex thing... I understand why you're obsessed."

"Oh, you do? You understand what it's like to have your parents murdered and the werewolf responsible free and living somewhere in the city?" Silas slid his narrowed gaze toward Meredith, probably wondering how much she knew about Alex. She knew. Everyone close to pack life knew.

The captain leaned back in his chair, bouncing against the backrest and threading his fingers over the mound of his belly. "Okay, let me rephrase that. I understand the pursuit of Alex needs to be your top priority. But there are other cases."

"Which I haven't neglected. Name one time I ever fell short on expectations."

The captain ran his tongue along his teeth, making a sucking noise like he was dislodging something caught behind his eyetooth. "Sleep. A personal life."

Silas snorted. "I haven't enjoyed either in years."

"Exactly."

A long stretch of silence unraveled between them. Meredith straightened in her chair. She crossed her legs and bobbed her foot. How long was this going to take? Silas needed to get his shit together on this. They had work to do.

"You're burning the candle at both ends," the big man continued. "The stress is getting to you. It's my responsibility to keep you safe, and that means until Alex is brought to justice, you need backup." Silas began to protest, but the captain cut him off. "Last week you busted down a door on Fifth Street. Significant property damage."

"There was a healer there I thought might know something."

"Yeah? Well, you're lucky she didn't know a spell strong enough to kill you."

"I had a rash for a week."

"I had a hell of a time calming her down. She threatened to sue us in human court. That's the last thing we need."

"It was a false lead. I should have handled it differently, I admit. But I'm close, Patrick. One of these days Alex is going to slip up and I'll have him. I can feel it."

The captain nodded. "No doubt. But until you hit the bull's-eye, Meredith will keep you from self-destructing. She's not emotionally involved."

Hmm. *Where did he get that idea?* Meredith took special interest in her fingernails and squirmed in her chair.

"You need an objective brain on this," he continued. "Listen to her. Let her help you. I have it on good authority that she's one of the best."

Silas gave an exaggerated sigh, rubbing his eyes with his thumb and forefinger. "I don't suppose I can talk you out of this?"

The captain shook his head. "She's already on the payroll." He snatched a manila folder off the corner of his desk and held it out toward Meredith. "Also, both of you need to check this out."

"What's this about?" Tentatively, she stood and accepted the folder he offered. She wasn't against working on other cases, but Alex was her top priority.

"Human murder. Shallow graves. Seemed like an open-and-shut abduction, murder, hide-the-bodies type thing. Only there's been some unapproved excavation at the burial site. Officer Brighton's undies are in a bunch over it. It could be ghouls. Better check it out."

"Ghouls. Right." Silas snatched the folder from Meredith's hands without a word. He violently flipped through the contents.

"Hey!" She tapped her foot, becoming increasingly agitated at the bossy asshole. Meredith regularly handled cases like this on her own. Ghouls loved to scavenge graves the way raccoons scavenge garbage cans. Luckily, they were relatively harmless and rare due to their incompatibility with consecrated ground. If ghouls were the culprits, a simple vial of holy water would fix the problem for good.

"I'll take care of it," Silas said, closing the folder.

"With Meredith," Manahan said firmly.

Meredith popped out a hip and snatched the folder back from him.

Silas sighed heavily. "With Meredith."

She offered him a forced smile dripping with I-told-you-so.

With a grunt, as if he found her repulsive, he rose from the chair and left the room.

Meredith scratched her temple and met the captain's apologetic stare. "Yeah. So that went well."

TWO

Only half an hour later, Silas found himself on a road outside Carlton City, driving toward the rural property where the murders had occurred, with his new *partner* at his side. *Son of a bitch.* This was the last thing he needed. Jesus Christ, to be so close to catching Alex and now saddled with a new partner? It was sabotage. If he hadn't known Patrick for going on fifteen years, he'd swear the man was intentionally trying to interfere with his progress. Not only would this chick slow him down, but she was also an intolerable distraction. Her scent lingered in his nose. He kept his eyes on the road and tried to ignore the strange feeling in his gut her presence elicited.

The worst part was she wasn't pack. He couldn't alpha her into submission. Which meant he'd need to work *with* her. Pain in the ass considering she had no idea what he was up against. Worse, she looked like the type who always followed procedure and couldn't go out without a coat of mascara. This was never going to work.

He double-checked the coordinates to make sure they were headed in the right direction. The crime scene was in the middle of nowhere, but they were almost there.

"Did you read this case? This is horrific." Meredith flipped through the folder on the seat beside him. "Five girls, young girls, lured away from home by one of their friends. Same age. They all lived on the same block. Looks like one of them murdered her friends and then killed herself."

"Humans." Silas snorted.

The feisty redhead huffed. "It's not like supernatural creatures don't kill each other."

Silas flashed her a lopsided grin. "Yeah, but we do it with style."

She snapped the folder closed. "How's this going to work? I propose we check the graves for ghoul droppings, take a spectral imprint of the area, and sprinkle holy water around the periphery if there's any evidence the graves have been compromised."

"I propose you stay in the car while I handle this." Silas pulled onto the side of the road beside an over-grown field. In the distance, police tape cordoned off a wooded area, the yellow ribbon twisting in the breeze. His words had come out harsher than he'd intended, but he wanted to start as he intended to go. Namely, he fully intended to be the one calling the shots in this relation-ship. Besides, his wolf was too close to the surface with her around. He'd work faster if she kept her distance.

Meredith pivoted her shoulders to face him. "I propose you go fuck yourself." She swept the holy water from the cup holder and exited the car.

"Hey, give me that!" He jumped from the unmarked car and strode after her. But she was already more than halfway across the field, her supernatural speed requiring him to break into a jog to keep up.

She paused abruptly a few yards out from the crime scene, pressing one long finger to her lips. "Shhhh."

Who did she think he was? He knew better than to scare away the ghouls before he had a chance to confirm their presence. He didn't need her treating him like a child. He caught up to her but couldn't give her a piece of his mind because something was moving between the trees about a hundred yards ahead.

A pale figure darted in the dim light. Silas sniffed, but the wind was blowing the wrong way. He wasn't getting anything but dirt, leaves, and Meredith. *Fuck*, he'd known she'd be a distraction.

As if to deliberately call more attention to herself, she ducked under the yellow tape and crept, holy water in hand, toward the movement. Silas had no choice but to follow. Ghouls could be dangerous, and she might need backup. He swore silently to himself for not being in front. He should be leading the way, not her, but addressing it at this point wouldn't be prudent. But the closer they got to the form hovering over the crime scene, the more he thought there was something familiar about the silhouette.

And it was too big to be a ghoul.

"Look out!" Silas bounded forward, knocking Meredith to the ground to place his body between her and the threat that loomed above the grave. He drew his gun. "Don't move!"

Alex, Fireborn Pack nemesis number one, scowled at Silas with unrepentant rage, his dark blond waves catching the moonlight with the quick turn of his head. Skin waxy and pale enough to glow in the dark, he hardly appeared human any longer. In his hands, he gripped a mesh bag full of bones freshly torn from the bodies, judging by the chunks of flesh still adhering to them.

Silas pulled the trigger, unloading three silver bullets toward Alex's heart. They wouldn't kill him, but they'd slow him down.

Pulse. The dragon fae amulet around Alex's neck blinked, and the man disappeared. There was a high-pitched squeal as the bullets passed through where Alex had been and landed in the body of a ghoul who'd been creeping up behind him.

Alex was gone.

"Oww," Meredith said, sitting up in the tall grass.

Silas glanced back to find her head was bleeding. She must have knocked it on something when he pushed her down.

"Meredith. Shit!" Silas holstered his weapon and jogged to her side. Removing his button-down, he pressed it to the scrape on her head, then cradled the base of her skull with his opposite hand for leverage. "I don't think it's deep."

She fixed him with a harsh glare, and he expected her

to tell him to fuck off. But as her dark brown eyes met his, she stopped, lips parted as if she'd forgotten what she was going to say. Silas's nostrils flared with the scent she was putting off. He closed his eyes. That was arousal. *Damn.* So he wasn't the only one experiencing the strange electric tingle at being this close. When he opened his eyes again, she was staring at his T-shirt-covered chest, and her cheeks had flushed a gorgeous shade of pink.

He cleared his throat and removed his hands from her head, handing her the bloody button-down.

"Who the hell was that?" she finally asked. "And where did he go?"

Silas's shoulders hunched forward as his thoughts shifted to Alex. So close. He'd been so close. "I should have fired sooner."

"Sure. Why follow protocol?" Meredith asked sarcastically. "Are you going to tell me who it was and why you practically bludgeoned me to shoot at him?"

"Yes," he said darkly. "But first, do you need a doctor?"

She removed the shirt from her head. The wound had already stopped bleeding. "No. I'm good. It's just a scrape." She got to her feet.

"Are you sure? You could have a concussion."

With a shake of her head, she waved him off. "I'm fine. Tell me who that was."

"I'll burn the ghoul's body," he said. "You sprinkle the holy water. I'll explain on the way back to the station."

Thankfully, she didn't argue.

As she headed for the border of the crime scene, he decided he owed her an explanation. If she was going to be his partner, she needed to know about the risks. And Alex was one deadly risk.

Meredith wanted to reach across the seat, grab Silas by the throat, and shake the information out of him. Her gut told her the man she'd glimpsed hunched over the grave was Alex, but she needed confirmation. She'd never seen the bastard in real life, and what she'd seen tonight was confusing to say the least.

"Okay, we're in the car, driving back to the station. Are you going to tell me who that was or am I going to have to force it out of you?" She stared at the side of his head expectantly.

Silas scoffed, raising an eyebrow as he gave her a once-over out of the corner of his eye. "How exactly would *you* force it out of me?"

Gritting her teeth, she reached between his legs and squeezed. The car veered wildly.

"Jesus, okay, I'll tell you!" Silas howled.

She released his balls, trying not to think about how full her hand had been. Silas had a lot going for him in that department. Damn it, was there anything about this guy that wasn't sexy other than his personality?

"Is that how you interrogate your perps, go around

squeezing their balls?" He glared at her like she was insane.

"If that's what it takes. Spill it." She reached for him again, and he knocked her hand away.

"That was Alex Ravien Bloodright."

"I thought so. I couldn't think of anyone else you'd shoot at without hesitation."

"You're familiar with the case then?"

"Yeah. Like I said, my father was a werewolf."

Silas nodded, dark clouds moving in behind his eyes as he hyperfocused on the deserted road.

"I'm sorry about your parents," she said.

"Thanks."

"There's more to this case than that though, isn't there? Alex looked strange. I thought he was a ghoul at first because of his complexion."

Silas scratched the back of his head but never took his eyes off the road. "He attacked me and my siblings a few months ago. He tried to kill me because he wanted to take my place as Alpha of Fireborn Pack and head of the Lycanthropic Society. He failed." Silas gripped the steering wheel so tight his knuckles turned white. "My sister delivered a deadly bite to his abdomen. We thought he was dead. The dragon fae he was working with healed him, but there were magical consequences."

Meredith tried to process all that. She'd heard rumors, but it was important to have the facts if she was going to help take Alex down. "Captain Manahan said you roughed up a healer. That was why, wasn't it? You think Alex is visiting healers because he's still sick or cursed or something."

He nodded. "That's exactly it. There are still a few healers in town I haven't investigated."

"Good, then that's where we go next."

"That's where I go next," Silas said adamantly.

She let it go, but if he thought for a second she was going to let him pursue this investigation without her, he was fooling himself.

"Well, at least you learned one thing tonight."

"What's that?"

"Alex doesn't want to kill you anymore."

"Huh?"

"He had a crack at you tonight. Hell, he had the advantage. That amulet around his neck could have blown you apart in a heartbeat. But he chose to run. That means there's something else going on, a reason he felt it was more important to conserve his energy for rather than killing you."

Silas frowned, his head jerking back in surprise. "I think you're right."

"I'm right a lot. You should listen to me." Meredith smirked, but he ignored her.

"Alex is still healing, and he was after human bones tonight. An odd quarry, don't you think?"

"Maybe he needs it for a healing spell?"

"Possible. Attacking me would take energy. Perhaps he was concerned he couldn't win a confrontation with me yet, even with magic, and that's why he ran. He avoided using the amulet before on my brother to conserve energy."

She picked at the side of her nail. "Hmmm. But what's he conserving his energy for then if not to take you out?"

"That is the question." Silas turned in to the CCPD parking lot and parked the car. "What's important is Alex is still vulnerable. Now is not the time to turn down the heat. Now is the time to press even harder to find where he's hiding and who's helping him."

Meredith unbuckled her seat belt, gathered her things, and popped the door. "I couldn't agree more, which is why I'll be going with you to question the next healer."

He grumbled something, but she'd already slammed the door and was halfway into the building.

CHAPTER

THREE

"Why does having a partner bother you so much?" Laina took a huge bite of her burger, studying him like he was a chess game and she was deciding on her next move.

Silas had asked his younger sister to lunch to catch up but was enjoying the opportunity to vent about Meredith.

"The woman is insufferable," Silas explained. "She refuses to listen to reason. Refuses to follow orders. Might have cost me my chance at Alex last night—"

"It sounds like she didn't cost you anything. The moment you shot, Alex dematerialized." As she spoke, a glob of sauce dripped from the corner of Laina's mouth and landed with a splat on the table.

"Hungry, sister?" Silas asked, snorting at the way she practically inhaled the half pound of meat in her hands. He handed her a napkin. "I don't think I've ever seen you eat like this."

"It's weird, isn't it? I've been craving meat constantly these days. Must be the stress of knowing Alex is on the loose again." She dabbed her lips with the napkin. "Anyway, don't change the subject. What's your beef with this woman? It sounds like she's exactly the type of backup you need. I think her theory about Alex's changing priorities is correct. He could have killed you last night."

"Don't take her side."

She leaned back in the booth. "There are no sides, Silas. You both want to kill Alex. She's a detective. You're a detective. You're both on the same side. The real problem is you don't play well with others. You're so used to being able to order people around you've forgotten what it's like to have to cooperate with someone toward a common goal."

"Last night was the closest I've ever been to bringing him down." He shook his head. "She's out of her league with this case. It's not that I can't cooperate. It's that I don't need any distractions right now."

"What's her name again?"

"Meredith Turner."

"Why does that name sound familiar?"

Silas shrugged. "Her father was pack, but she was raised by her mother. Shifter. Usually a fox. I told her about Alex after I shot at him last night. She knew who he was, that he shot our parents, but not about our recent confrontations with him."

"Wow, so not only is this woman an experienced detective, she's familiar with Alex and the pack and wants to help. Seems like the perfect partner."

Someone had put pepper in the saltshaker. Silas unscrewed the top. It wasn't mixed together yet. This could be salvaged. He picked up his spoon and started carefully scooping out the black grains. "I like to work alone. You can't trust anyone these days. Everyone has hidden agendas. She shows up out of nowhere and I'm supposed to trust her with the biggest case of my life, a case that affects my family and my pack? The only person I trust is me. I'm meticulous. I have a stellar memory. My hunches are ninety-eight percent accurate. A partner throws all of that off. Like last night. If I hadn't wasted time pushing her out of the way, I might've sunk a silver bullet between Alex's eyes."

Laina leaned back against her seat. "Well, I think it's a good idea."

"Why?"

"Because you've been alone too long. You work all the time. We never see you anymore. And frankly, Silas, everyone needs someone. You're not an island, even when it comes to detective work. You'll burn out if you don't accept help."

"I've been doing this for years." He scooped more tainted salt onto his plate.

"Look at you! You took it upon yourself to clean pepper out of the saltshaker."

He spread his hands in disbelief. "It's rude."

"You didn't do it."

"Yeah, but I noticed."

"It wasn't your responsibility."

"Of course it was. I saw it. Honestly, Laina. What is this all about?"

"It's about you. You think it's your responsibility to save everyone and that only you can do it. Ever since Dad died and you became alpha, I've watched you slowly lose your smile."

"I have not lost my smile."

"You walk around like the entire world rests on your shoulders. When was the last time you had any fun? Or laughed? Actually laughed."

Silas shrugged. "I'm a busy person. There's a killer on the loose. That's not a laughing matter."

"You don't need to remind me." She picked at her fries. "Any one of us could be Alex's next victim."

"Exactly."

"Even you."

"This is why I work as much as I do."

"But wouldn't you hate to die knowing you never fully lived?"

Silas rolled his eyes. "Did you get that from a greeting card?"

"No, really, brother. What kind of life is this?" Laina leaned forward and placed her hand on top of his. "Use this new partner. Even if she can't help you bring Alex down, she can share in the struggle. Be someone to talk to. Let her help you. And for the love of the goddess, find your joy again. I miss it."

DAMN WOMAN WAS A PAIN IN THE ASS. DESPITE HIS SISTER'S encouragement, Silas hadn't felt the urge to welcome Meredith onboard with open arms. The next morning, he tried to appeal to her logical side when he asked her to stay behind as he investigated the next healer on his list. It was hard enough to get these people to talk to him when he was alone. With another detective in tow, he'd never get a true word. Plus he might have to rough someone up, and he didn't need Miss Goody Two-shoes messing up his interrogation tactics. Besides, after last night, he didn't want to risk her getting hurt again if something did go down. The Band-Aid on her head was a good reminder of why that would be a bad idea.

"I put people at ease," she said as she slid into the passenger's side of the unmarked car, ignoring his request. "They like to talk to me. Always have. I think it's because I come across as vulnerable."

He stared at the side of her head for a solid minute. "You're not going to get out of the car, are you?"

"Nope." She popped the p at the end of the word and stared at him with a steely gaze.

"Hardheaded, irrational...," he mumbled under his breath as he put the car into gear and drove to the address.

"You can wait here," Silas ordered once he'd parked the car.

"Okay," Meredith said flatly.

At least she was agreeable. He climbed out of the car and crossed the street. Surprisingly, this healer wasn't in the vampire district. The address was an apartment above a busy Starbucks in the heart of the city.

"Where did you get this list anyway?" Meredith said, appearing slightly behind him.

Silas stopped abruptly, tipping his head back to stare at the bright blue sky. "I thought I told you to wait in the car?"

"You said I *could* wait in the car. I acknowledged that, yes, okay, waiting was an option. Then I chose to come with you. See how that works? When we're done here, can you insist I don't drink your coffee? I'm feeling a little thirsty." The toothy grin she flashed was worthy of a car salesman. "Now, how did you come across this list of suspects?" She ran her fingers through her hair and pulled it into a ponytail, tying the thick red mass back with an elastic from around her wrist.

He stared at her for a moment, ushering her onto the curb to avoid traffic. "After what happened last night, don't you think you should stay where it's safe?"

"Hey, the only person who hurt me last night was you. Don't push me down and I should be okay." She glanced at him first, then peered at the slip of paper with the address he was holding.

"Seriously. Your head isn't even healed yet. Maybe you should take the day off." *And free me from the pressure I feel in my chest whenever you're around.* His inner wolf chuffed at that thought, giving a little twist behind his sternum.

"I'm not going anywhere," she said. "If you want to do this, you'd best let me in on the plan."

With a sigh, Silas contemplated how much to share with her, then figured it would be less hassle to tell her the truth. He gestured with his head in the direction of the Starbucks about a block away and started walking again. "All these so-called healers were mentioned by clients of a fae bordello, Maison des Étoilles, as places where one could receive healing services that require dark magic. We know Alex is recovering somewhere in the area. One of these names is likely helping him. No reputable healer would become involved with Alex voluntarily."

"I see." Meredith glanced in his direction. "Why do you think you can trust a list of names originating in a bordello? Don't prostitutes have a conflict of interest reporting on their johns?"

It was a legitimate question, one Silas would ask if the roles were reversed. "There are extenuating circum-stances. The fae at Maison des Étoilles can read minds. Plus the madam is my ex-girlfriend."

Meredith sucked air through her teeth. "Didn't see that one coming. So you two aren't an item anymore, but you still bump uglies every now and again, eh?"

"No. No bumping uglies. We're just friends. Good friends. I trust her."

"Ended things on a positive note. Mm-hmm. So how many dark practitioners are left to investigate?"

"Three."

"Down to the wire. Do you have a search warrant?"

Silas cast a sideways glance in her direction. "No."

"Hmm. Then you better let me go in first."

"Are you high?" Silas stopped abruptly, a muscle in his jaw tensing to the point of pain. "Did you learn nothing from last night? Why would you think that's a good idea?"

She shrugged. "If Alex is up there, he'll be expecting you. Me, he won't see coming." She grabbed the address out of Silas's hand and took off toward the café.

Silas protested all the way past the crowded Starbucks to the foreboding stairwell that led above the bustling coffee shop. An illustration of a finger pointed toward the second floor.

"This looks cozy." Meredith climbed the dim and dirty stairwell two steps at a time.

"Wait," Silas protested.

She glanced back and pressed a finger to her lips. "Shhh."

Why was she always hushing him?

On the second floor, a frosted glass window inscribed with the Eye of Horus read COPPER HERALD HEALTH & WELLNESS in a script font.

Silas bit his tongue as Meredith tried the door and found it locked. He pointed at a handwritten note taped to the glass: KNOCK FOR SERVICE. She rapped three times.

They waited. She knocked again.

Footsteps. Silas flattened himself against the wall just as the door opened.

"How can I help you today, young lady?" an old man's voice asked.

Meredith rubbed the bandaged bump on her head from the night before as she notably lowered her gaze by two feet. "I've been having a lot of pain in my shoulder and neck area since I fell yesterday. I was wondering if you had any therapies for that."

"Is this pain with you all the time or only after you shift?"

Meredith raised both eyebrows. "Only when I'm walking on two legs actually."

"You've come to the right place. Come in, and bring your werewolf friend with you."

She glanced behind the door at Silas and gestured with her head. So much for the element of surprise. He came out of hiding and stared down at the wrinkled man inside. Based on his height alone, he would guess he was a troll, but the shape of his ears and nose suggested part elf. The medicinal herbs hanging in the office masked his scent, but Silas thought he caught a whiff of elf under it all. Whatever he was, he must be sensitive to the light: he wore sunglasses in the dim room.

"Over here then. Lie down on the table. Please remove your blouse."

A deep growl came from Silas's chest. It was an involuntary thing, like a hiccup or a sneeze. Mortified, he coughed into his hand and turned away to try to cover it up.

"There's a gown on the table," the doctor said, ignoring the interruption. "Although I can't see anything but your aura anyway. I'm blind as a bat."

With a pointed glance toward Silas, Meredith walked deeper into the room. Silas turned his back until the rustle of her undressing stopped and he heard the crinkle of her lying down on the paper-draped medical table.

"I'm Dr. Copper by the way. If you come by another time, you might see Dr. Herald." The little man selected a bowl of stones from a shelf along the wall.

"There are two of you?" Silas asked.

Dr. Copper made a face and began placing stones carved with ancient runes along Meredith's solar plexus. "You obviously don't keep him around for his brains," he murmured to her.

Silas scowled. After a few moments, he decided to make use of the silence. "Do you treat many shifters here?"

"I don't, no. My specialization is vampires. But Dr. Herald does. He's fascinated by shifter anatomy. I daresay if you'd phoned first, he'd be the one treating you today."

"What days does he work?"

"He'll be in later tonight. He tends to come and go. Make an appointment if you're interested."

If Dr. Herald specialized in shifters, Alex definitely would have sought him out. Silas inspected the room for any clues that the bastard might have been there. The walls of the examination room were lined with skins, skulls, teeth, and clay bowls of assorted magical items. There was a hook laden with amulets on one wall. He scanned the papers on the desk. Nothing stood out. There was only one other door in the place, and it was behind the desk.

"Can I help you find something?" Dr. Copper said. "Or is there an alternative reason for your fidgeting?"

Silas cleared his throat. "Bathroom?"

"Out the door and to the left."

He wasted no time. He strode to the door behind the desk and threw it open, only to have a small body rush in front of him and catch the knob.

Dr. Copper sneered at him from below. "Not that door, you fool! The one you came in."

The doctor pulled the door closed again, but not before Silas saw a small bedroom with a pair of mud-caked boots beside a twin-sized bed. He remembered Alex wearing a similar pair, and the dirt could have come from the crime scene. Otherwise, the room was empty. He took a deep breath through his nose but couldn't detect even a hint of Alex. Maybe it was a coincidence, but he intended to find out for sure.

"You know, I think I'll just wait for you in the car," Silas said to Meredith.

Her eyes darted between him and the door, her red brow arching in question.

Silas winked at her and gestured toward the door with his head. Hopefully she'd get the hint and excuse herself after he was gone.

"Sounds good," she said. "This won't take long, will it, Dr. Copper?"

"Hold still," he said gruffly, positioning the next stone.

Silas exited and descended the stairs two at a time, drawing his phone to his ear. Laina's number went to voicemail. As he spilled onto the bustling sidewalk, he left her a quick message. His gut told him this was the lead he'd been waiting for. He'd case the place tonight and find out if it was Alex staying in that room.

He was about to return the phone to his pocket when it rang. Unknown number. He answered.

"Is this Silas Flynn?"

"Yes."

"This is Saint John's Hospital calling. Your sister Laina is here."

"Laina? What happened?"

"I'm sorry. We can't give out that information over the phone. But we need you to come to the hospital right away."

FOUR

"I'm looking for my sister, Laina Flynn," Silas told the woman behind the desk. He'd texted Meredith that he had an emergency and that she should take a cab back to the station, then raced for the hospital as fast as he could. He had a bad feeling about this.

"You must be Silas. I've been expecting you. I have a note here that one of our nurses wants to meet with you directly about Laina's condition. I'll page her for you."

A nurse needed to talk to him directly. He bet his life he knew who it was.

"Silas, thank the goddess!" Grateful Knight grabbed him by the elbow and ushered him away from the desk, her massive belly leading the way.

"Whoa," he mumbled. "You are exceptionally pregnant." He couldn't help but stare. Her stomach seemed to have popped out overnight.

"I won't take that personally." She lowered her voice. "Between you and me, I've been using a spell to help conceal it, but I'm so far along now the magic won't work anymore." Grateful paused, looked both ways, and pulled him into a consultation room.

"So what's going on with my sister?" Silas asked. It always fascinated him that Grateful, one of the most powerful witches of her time, chose to keep her job as a nurse. Then again, working in the intensive care unit gave her access to insider information on human injuries caused by supernatural beings. As a Hecate, judge and jury of all things not human, that was useful information.

"She's in surgery."

"Fuck. Is she going to be okay? What happened?"

"She was attacked. Stabbed four times in the abdomen about an hour ago outside Four Paws Animal Hospital."

"During daylight hours?"

"Yeah. That's not even the weirdest part."

"What's the weird part?"

"The stab marks... The flesh around the entry points is singed as if they stabbed her with a hot poker."

Silas swallowed hard. "In the parking lot? I thought we had the place warded against supernatural threats?"

"We did. We do. I had Rick check, and both my wards and Gerty's are still up. Whoever did this walked right through them."

"Fuck. So a human did this?"

"That was my first assumption too, but there was a substance in the wounds. I'm not sure what it is yet, but I took a sample and let's just say it made Nightshade light up like a laser beam. The person who stabbed her might be human, but the poison on the blade definitely had a supernatural source." Nightshade was Grateful's sword, a magical blade that served as a supernatural lie detector, sniffing out evil intent in both supernatural creatures and enchanted objects. The thing could destroy curses too, as it had for the cursed ring his brother had been using that spring. It was never wrong.

He rubbed the back of his neck and shoulders where the muscles had tightened to the point of pain. "You used the word *poison*. Is there an antidote?"

"Honestly, I was using the term loosely. I'm not sure exactly what it is yet. Not even a guess unfortunately. But I'll find out, and as soon as I know, I'll do whatever it takes to heal Laina. But Silas, the stab wounds... You need to know they weren't random." She pulled out her phone and slid her finger across the screen to bring up a picture.

"The letter *A*. Alex did this." Silas's stomach pitched. He'd promised to keep his sister safe and he'd failed again. "I got too close last night. This is his warning to me. He wants me to back off."

"You saw Alex last night?"

"Yeah. Almost shot his ass. He was collecting bones at a crime scene I was investigating."

"Bones?"

Silas shrugged. "I have no idea what he plans to do with them."

Grateful shook her head. "Alex *couldn't* have done this himself, Silas. Those protective wards are impenetrable. They're the same ones we laid around Rivergate. Nothing supernatural can get in there without our knowledge. It's sealed so tight that Laina has to call me if a witch or fae wants to bring their dog in for an exam. And before you ask, she hasn't added any new clients recently."

Silas closed his eyes tightly. "So Alex has a human doing his dirty work."

"That's what I'm thinking. Someone who knows enough about magic to activate a spell or magical substance once they were inside the wards."

"*Fuck.* Does Kyle know?"

She nods. "We called him first. He's waiting outside of surgery."

"Tell me the truth, Grateful. What's the expected outcome here? Don't sugarcoat it. What's going to happen to my sister?"

Grateful's entire body seemed to sag, and she slipped her hands into the pockets of her scrubs. "Honestly, if she were human, she'd already be dead. But she's not human. Her heart is still beating, and Gerty is asking permission of the fae council to bring fire lily juice here. I'm going to make a healing potion based on what I determine was on the blade. She's not out of the woods, but she's got some powerful people pulling for her."

Silas swallowed around a fist-sized lump that had formed in his throat. "Thank you. Just do your best."

Smoothing a loose strand of blond hair back into her ponytail, Grateful frowned. "There's one more thing I need to tell you."

"Go ahead and say it." Silas scratched his jaw. "Nothing can make this situation worse."

"They ran her blood work before surgery."

"Yeah? And?"

Grateful ran a hand over the mound of her abdomen. "Laina's pregnant."

THE STEADY BEEP OF THE MACHINES IN LAINA'S ROOM WAS almost hypnotic. Even though her surgery had gone as expected, for still-unknown reasons, she hadn't woken up. All the human doctors were calling it a coma. Grateful quietly declared it a curse.

"She's going to be all right," Silas said to Kyle. "Grateful will figure out the nature of what's doing this to Laina, and she'll undo it."

"I called Jason," Kyle said. "He and Selene are flying back from Italy. They'll be here tomorrow."

"Good. Laina needs all the support she can get right now."

The men sat in silence, Silas on Laina's right, Kyle on her left. Laina looked small in the bed, small and thin. He thought of the way she'd packed away the burger at Valentine's and wondered if it was because of the baby. Goddess, he was going to kill Alex for this. For this and for everything else the bastard had done to their family.

"Did Grateful tell you?" Kyle asked eventually. "About what they found when they tested her blood?"

What should he say? Congratulations seemed inappropriate given the circumstances. Silas decided a nod would be enough.

"They say the baby is about seven weeks along. We didn't even know." He took Laina's hand in his, his thumb rubbing gently over the back of her hand. "I guess she still doesn't know."

"She'll be so excited, Kyle. The entire pack will be."

"I hope so."

Silas rubbed the back of his head. His hair was too long and bushy and it caught in his fingers, but who had time for haircuts when you were hunting down your mortal enemy?

"We've got to find him," Kyle said, his voice low and threatening. "Alex needs to pay for this."

"I won't stop until he does," Silas said.

"What's taking so long? Jason said Alex was so weak he could hardly use the amulet. That was weeks ago."

"I know. Alex has to be working with a healer. Has to be." Silas scratched the stubble on his jaw. "I'm getting closer. I'm staking out a new place tonight."

Kyle rose from his wife's side and paced the room. "Maybe. Maybe you got too close and that was why he targeted Laina."

"Yeah. I was thinking the same thing."

"So what are you going to do about it?" Kyle's voice rose in pitch. "You have a Hecate on your side, a best friend who's a caretaker. Fuck, we've got a fairy godmother in Gerty, for Pete's sake. Do you need money? I can give you any amount you need."

"It's not money or power." Silas sighed. He understood why Kyle was frustrated. He was frustrated too.

"You need something, Silas," Kyle gritted out,

pointing a finger over Laina's body. "Fucking stop trying to do this on your own and get the help you need to get it done or so help me God, I'll hunt and kill Alex myself. I'll do it with my bare hands if I have to."

Silas's blood heated. He felt for Kyle, he did, but he'd had about enough of being indirectly blamed for what happened to Laina. He was pondering how to respond to the man without losing his shit when the door flew open and Meredith stumbled into the room, panting and doubled over. She looked like hell. Half her red hair spilled from her ponytail, her clothing was disheveled, and her eyes bulged.

She grabbed Silas by the collar and shook him. "You... you left me there. Why did you leave me there?"

"I... Uh..." Goddess, he felt like an asshole for leaving without her. But he'd had no choice. "I did text..."

"Do you know what cupping is?" Her voice was quiet but held a tinge of venom.

Slowly he shook his head.

"After you left, Dr. Lucky Charms decided the therapy I needed involved suctioning heated glass cups to my skin." She pulled the neck of her blouse aside to reveal an angry red welt. "Not only did it hurt like hell, he charged me five hundred dollars!"

"We'll submit that to the department for reimbursement," Silas mumbled.

"And then... And then..." She shook him harder. "By the time I left, my invented condition was a real one. I feel like I've been hit by a frickin' truck. You abandoned me. I had to call for an Uber. An Uber, Silas, covered in welts! I can barely sit down!"

He swallowed, not knowing what to say. "Did he do that to your butt too?"

Meredith bared her teeth. "My entire backside from neck to ankle looks like an infection of megasized adult acne."

Kyle snorted, then broke into a full-out laugh despite himself.

Meredith raised her head, seeming to notice Laina in the bed and Kyle by her side for the first time.

"My sister," Silas said. "She was stabbed today. We think it was Alex. That was the emergency. I'm sorry I left you."

Lips parting, Meredith shoved against his collarbones and staggered backward, glancing between him and Kyle. "Manahan said you were here for your sister. I had no idea."

"Who is this person?" Kyle asked Silas.

"Meredith." She held out her hand in Kyle's direction. "I'm Silas's new partner."

"She's not really my partner," Silas said. "Well, technically she is, but temporarily... and not really."

Kyle raised his eyebrows. "I'm Silas's brother-in-law, Kyle."

Meredith paused a moment as if she were processing the family dynamic, then said, "I'm sorry."

With a grim smile, Kyle turned back to Silas. "You were saying something about a stakeout?"

"I'm going to stake out Dr. Copper's office. He said

his partner specialized in werewolves, and there was a small bedroom off the office. It looked like someone was sleeping there." Silas took a deep breath.

"I'll tell you one thing, Dr. Copper has some secrets," Meredith said.

Silas peered at her expectantly. "Yeah?"

"Look how he signed my take-home instructions." She pulled a folded paper from her back pocket and handed it to him.

"Dr. Herald?" Silas squinted at the signature.

"There was only one desk, one examination table, one set of equipment, and one nameplate I could find anywhere. Copper Herald. One name." Meredith rested her hands on her hips. "I think Dr. Copper started my exam and Dr. Herald finished it."

"So…"

"He's both men, a Jekyll and Hyde, and you know what else? After my exam, I barged through that door behind his desk, and you were right." She gave Silas a knowing grin. "I'm not sure it's Alex, but someone is living there. Someone with a pair of muddy boots."

CHAPTER
FIVE

Meredith watched Silas closely as he processed her revelation about Copper Herald and knew the instant he agreed with her assessment of the doctor, because those insanely intense eyes of his sharpened under the dark slashes of his brows and he gave her an almost imperceptible nod.

"Uh, thanks. I'll check it out tonight." He folded the evidence she'd handed him and tucked it into his pocket.

"We'll check it out tonight." She offered a sweet smile and leaned a shoulder against the wall.

"I'm going to head down to the cafeteria for a coffee and to call Gerty," Kyle said. "Either of you want anything?"

"No, thank you," Meredith said without taking her eyes off Silas.

"She's not staying," Silas added. Kyle had already left the room.

With a wry grin, she crossed to the seat beside him, lowering herself gingerly into it. Part of her did it with the sole purpose of vexing the bastard. Another part, maybe a bigger part if she was being honest, did it because she genuinely liked the asshole. He was an asshole, no doubt about it, but there was something about his confidence that did funny things to her insides. When Silas commanded her to do something, her inner beast wanted to do it... at first. But denying him the satisfaction was far more fun. It didn't hurt that he was pleasant to look at. Standing up to him and trying to manipulate him to her will was becoming her favorite new addiction.

Beside her, he sighed heavily. "This is family business. There's no reason for you to stay."

Game on. "I'm supporting my new partner."

"No support needed. I'm good. Holding up fairly well actually." He crossed an ankle over his opposite knee, trying to look casual.

"Must be because I'm here."

He sank deeper into his chair, bobbing his foot.

"So, what's going on with your sister? Is she going to be okay?"

He looked down at his fingers threaded across his belly, seeming to deliberate on whether he should share anything or not. She was relieved when he spoke again. "There was a poison, some kind of cursed substance, on the blade she was stabbed with. I have a witch analyzing it for the antidote."

"Jesus."

"The supernatural medical staff here is doing all they can. It's complicated because she's... pregnant."

All levity drained from Meredith's soul. "Oh Silas, I'm so sorry." A heavy weight formed deep within her. She hadn't known how serious things were when she'd walked in the room. Maybe she should leave. Give Silas his space. She scooted to the end of her seat.

"Do you have any brothers or sisters?" he asked her quickly, before she could get up.

She slid to the back of the chair again, wincing at the pain it caused her backside. Guess she'd be staying after all. "No. Only child." She wondered if Silas remembered her father, but this wasn't the time to bring that up. "Do you feel responsible for what happened to Laina?"

He snorted. "I don't feel responsible. I am responsible."

"Because you're alpha."

"Because she's family. My little sister. My parents are gone. She's my responsibility."

She leaned toward him and placed her hand on his arm. "She might be your responsibility, but this isn't your fault. You've done everything within your power to stop that evil bastard."

Silas's eyes locked with hers and held. Damn. She had no explanation for the heat that rose in her blood or the intense urge to move her hand along his arm, maybe to his chest. Her heart sputtered.

The door opened and Kyle walked in. She pulled her hand away, breaking the spell. Good thing too. That was far too intense. She rose from the chair, glancing between

Silas and Kyle as she tightened what remained of her ponytail. "I'd better go."

"Yeah," Silas agreed, shifting in his seat.

She paused to look at Kyle as she passed him on the way out. "We're going to get the bastard. I promise you that."

LATE THAT AFTERNOON, SILAS SLIPPED HIS KEY INTO THE LOCK of his tiny brick bungalow, gaze sweeping up and down the street for lookie-loos before he pushed inside. It was a relatively safe neighborhood. Mostly parents with young children and retired folks. But old habits died hard. It was always best to change up your routine, make sure you weren't being watched coming and going.

He'd barely closed the door behind him when something flew at his knees. He caught the brown-and-white blur by the head. "Now that's a welcome home," he said, scratching the mutt behind the ears. "How's my Maggie girl? You hungry?"

The medium-sized fuzz ball panted up at him, tongue lolling out the corner of her mouth. The spaniel had a doggie door to do her business but hadn't been fed since early that morning before he left for work. Come to think of it, he hadn't been fed either. His stomach rumbled as, with one last ear-flapping rub of her head, he moved for the kitchen. He dug a bag of kibble out of the cupboard and filled her food and water bowl, then opened the door to the fridge and stared as she chowed down.

There was nothing inside but a half gallon of milk that was two days past its expiration and some leftover takeout that was old enough to take itself out. He closed the door again.

A streak of black moved past the kitchen window. Silas froze. He'd definitely seen that, and it was fast, too fast to be human. He sidestepped into the shadows, out of direct sight of the window, and dug in the silverware drawer for the large knife he used to carve the Thanksgiving turkey. He'd have much preferred his Glock, but he'd left it locked in his glove compartment when visiting Laina in the hospital. His other gun was in the safe in his bedroom at the back of the house. No time for that one either. Anything that moved as fast as what he'd seen was an immediate threat.

He skimmed along the wall, jogging past the breakfast nook, and flattened himself next to the front-facing window. *Knock. Knock. Knock.* Maggie woofed once at the door, then backed up, growling.

Someone was out there. With two fingers, he moved the curtains aside a fraction of an inch and peered through the window at the front porch. There was no one on the front stoop. He frowned.

Maggie barked again, and Silas whirled as a column of black smoke filtered under the door and into his foyer. He hurled the knife at the center of the thing, knowing damn well the steel blade would barely damage anything that moved like that but hoping it would give him time to reach his gun.

He was halfway to the bedroom when a familiar voice said, "This is a fine how-do-you-do."

"Logan. Thank the goddess." Silas ran a hand down his face, profound relief flooding him.

His best friend stared down at the carving knife protruding from his sternum. He grabbed the hilt and tugged it from his flesh with a grunt. A spurt of blood landed on the wood floor of his entryway with a splat, but the wound healed almost immediately. It was a good thing Silas's formerly human friend had become Polina's caretaker last year or that knife wound might have been fatal. Of course, if he had been human, he wouldn't be misting out and sliding under his door.

"What the hell do you think you're doing breaking into my house like that, Logan? Alex is still at large. My sister was almost killed today."

Logan handed him the bloody knife, then squatted down to pet Maggie, who ran up to him, wagging her tail, as soon as her doggie senses picked up who it was. "I heard. That's why I'm here. Polina suggested you'd be at the hospital and I should feed Maggie dinner. I knocked first. When you didn't answer and your car wasn't in the driveway, I assumed you weren't here."

Silas strode into the kitchen to ditch the knife in the sink, then grabbed a towel and returned to clean up the blood. "I park in a different place every night. If someone's watching the house, I don't want them to be able to establish a pattern."

"Oh." Logan frowned. "That's a hell of a way to live."

"Yeah." Silas stood and walked the towel to the small laundry room behind the kitchen. "Actually, I was just about to swing by Valentine's for some dinner before heading back to work. Stakeout. I think I have a lead on Alex." Silas rested his hands on his hips.

"Did Soleil's list finally pan out?"

"Maybe. We'll know tonight."

"I talked to Polina. Alex's amulet is blocking her from seeing his future. But she thinks she can do a locator spell if you have something of his. Something he's touched recently. The more important to him, the better."

"Should be easy enough. Alex lent me his shampoo yesterday, and tonight we're reading to each other from our diaries."

"Cynicism is a sign of an addled mind."

"It's not that I don't appreciate your offer, and believe me, if I come across something of his, you'll be the first to know. It's just the guy is a fucking ghost. I'd like to think I'm an above-average detective. I've done the footwork. I keep coming up empty-handed. Last night I had him. He was right in front of me—"

"You saw him? Where?"

"In the country, off Route 9. He was digging up bones at a crime scene. I shot him, but he dematerialized. I have a lead though. A healer."

Logan leaned a shoulder against the kitchen door-frame, his jaw hardening and his gaze drifting toward the floor. "The list of healers you're working off, it came from Soleil and the bordello?"

Silas shrugged. "Yeah."

"Hmm."

"What are you trying to say?"

Logan scratched behind his ear. "I saw her with someone."

Silas crossed his arms over his chest, a weighty silence making his kitchen feel small and stuffy. He forced himself to shrug. "We're not a couple anymore. It's none of my business."

"It is if the guy she was with might influence the accuracy of the information she's giving you."

"Who was it?"

"I don't know who. I didn't get a good look at his face. But I do know what. He was a demon, Silas. I could smell him across the restaurant. Soleil came into Valentine's for lunch with a demon, and they were mighty cozy."

"Just because she's dating a demon doesn't mean she's misleading me about Alex. This latest lead seems to be panning out."

"You're right. It doesn't. But I thought you should know."

Silas turned toward the window, letting his eyes drift with his thoughts. "She was never fully monogamous, not even when we were together."

"No. She wasn't."

"I need to let it go. I need to let her go."

"But you don't want to." Logan frowned. "You told me you wanted to marry her."

"I did, once. I think I'm over it."

"I'm sorry, man. That's some tough stuff."

If his friend only knew the half of it. How much he'd thought about her when they'd first split. The extent of his sleeplessness. How the very idea that she was with another guy had made his skin crawl. Sure, he'd known she ran a bordello when he met her, but she didn't see patrons. He'd thought he could change her. He'd thought he could be enough for her to leave the lifestyle. Only she didn't want to leave and had no interest in commitment.

At any rate, he was over it now. He wasn't sure what had changed exactly, or when, but life was too short to dwell on a failed relationship. It was long past time to move on. "I'll finish investigating her list. If I come up empty, I'll entertain the idea that she's not a reliable source."

"And then you'll work with Polina?"

"I still won't have anything of Alex's to use to find him, but yeah, I'll pursue other options." Silas rubbed his eyes, suddenly feeling exhausted. "Hey, speaking of Polina, considering what happened today to Laina, do you think she could refresh the protective wards around this place? Gerty and Grateful are busy with Four Paws and Rivergate."

Logan nodded. "Yeah. I'll ask her tonight." Without warning, he pulled Silas into a one-armed hug. "We're going to catch him, Silas. You're not alone in this."

"Yeah." People kept telling him that, but no one else would be heading to Copper Herald's tonight.

"I should be going." Logan glanced at the darkening window. "Almost time for Polina and me to get to work slaying the bad guys. Stay safe, my friend."

As he watched Logan dematerialize from his kitchen, Silas desperately hoped that he would *not* be safe tonight. He hoped he'd come face-to-face with Alex. And there was nothing safe about that.

SIX

Every stakeout was a game of hide-and-seek. The goal was to be close enough to see without being seen, to hear without being heard. Tonight Silas had picked out a Ford Transit in prisoner-of-suburbia blue from the department's fleet of unmarked cars. He parked on the street outside Starbucks and moved into the windowless back, relying on surveillance equipment connected to his laptop for a visual. The tiny but high-powered microphone and camera were expertly hidden in the grill of the van. Donning his headphones, he leaned back and adjusted the camera to zoom in on Copper Herald Health & Wellness.

A sudden knock on the passenger's side door made him jump. He whipped his headphones off and drew his gun, training it on the door.

"Silas!" came a loud, female whisper. "Let me in."

Rolling his eyes toward the roof of the van, Silas

cursed. "By the goddess." He leaned across the seat and unlocked the door for Meredith.

"I brought coffee and blueberry scones." She ducked inside, pulling the door shut behind her and locking it. "I prefer maple walnut, but the blueberry is healthier because of the fruit." She climbed into the back and plunked down on the seat beside him. "I'm trying to eat healthier, you know, because I drink like six cups of coffee a day. And it's not only the caffeine but the cream and sugar. Plus, oh my goddess, I do not *ever* want to see a healer again, I'll tell you that."

"What the hell are you doing here?" Fuck. There went his wolf again. He gave his head a hard shake. Not gonna happen.

"Waiting for Alex." She looked at him in confusion. "The stakeout. Staking. Out. Copper Herald. The muddy boots? Alex?"

"I don't need your help tonight, Meredith. Honestly, you'll just be in the way." Definitely a distraction he didn't need tonight.

"You think you're on your own in this because it's personal for you. Alex Bloodright killed your parents and came very close to taking your life. But he killed other members of the Lycanthropic Society too, almost wiped out an entire pack in fact." Meredith leaned forward to remove her leather blazer and started unbuttoning her blouse. "I need to show you something."

A rush of blood flowed due south in Silas's anatomy, and he shifted uneasily in his seat, his inner wolf pacing and whimpering as his attention hyperfocused on the skin quickly being revealed. His mouth went dry and his tongue felt thick as he said, "Stop, Meredith. What are you doing?"

"Relax, this isn't what you think."

He tried not to be disappointed at that revelation. She pulled the neck of her blouse aside. A tattoo of a crescent moon with a five-pointed star in its hollow was in residence on her right shoulder.

"Crescent Moon Pack?" He'd known she was half werewolf but considering she didn't shift with the moon, he figured she'd eschewed pack membership.

"My father was a werewolf. I shift into a fox. When a madman murders three-quarters of your pack, shifting at all is enough to bring you into the ranks. I'm a beta for the pack."

"I'm sorry. I didn't know."

"How could you? I don't have to shift if I don't want to. I don't use Rivergate, and we barely have representation on the council anymore. There's too few of us."

"So this is personal for you too."

"More than you know."

"Why didn't you say anything before?"

She sighed. "When I came to the department, I knew who you were and that you were hunting Alex. I wanted to be part of it. I was afraid if I told you too much, you'd shut me out. Manahan stressed that he hired me to be emotionally uninvolved." She played with the plastic tab on the lid of her coffee. "And then last night, I didn't recognize Alex. I only saw a glimpse before you pushed me down, and I've never seen him in real life."

"He changes his appearance slightly on a regular basis."

"Anyway, I didn't mention it then because I was in shock, and then in the hospital it didn't seem like the right time to bring it up. But you need to understand: I want him dead as much as you do." She buttoned her blouse. "Alex murdered my father."

"Turner. Your father was Grayson Turner. Second-in-command."

"First to die."

A sharp breath whistled through his teeth. "And your mother?"

"Shifted into an eagle and flew away. She survived. Physically anyway. It's been a long time since I've seen her smile. She never forgave herself for leaving my father behind." A ghost passed behind Meredith's pupils—a fleeting shadow of pain temporarily escaping from a well-guarded cage. But it was enough for Silas to recognize its face. That pain had taken up residence in his heart when Alex murdered *his* parents. It was a fire that could only be extinguished by blood, Alex's blood. "I was away when it happened. Working on a case in Merrimack."

Silas stared at her as if seeing her for the first time. "How long have you been a detective?"

"Ten years. Before that I did active duty for six. "

"No shit?"

Maybe she did belong here. She carried the kind of grief Silas had been dealing with for years. And like him, she'd risen above it and was doing something about it.

He could respect that, and maybe Laina and Kyle were right about things going faster if he accepted help. As for his wolf's interest in her, he was strong enough to keep the beast in check if it meant stopping Alex.

Abruptly, he shoved his laptop onto her knees and tossed the headphones at her. Reaching across her body, he grabbed a coffee and blueberry scone then nodded toward the equipment. "Get to work. You don't want to miss our big break."

SEVEN

"Silas! Goddess, Silas, I think it's him." Meredith pressed the headphones to her ears and squinted at the screen. Fuck, it was almost midnight. A man she thought was about Alex's size, dressed in jeans, athletic shoes, and a dark hoodie, looked both ways before entering the Copper Herald stairwell. Was that him? She needed Silas to confirm.

He must have dozed off.

Meredith shook his shoulder. "Silas!"

He shifted in his seat and blinked at the laptop screen. But if it had been Alex, he was already upstairs.

"I didn't see his face, but his movements were what I remembered," she said.

"Let's go." Silas unsnapped the thin strap that secured his gun inside his shoulder holster and shrugged into a Boston Red Sox jacket. Weapon concealed but with easy access. Smart.

"I loaded silver bullets," she said, adjusting her gun

at the small of her back. It was common knowledge that silver caused the most injury in werewolves, wood in vampires, and iron in anything fae. She had a little of everything in her bag, but she planned to travel light.

"Even silver won't kill him. Not while he's wearing the amulet. But it'll slow him down." Silas cracked his neck. "That's what I have loaded."

Meredith quietly slid the door open and climbed out of the van, tossing on her leather blazer to completely conceal her weapon. With a nod of her head, she confirmed she was ready. Silas led the way toward Copper Herald's. This time she allowed him to go up the stairs first, ready to back him up, her hand on her gun.

The door to the Health & Wellness facility was partially open. Suspicious. A shiver traveled the length of her spine. She drew her gun.

Silas gently pushed the door and slid in sideways through the opening. The office was dark, vacant. The door to the small bedroom was also cracked, a light on inside.

Every hair follicle on Meredith's body tingled with her unease. "Silas...," she whispered.

A dark shadow interrupted the steady glow from within.

Silas burst forward, kicking open the door. "Stop!" He chased the man in the dark hoodie through the window, down the fire escape, and into the alley. Was it Alex? The man was Alex's height and weight and too fast to be human. But she couldn't see his face, and he wasn't using the amulet.

Meredith sprinted after them, crawling through the window and throwing her legs over the side of the fire escape rather than bothering with the stairs. She landed easily on the balls of her feet and chased Silas and the hooded man around the next corner.

"He went inside ZeroHour," Silas said, heading for a packed nightclub. The music inside thumped in Meredith's ears.

Damn. Humans. Just what they needed. She pulled her jacket tighter around herself and slipped inside, following Silas. The shoulder-to-shoulder crowd pulsated on the dance floor, the scent of humans burning in her nostrils and the volume of the music rendering her deaf.

A flash of black hoodie in the crowd drew her forward, and she nudged her way into the throng. Meredith swept past Silas, her smaller body weaving between the dancers faster. Among the gyrating bodies, she homed in on her target, her fox senses tracking him to the back of the club.

"Hey!" a girl yelled as Meredith shoved her aside.

There was no time for apologies. She chased the hooded man up a set of stairs and into a private room near the back of the club. By the design of this building, there wasn't a way out aside from the way in—no windows. Which meant either Alex was stupid or this was a trap. And she knew for a fact Alex wasn't stupid.

But Meredith forged ahead, suppressing her fears as she ducked inside and drew her weapon. "Hold it right there!" she yelled.

She heard Silas enter the room behind her, saw his weapon in her peripheral vision.

"Finally, someplace we can talk." The voice wasn't Alex's.

The lights came on, and the man pushed the hood from his shaved head. A vampire. Without a doubt. His fangs were fully extended, and his eyes were red-rimmed with the need for blood. There was a large tattoo of an ankh on the side of his neck.

"Who are you?" Silas asked.

The man raised his hands, palms out. He was unarmed. Of course, with superhuman speed and razor-sharp teeth, he was absolutely lethal anyway. The bite of a shifted werewolf was deadly to vamps, but any other time of the month, vampires were stronger and faster. Meredith's finger twitched on the trigger.

"I have a message for you from Alex," the vamp said to Silas, ignoring her.

"Where is Alex?" Silas asked.

"Alex warns you to stop looking for him. Laina was only the beginning. If you don't stop, everyone you love will die a slow and painful death."

"Where is he? Who's helping him?" Silas took a step forward, aiming at the vamp's head.

The vampire shivered violently. "Everyone helps him," he mumbled. "We have to. All of us." He took a step back, avoiding one of the cocktail tables. There was nowhere for him to go. No way out but the door he came in through.

"Who, vampires? Why? Why are you helping him?"

"Just stay away from him or Laina dies and Jason is next." The vamp reached inside the zipper of his hoodie.

"Hands in the air!" Meredith yelled.

But the threat went unheeded. The vamp pulled a stake from inside his sweatshirt and thrust it into his own heart. Meredith's gun discharged, although she hadn't consciously pulled the trigger. The bullet passed through the vampire's stake-holding hand, but it was too late.

The stake retracted into the vamp's chest cavity, his body shaking around it, vibrating harder and faster until one arm and then the other dropped and shattered on the floor. The vamp's legs followed, crumbling to dust and causing the head and torso to collapse. A shower of sparks sprayed forth as the remaining pieces of the vampire decomposed into ash right in front of her.

She stepped forward, her gun still trained on the pile of soot even though not a single bone remained. She kicked the gray dust with the toe of her boot.

"Fucking bastard. Some guys would rather implode than tell the honest truth." Meredith groaned. "Can the dragon fae amulet control minds?"

"Not that I know of. And this wasn't just any mind. Vampire minds are far more resistant to fae magic than human ones."

"You saw that symbol on his neck, right? You think that's some kind of spell marker or sigil? Maybe there's more than fae magic involved."

"I don't know. But I'm sure of one thing," Silas said.

"Yeah?"

"We're getting closer. Alex wouldn't have sacrificed one of his pawns to warn me off"—Silas pointed at the mound of dust—"unless he felt threatened. Which confirms what we suspected before—he's vulnerable and we're close."

Silas could barely keep his eyes open. By the time he'd confirmed, with Meredith's help, that the small bedroom at Copper Herald's had been completely cleaned out while they were chasing the vampire, a soul-sapping exhaustion had settled over him. Alex *had* been staying there. The vampire was a decoy. And now both were gone.

The hollow gong of defeat accompanied him through his front door. Even the wag of Maggie's stubby tail didn't serve to lighten his mood. He locked up and flopped onto his bed, fully clothed. What if he wasn't strong enough to catch Alex? Or cunning enough? The pack was counting on their alpha. Worse, Laina might pay for his ineptitude with her life.

He closed his eyes and groaned. He could use a drink, but he was old enough to know that this type of self-loathing didn't mix well with alcohol. He wasn't above drowning his sorrows, but he understood when he was flirting with dependence. He had no intention of going down that road. Too many people were counting on him. Or maybe he was too tired to lift a bottle even if he had one. He closed his eyes and let himself slip away.

Too soon, bright sunlight filtered through the cracks beneath his lids and warmed his face. Morning already? He rubbed his eyes and opened them slowly. The light was blinding, his view of the room coming together from the edges as his vision adjusted. And then she was there. Soleil, blinking at him from the center of the glow, her hair down in loose waves around her golden shoulders.

"I'm sorry to wake you," she said softly. "I heard about Laina and needed to see for myself that you were okay."

He pushed himself up on an elbow, shading his eyes with one cupped hand.

Her light dimmed. "Better?"

"Better." He hadn't told Soleil a thing about the case in days. He still trusted her, but after what Logan had said about her date with a demon, he'd decided to be careful. She might be benevolent, but the wrong secret passed between her and one of her lovers could ruin him.

"How is she?"

"Still in a coma. It was Alex. For sure. He's threatening me because I'm getting close."

She covered her mouth with her hand. "Will she be all right?"

"I don't know. Grateful is working on a spell to counteract the dark magic she was infected with when he stabbed her."

"Goddess help her."

He nodded. "What else is going on here, Soleil?"

"What do you mean?"

"You hear my sister was hospitalized, and instead of

calling, you come over on a whim. It's been a long time since we had the type of relationship where you could just pop over in the middle of the night."

"Morning. It's almost six."

"You haven't let yourself in since we were seeing each other," Silas said more firmly. "It's been over a year."

"You haven't changed the locks."

"I didn't think I needed to. Why are you here?"

She'd been sitting on the side of his bed, one leg curled under her, but now she rose up onto her knee and crawled toward him like something out of an erotic dream. Her short white summer dress lifted on her thighs. "I miss you, Silas. I wanted to see you." Her warm hand came to rest on his forearm. "Don't you miss me?"

He'd always been fascinated by her fingers. She had tiny, delicate hands with long, tapered fingers that ended in perfectly manicured nails. Everything about Soleil was decidedly feminine. Soft. Warm. Sensual. The delicate oval of her face and the angle of her nose reminded him of a Botticelli painting. As she played with the thick, dark hair on his arm, he remembered what it was like to touch her, to make her purr until light poured out of her skin.

But his wolf recoiled. She wasn't what he hungered for. Not anymore. An image of red hair and brown eyes flashed through his brain. He pushed the unwelcome thought aside.

"I think you should go," he said.

"Is this about the monogamy?" Her features contorted painfully, the corners of her mouth tugging downward. "You know I can't. It's not in my nature."

He scowled. "What is that even supposed to mean?"

"Wolves mate for life. But many planets revolve around a sun."

"So you're a slave to your nature?" he said cynically. "Give me a break."

She moved closer, the heat she was putting off raising the temperature in the room. "I am what I am, Silas. You knew I was a madam the day you met me. Why do you want to change me?" She leaned toward him on the bed. "Darling, don't you think we've played this game long enough? Can't we take things back to how they used to be?"

She'd taste like a fresh-picked peach, and she never said no. He could have her ten different ways a night if he let himself. And maybe he could. Maybe he could lose himself in her buttery flesh one more time.

Only, he wasn't interested. He respected her. He cared for her, but anything more than that was long over.

He met her intense blue stare. "I didn't want to change you, Soleil. I wanted you to want to change. I wanted you to want something better for yourself. Something real and permanent. To have a family. Be loved... not just fucked." He was careful to use the past tense. At this point, this was ancient history.

She scrambled off the bed as if he'd insulted her deeply. "Is that what our relationship was to you? Fucking?"

He tossed back the comforter, bounded from the bed, and pointed a finger at her chest. "No Soleil. That's my point. We were *always* more than sex. And we couldn't go back because for me, going back meant there was no way forward." He shook his head. "Fuck. Why are we even having this conversation?"

"Because I don't want you to give up on us," she whispered.

He lowered his gaze to the floor. "Us? There is no us. Besides, I heard you're seeing someone else."

"It would be inappropriate for me to discuss."

"Why?"

"Would you like to think I spoke about you with him?"

"I'd like to think you wouldn't let yourself into my house and tell me not to give up on us if you were seeing someone else."

Her gaze flicked toward the door. It was a long time before she spoke again. Or maybe it was only seconds, but those seconds felt long, like time was giving them the benefit of the doubt. Something was supposed to be said. The universe wanted closure.

"I should get back to work," she said.

"Yeah. Me too. Alex is still out there."

"Is there anything else I can do to help?"

He narrowed his eyes for a moment. "Do you know of anything that can be used to control vampires? Like control their minds?"

"Only a sire bond."

"No, I mean for someone who is not a vampire to control a vampire."

She shook her head. "No. Why?"

"Just curious. Something I heard. Don't worry about it."

She smiled and drifted toward the door.

"Goodbye, Soleil."

She gave one last beaming smile as she slipped out the front door. "Don't say goodbye, Silas. It sounds too final."

Goodbye did sound final, but the three-ton weight on his chest told him that was exactly what this was. He watched her slip into the early-morning light and wasn't sorry to see her go.

He needed to call Logan. It was time to change the locks.

EIGHT

Every once in a while, Silas wondered if he'd chosen the right profession. Usually those thoughts occurred when he was doing desk work, like now, leaning over a massive tome titled *Dr. Mortimer's Potent Spells and Balms*. He had skimmed the ancient text for the better part of three hours and had yet to find a single potion that could make a vampire stab himself in the heart.

"Knock, knock." Grateful Knight poked her head into his office, looking like she'd fought through a crowd of angry cannibals to reach him. Her honey-blond hair was tied up in a messy bun that was messier than usual, and the skin under her eyes was a spectrum of purple hues.

"You look like hell," he said.

"Thanks," she said dryly. Her hand rubbed the top of her pregnant belly rhythmically. "Lucas won't stay in his crib anymore. And he never sleeps. Ever. And the diapers.

Oh gawd, the diapers. And I am so ready to pop this kid out. What's your excuse?"

"I was up late last night." He told her about the stakeout and the suicidal vampire.

Her eyes widened. "Suicidal vampires are serious business, as is what I came here to discuss with you."

"Do tell."

She pulled a small vial out of her purse, filled to the brim with a black, powdery substance. "This is what I collected from your sister's wound."

"Uh-huh. So what is it?"

"This is a rare mineral. So rare that most humans don't know it exists. It's called sulfralite."

"Sulfralite? So where'd it come from?"

"I couldn't figure it out. But Rick remembered the smell. Sulfralite is only found in one place—a place none of us ever want to go. The underworld."

"My sister was injected with a mineral from hell?"

Grateful nodded. "My hellmouth—the cemetery behind my house, the place I send supernatural criminals who break the natural law—opens at night. It's why Rick and I have to police the gate. All manner of supernatural baddies emerge from the underworld after sunset. And they sometimes smell like this."

"Do you think something escaped? Maybe a demon?"

"Rick and I weren't aware of any breach from our hellmouth, and we followed up with a few witches in our network. No one is aware of any escapees. However, the Hecate from New Orleans passed on some interesting information on the properties of sulfralite, properties that are leveraged by the vast community of voodoo practitioners in her area. When sulfralite enters your bloodstream, it has a toxic effect on the nervous system. It makes you tired, disoriented, and extremely vulnerable to suggestion. In high doses—"

"It can put you into a coma."

"Exactly. I don't think your sister is unconscious because of the stab wounds. I think the sulfralite in her bloodstream is keeping her from healing. And I believe your vampire may have been infected with the same stuff. It's very possible that Alex is combining the natural properties of sulfralite with the power of the dragon fae amulet to perform some serious mind control on his victims."

"So who did the infecting? You said this stuff is rare. I assume Alex couldn't get it on any street corner."

Grateful shook her head. "The New Orleans witch said there's only one way to get it. You must conjure a demon from the underworld and ask it to bring the element into our world in hand. As you might imagine, that is risky magic and only delivers a limited amount. Ripping open a portal to the underworld dimension requires a blood sacrifice, and the one performing it better be up to the task of controlling what passes into their realm."

Silas's stomach twisted. *She's dating a demon*, Logan had said. He hadn't seen Soleil for weeks and suddenly she shows up in his bedroom. She gives him a list of healers possibly helping Alex, but by some miracle, Alex always seems one step ahead of him. What if the demon was the source of the sulfralite? What if Soleil was under his spell?

"Does sulfralite work on all supernaturals?"

"Only the ones who have remnants of human DNA. Vampires, because they were once human. Werewolves and other shifters who were born human. Witches like me."

"But it wouldn't work on a fae?"

"Fae, sprites, leprechauns. Anything born or created supernatural is immune according to my source."

"Humans?"

"Susceptible, although New Orleans said sulfralite is frequently fatal to humans and therefore has limited applicability. Infected humans are often mistaken for zombies until they kick the bucket."

Silas groaned. Grateful stood and set her hand on his shoulder. "What's going on, Silas? You went green on me. Do I need to get my medical bag?"

"Can you save my sister?" Silas swallowed the lump in his throat. He could think of several reasons Alex might put that shit in Laina's body, and none of them were good.

"I can. There's a spell that will extract sulfralite from the body, but it requires a feather from an angel."

"An actual heavenly angel? Are they real?"

Grateful shrugged. "I've never seen one. Luckily, New Orleans has a feather she's willing to lend me in exchange for a future favor. I'm heading down there tonight. If everything goes as planned, I should be able to heal your sister by the end of the week."

He reached across the desk and squeezed her hand. "Thank you, Grateful. I don't know what I would do without you. You know you can always count on me, don't you? For anything."

"Careful. I may take you up on that, and it will almost certainly involve babysitting."

Silas smiled. "I'll take care of the little guy. How hard could it be?"

Grateful closed her eyes for a moment, then gave a slight shake of her head. "I'll be in touch." She adjusted her yoga pants and smoothed her tunic-style T-shirt on the way out the door. He noted she took the vial of sulfralite with her. Good thing. He didn't want the responsibility of guarding the stuff.

Leaning back in his chair, he thought about what Grateful had said. Sulfralite came from demons. Soleil was dating a demon. Influenced or not, something was up. Tonight he wouldn't scrutinize the next healer on the list. Tonight he'd follow Soleil.

MEREDITH REFUSED TO BE MARGINALIZED. AFTER WHAT happened to her family, she had the same right to take revenge on Alex as Silas did. She'd thought they'd had a breakthrough yesterday when he handed her the surveillance equipment. It seemed like he'd fully accepted her partnership and wanted the help. Only today, Silas had been distant and secretive, avoiding her at every opportunity. She hadn't become a detective by allowing things to go unnoticed. After tailing him all afternoon, her effort paid off when she caught him crossing the parking lot to the unmarked vehicle.

"Hey! I thought you were going home for the night. Don't you think you should take your own car?"

He groaned and tipped his head back, rolling his eyes toward the heavens. "There's something I have to do, Meredith. Alone." Silas refused to meet her gaze.

She planted her fists on her hips. "Because you don't need my help, just like you didn't need me last night when that vampire staked himself? You're cutting me out again, aren't you? I thought we were beyond this!"

He sighed, staring down at his feet. "No, I'm not. You have as much right to revenge on Alex as I do. If you must know, I'm taking the night off from Alex-hunting."

"Then why are you standing next to the Family Truckster?" She tapped the side of her fist against the Ford Transit. "I have to warn you. Every time you drive this thing, your sperm count drops. You're flirting with disaster here."

The corner of Silas's mouth twitched. The guy had perpetual stubble thanks to his werewolf genes, and the effect was annoyingly sexy. She internally slapped herself for noticing.

"I'm following up on a long shot. Trust me, you don't want to get involved."

Meredith crossed her arms over her chest. "Does this have to do with why Grateful Knight came to visit you today?"

Silas squinted. "Were you listening outside the door?"

"A lot of good it did me. She must have used an enchantment. I couldn't hear a thing."

He snorted. *Good one, Grateful.* "This doesn't concern you. It isn't even police business, to be honest."

"Listen, if you're doing something shady to find Alex—"

"It's not shady—"

"Whatever it is, I'm in. This is more important than the law. We've got to try everything." She blocked the door to the Ford with her body. He was *not* going without her.

Silas glanced at his watch, apparently calculating how long it would take to get rid of her against how much time he had to waste. "Okay. Get in."

With a tempered squeal, she danced around the car and jumped into the passenger's seat. Silas climbed behind the wheel and started the engine, wasting no time exiting the lot.

"So... who are we staking out if not Alex?"

"The bordello."

"Maison des Étoilles?"

He hummed in affirmation.

"You're checking up on your ex-girlfriend!"

Knuckles whitening atop the steering wheel, he said, "Additional information came to light that makes me believe my source may have been compromised. Tonight I'm attempting to verify or disprove that theory." He sounded defensive. Why was he defensive?

"Right." Meredith leaned back in her chair and fumbled with the edge of her blazer for a moment. "I could see this coming a mile away. Last night Alex knew we were coming."

Silas groaned. "Yes, Meredith. My ex-girlfriend may have given me tainted info, and yes, I should have suspected it earlier. 'Kay?"

She smiled smugly, then fought the wave of guilt that flooded her. Way to kick him while he was down. Goddess, she could be a pain in the ass.

"Sorry," she said. "That's a tough thing."

Silas leaned an elbow against his window. They drove the rest of the way in silence. He parked around the corner from the bordello and was quick to get out of sight. Meredith followed his lead and climbed into the back.

"How did you meet this chick anyway?"

"I investigated an attempted murder in the alley behind the bordello. Part of the investigation required me to interview the madam. The attraction was... well... stellar." He laughed at his own joke. She did not. "You know, because they're celestial fae."

"Oh, like the source of their power is the planets and stars and such? Mansion of the stars. Huh."

"Right. Soleil draws her power from the sun, so my attraction to her was inevitable."

Meredith's mouth twitched. "Why?"

"When I was with her physically, it was never night. I avoided an entire shift once. All three days."

"You don't like to shift?"

"You do?"

"Hell yeah. I shift every month, and I don't even have to. If I wait too long, I start to feel claustrophobic."

"But the loss of control, the inconvenience of losing yourself, you don't think of that as a curse? I mean, before we perfected the Rivergate boundary, I used to wake up worrying I might have hurt someone."

"You hate who you are, and you love her because she makes you not you. That's understandable, I guess. But surprising. You seem so confident." Meredith crossed her legs at the ankle.

"I don't hate who I am!"

"But you'd change it if you could. You'd give up the night air in your nose and the thrill of running as fast as your four legs will carry you. You'd give up the freedom and the intimacy with your packmates."

Silas thought for a moment. "No. I wouldn't give it up. Not permanently."

"Then what's the draw for you? Is it because she's... you know..." She turned toward him and bobbed her eyebrows lasciviously. "Experienced?"

Silas did a double take. "I am not talking about this with you."

"Truly, why did you love her? You're an alpha werewolf, and she's a prostitute. You could have anyone. Why her?"

Taking a deep breath, Silas parted his lips to answer but ended up sighing heavily. "What does it matter? It's over. A year ago, I asked her to marry me, and she said no. That's all she wrote."

Meredith tucked her chin, her expression morphing from smug and teasing to horrified. "Can you even marry her? Would the pack allow that?"

"It's a moot point, isn't it?" he said harshly. "She said no. And honestly, I think it was for the best."

Meredith grimaced. "I am the world's biggest asshole," she said. "I'm sorry, Silas. I didn't realize it was that serious between you two."

He nodded slowly. "*Was* is the key word in that sentence. I'm glad it didn't work out. The further I get away from it, the more I realize it wasn't meant to be. And yep. You are *the* biggest asshole."

She flipped him the finger. A beacon of light washed over them—light that came from a woman who was descending the steps of the bordello.

"That's her, isn't it?"

"Yes."

"She's beautiful. It's like... It's like..."

"Staring into the sun," Silas murmured.

"Yeah."

A limousine had pulled up to the curb at the end of the walkway. The demon? The door opened without any assistance from the driver or anyone else for that matter. Soleil slipped into the back, and the limo took off. Silas closed the laptop. Behind the wheel again, he tailed the limo, careful to keep his distance.

"I had a boyfriend like that once," Meredith said.

"You had a boyfriend who glowed in the dark?"

She snorted. "No. He wasn't fae or anything. Just a shifter. But he had this sort of charisma. Like, you looked at him and everything just seemed easier. It was like you weren't in reality anymore but in a movie where every-thing was scripted, and you knew things would turn out all right because this guy... this intensely attractive guy... loved *you*."

"So what went wrong?" Silas asked.

"Oh, he was as dumb as a box of rocks. Accidentally lit himself on fire."

Silas raised an eyebrow at her.

"Okay, I set him on fire."

"You set—"

"I set myself on fire."

Silas curled his upper lip.

"Figuratively. He broke up with me for someone pret-tier and more agreeable. I imploded."

"But no one actually burned?"

"It was a metaphor for my emotional pain. No. No one was burned in this story." She rested her forehead against the window. *Why couldn't she keep her mouth shut?*

The limo turned in to the circle drive of a brownstone deep within the vampire district.

"There's no sign," she said. A wooden panel swung from a hook over the door, displaying a symbol of three overlapping red triangles. "Oh wait. There's a symbol. What does that mean?"

Silas didn't answer. Soleil and a man in a dark suit exited the limo and were ushered inside the stone building by three security guards. Meredith strained to see the man's face, but it was hidden by shadows that clung to him despite Soleil glowing on his arm.

"We'll have to go inside." Silas unbuckled his seat belt.

"What is this place?" Meredith asked, squinting at the building. The historical architecture was stunning. Had to be a hundred years old.

"I have no idea." He climbed from the van and straightened his clothes.

She followed his lead, hooking her arm into his as they rounded the corner together on foot. Silas glanced down at her hand around his elbow.

"To look the part."

He nodded once.

A man in a black suit stopped them at the door. "Observing or participating?"

A chill coursed through Meredith. She still wasn't sure what this place was, but with options like that, she could guess. "Observing," she said quickly.

Silas flashed her a completely confused look.

"That'll be fifty," the man said. "Strict confidentiality is enforced. No pictures or recording devices of any kind. There's a spell on the place, so don't even try it."

While Meredith accepted two red wristbands from the man, Silas pulled out his wallet and handed over the cash. Her heart sank. He had no idea what he was in for. She took him by the elbow and led him inside.

"You may not want to see this," she whispered in his ear.

The dark paneled walls and dim lighting reminded her of a reception hall or maybe a funeral parlor. It had the quality of an ancient castle or the type of old building you would find on Ivy League campuses. High end. Above the fray. Classical music played in the background. Several other guests strode past them in suits and gowns, seeming to know exactly where they were going.

"Do you know what this place is?"

"No. What is it?" he asked. By his expression, he didn't have a clue. "We're underdressed, that's for sure."

They came to two doors. Most of the guests filtered through the one with a red X carved into the wood. But Meredith tugged him in the opposite direction, to one labeled with a carving of an eye. As she opened the door, an elderly man behind them chuckled and whispered to the woman next to him.

She flashed a little fang and adjusted her fur stole. "Enjoy the show," she crooned.

Meredith nodded dumbly and ushered Silas up a flight of narrow steps and into a dark room. "Thank the goddess, we're the only ones up here."

"Why? What the hell is this place? Why would Soleil come here with that guy?" Silas glanced around the room, taking in the red velvet seats, the floor-to-ceiling observation windows.

"I wasn't sure at first. I've never actually been to one, but you hear things as a woman." She pointed to the windows. One-way glass like the kind they had in the interrogation room at the station. She could see out, but the people on the other side would only see a mirror.

Silas shuffled to her side, looking stiff. They peered down into a circular room with a narrow padded bench at its center and multiple racks of instruments: floggers, canes, chains, and cuffs.

"It looks like a torture chamber."

Meredith sighed. "Not torture. Sex."

Silas whirled to look at her.

"And blood," she said. "This is a fetish club. A vampire fetish club."

She'd never seen the warmth drain from someone's eyes so quickly. The deep green went stone cold. He stared at Meredith for a beat, all levity vacating his features, then turned back to the room.

Soleil was there now, at the center of it all. She wore a silvery white mask, but there was no disguising her glow. A dozen or so couples fanned out, taking seats on the bench that lined the periphery of the room. They'd donned masks of all shapes and sizes. Black, all black, aside from Soleil's. When the crowd had settled in, a man entered the room and approached Soleil, wearing a mask of red silk. He took her hand. The demon, Meredith presumed.

"We don't have to stay," Meredith whispered. "She's a prostitute, Silas. She's working."

Silas seemed to hear her, but he didn't look away from the scene below. He'd gone still as a statue. Meredith thought he looked vacant, impassive. She wondered what he must be thinking. Soleil was his ex, but he'd cared for her once.

The demon kissed Soleil on the mouth in a greedy, violent way that made Meredith's stomach turn. His barbed tail wagged behind him like he was a dog with a bone. This was not going to be pretty.

The demon pulled the tie on Soleil's wrap dress and slipped it from her body. The woman was stunning. Meredith had to stop herself from going down the rabbit hole of self-deprecation. Soleil's body was perfect—long, lean, with the straight spine of a ballerina. Every inch of her golden skin was flawless. There wasn't a wrinkle, freckle, or mole anywhere on the woman. Well, that was that, she thought. She had no chance with Silas. What man would want her after having that?

Meredith shifted uneasily. *Of course*, she had no future with Silas. He was her partner. She had no business even considering the possibility of a romantic relationship. She shook her head and forced herself to watch the train wreck below.

Now completely nude aside from stilettos and stockings, Soleil allowed the demon to lead her to the padded bench. He spun her around violently and shoved her between the shoulder blades.

"Yes, sir," Soleil said, although Meredith had to read her lips; she couldn't hear through the thick pane of glass.

Soleil's abdomen slapped the brown leather, her breasts dangling on the opposite side from her feet. Methodically, the demon bound her wrists behind her back with a red silk rope. He tapped the inside of her stilettos. Soleil smiled as she spread her feet, giving the room a clear view of everything between her legs.

The vampires in the room dropped fang. Other

guests, young and old, began touching each other, shedding clothes and locking lips.

Meredith touched Silas's arm. "Silas, what else do you hope to see? This isn't healthy. We should go."

Silas didn't respond. He stared absently through the glass, a look of disgust on his face.

The demon dragged a pointed nail down Soleil's spine, leaving a red trail behind. When he reached her tailbone, his hand drew back and connected with her backside in a slap that Meredith could hear through the glass. Soleil arched slightly from the pain, tugging against her restraints, but if it was painful, Meredith couldn't tell from her expression. She was smiling, a sultry, heated grin. Her lips formed the word *more*.

With a wicked smirk, the demon selected a flogger from the wall to his left. That seemed to excite the crowd. A vampire at the back of the room sat on one of the benches and pulled his middle-aged human escort onto his lap. The human's lips parted as he entered her, and the vampire ran one fang along her throat. He continued to watch the show over the human's shoulder.

As the demon whipped Soleil, her nipples extended and she arched with pleasure. Until, with his last thrash, he broke her skin. A bead of sunlight dripped from her flesh. The vampires in the room cringed. But the demon rubbed the light away and licked it off his thumb. He tossed the flogger aside.

One of the vampires sank his teeth into his human escort, spraying blood across Soleil's back. The demon was far from disturbed. He untied the belt of his robe and allowed it to fall open. As he entered Soleil from behind, more red droplets sprayed across his chest. Blood and sex filled the room. Couples joined other couples. Vampires fed on multiple hosts. The entire room became an orgy of pleasure and pain. Only Soleil and the demon remained exclusively with each other, showered in the blood of the surrounding guests.

"Silas, please." Tears had formed in Meredith's eyes, spilling over and trailing down her cheeks. It was all too much. She didn't want to be here anymore. She shook him by the elbow, hard.

He turned then, blinking his eyes like he'd just woken up. He lifted his hand, touched her face, and stared at the tears on his fingertips like he didn't know how they got there.

"I can't take it anymore," she said. "This is not my thing." Although she held no judgment against the consenting adults in the room below, there was too much pain here for her taste. Too many head games.

He nodded, then gestured toward the staircase. The air felt dense as they exited the building, the men in black at the entrance giving them a strange look. Silas tugged at his collar. Meredith took a full, deep breath, the cool night air flowing into her lungs, bolstering her. She wiped the tears from her face.

Wrapping one arm around her waist, Silas tugged her to his side. "I'm sorry." When she didn't respond, he hooked a finger under her chin and made her look at him. "Meredith, I'm sorry." He wiped away her tears with his thumbs.

She nodded. They climbed into the van. For several minutes, they sat beside each other, staring out the windshield without making a sound.

"Hey, you want to get a drink?" Meredith finally asked.

Silas answered immediately. "Yeah. I know a place."

"It didn't seem real at first." Silas sipped his vodka and tonic within the confines of a booth in the bar area at Valentine's. "I'm not a prude, Meredith, but I've never seen anything like that. You hear about things, you know, doing the work we do. You interview people. You know it happens. But there's a difference between knowing and seeing."

"I know what you mean. I thought I could handle it… until…"

Silas lifted a brow. "Until?"

"Until I thought about what it must be doing to you. It's obvious you cared for her. If I'd seen someone I loved, even in the past tense, doing something like that, it would be like enduring open-heart surgery without anesthesia."

He snorted. "Maybe. But not for the reasons you might think." He finished his drink and motioned to the bartender for another. "You want another wine?"

"No, I'm okay."

He held up a finger. "I thought about stopping it."

"They would have killed you. The place was full of vampires and demons. If you survived, it would have been a bloodbath."

"Part of me wanted to believe she'd been drugged. Part of me felt responsible for defending her."

Meredith swallowed hard and whispered, "She looked like an eager participant to me."

"Yeah. I eventually came to that conclusion too." Silas scrubbed his face with his hand, a shiver running through him. "Laina says I clean the pepper out of the salt shaker."

"What does that mean?"

"Long story."

"So I take it, it wasn't like that with her before?" Meredith's eyebrow quirked.

"Hmm? No. Not with me. I'm a simple guy. I like to keep things simple. Too many people and devices just complicate everything. Why do people need that stuff? Keep it simple, that's what I always say." The tip of his nose had started to tingle, and he had the distinct impression that he was oversharing. *Fuck.* He was drunk. "Sorry. I mean no offense if you're into that sorta thing. Whatever floats your boat." He gave a deep chuckle.

She laughed. Goddess, she had a cool laugh. It made you want to laugh along with her. "Uh, no. Not my cup of tea. When it comes to sex, I'm more about what's happening up here." She pointed at her head.

"Your mouth?" Silas whispered. Yep, he was drunk. Definitely drunk.

"No, my brain." There was that laugh again. "How many of those have you had?"

"I just think it shouldn't be that complicated, you know?"

"You're a werewolf. You're a creature of habit, of instinct. You want a permanent bond to raise young. It's in your nature. What we saw tonight was not it."

He nodded, pointing his pinky finger at her as he gripped his now-empty glass. "You get me."

The bartender plunked another drink down on the table and took his empty. "Danke schoen." Silas raised the glass in thanks to the bartender and took another sip, knowing damn well he should quit for the night.

Meredith took a microscopic sip of her wine. "When I was dating Dave, I thought he was the one. I pictured us living in the suburbs with our 2.5 kids. Turns out he pictured it too, but not with me. He married the girl he cheated on me with. They're expecting their first young in October. So as bad as today was, at least you know she wanted something different. It wasn't that she rejected you like Dave rejected me. She rejected the future you wanted with her."

"Is that better or worse?"

She shrugged. "Now that I think about it, I'm not sure. Sorry."

A shadow passed over their table. Logan. "Hey, buddy. What's going on? Dustin tells me you've been drinking the well dry."

"He's had a rough night," Meredith said. "I'm Meredith, Silas's new partner." She shook Logan's hand.

"Shee'sssss *not* my partner," Silas said. Okay, now he could hear it. He was definitely inebriated.

"Nice to meet you," Logan said, ignoring Silas's protest. "I'm Logan. Are you okay getting home on your own?" he asked Meredith, "because I'm going to take this guy's keys and set him up in my office for a long nap."

"Gotta get home and feed Maggie," Silas blurted. He was suddenly very tired.

Meredith's lips twitched like she was suppressing a good laugh. "Actually, we came here together," she said to Logan. "I'll drop him off at home. I'm good to drive." She pointed at the single glass of wine she'd been nursing the entire night. It was still half-full.

"Good enough for me." Logan grinned like he found the entire situation amusing. He reached for Silas's keys and handed them to Meredith.

Silas grabbed his best friend's wrist. "I've decided to take you up on your offer. You were right about that situation we discussed."

"Okay," Logan said. "We can talk about it tomorrow."

Silas squeezed. "The Soleil situation. She's been playing me. Playing me like a harp the entire time."

Grinning from ear to ear, Logan took him by the shoulders and shook gently. "I'll help you. We will figure this out. But right now I need you to go with Meredith. You need to lie down."

"Ooookay." Silas allowed Meredith to help him from

the booth, losing the murmured conversation between her and Logan.

She was a beautiful woman, Meredith. Her hard-ass attitude made her seem uptight, but now, as she buckled his seat belt around him, he realized how soft her hair looked, how the square jaw and athletic build gave her a strong but feminine mystique. She wasn't a girly girl. No makeup. No jewelry. A practical dresser, for sure. But there was something about her. She was funny and smart. Smart-mouthed. He loved her mouth.

"You gonna make it?" she asked, finally succeeding in clicking the seat belt at his hip. "You look a little—"

He leaned over and spewed out the open door. In his defense, he tried his best to miss her shoes.

TEN

Elven brain torture. The slicing pain that ran from Silas's right eye through the back of his head must have had a supernatural cause because it was sheer torment. His mouth tasted like he'd eaten his own dirty socks, and his stomach... He didn't want to think about his stomach.

He raised his hand to rub his aching temple and blinked his eyes. He was in bed, in his bedroom. A warm body shifted next to him. He looked over to find Maggie curled into his side.

"Hey, girl." He scratched her behind the ears.

The canine licked his hand and nuzzled his palm. He noticed she was lying directly on the sheets. That was odd. The comforter was pulled back as if someone had gotten out on the opposite side of the bed. Silas frowned. What had happened last night?

He glanced down at himself, lifted the covers. Naked. Naked as the day he was born. He closed his eyes. He remembered Meredith buckling him into the seat of the unmarked van. He'd gotten sick all over the parking lot. What happened after he threw up?

Nothing. He couldn't remember a thing.

What time was it? He turned his head to check his alarm clock, only to have a glass of water and two pills block his view. Painkillers. He sat up the rest of the way, shoveled the pills into his mouth, and swallowed them with an entire glass of water. It was a nice thing to do, leaving him the pills.

Meredith had driven him home. Had she undressed him? Why? He climbed out of bed and headed for his dresser. His gaze caught on the chair in the corner of his room. Folded neatly on the seat were Meredith's slacks and royal-blue blouse, topped off with her gun like the cherry on the she-got-naked ice cream sundae.

"Fuck me," he whispered. Meredith had spent the night!

He glanced down at his dick, but little Silas wasn't talking. His eyes darted between the bed and her clothes, his fingers digging into his hair. Why couldn't he remember?

Wild squawking traveled through his bedroom window. He spread the blinds with his fingers. A red fox jogged across his large backyard, sending a flock of birds into a tizzy. The fox seemed less than interested in their flight. It moved toward the house, transforming as it neared, one moment animal, the next human. Meredith. Her long red hair gathered in waves around her shoulders, over pert breasts, a long waist, well-muscled thighs.

Meredith was solid muscle, almost like there was something more than flesh under her skin. Bricks maybe. Concrete. Yet she was ultimately feminine with curves that would inspire him to paint if he were the artistic type. Goddess, she was beautiful. He couldn't have had sex with her last night. He would've remembered that body. Holy hell, he would have remembered.

As she neared the house, Silas frantically opened his drawers and threw on a CCPD T-shirt and a pair of black sweats. What was that smell? He breathed into his hand. *Fuck!* He sprinted to the bathroom to freshen up. He was still brushing his teeth when he heard her enter through the back door.

"Hey, Maggie girl," she whispered. There was a thud as the dog leaped down from the bed, then danced across the wood floor. "That's a good girl. Where's Silas?"

The brush of cloth on skin was followed by the clink and rattle of her gun holster. She was dressing. He finished brushing his teeth but waited until the movement quieted before coming out of the bathroom.

"How are you feeling this morning, slugger?" she asked him, grinning like the cat who ate the canary. She was fully dressed, scratching Maggie behind the ears.

Silas sniffed, picking up the scent of the outdoors on Meredith's skin. "Like the south end of a north-facing pig."

"After the night we spent together?" Meredith winked. "You were an animal. It was like an entire circus going on in here. I've never had anyone like you my entire life. You've ruined me for all other men."

He stopped breathing, his jaw going slack. After a moment of staring dumbly in her direction, Silas muttered, "Uh…"

She snorted, then burst into full-out laughter. "Relax. I brought you home and put you to bed. Then I spent the night in the woods in my fox form. I needed to burn off a little energy after what we saw last night."

He let out a relieved breath. "Thank the goddess."

Her face twisted. Fuck, he'd offended her.

"Not that it wouldn't have been great. I mean, I'm sure sleeping with you would be a really fun time." Her face continued to fall. "Not fun like carnival fun, like sexy fun. You are obviously a fun, sexy woman who is probably very good in bed. It wouldn't be a total disaster to sleep with you." He held up a hand. "Although it would be because we work together, but not because of you or your body or anything like that. Not that I'd ever have sex with you sober. I mean, anyone would want to have sex with you. Just not me. Given the circumstances of us working together."

He stopped talking.

"Okay then. No sex. Got it." She nodded her head slowly. "Sooo, I'll bring the van back on my way in, and I'll see you at the station. Oh, and you spewed all over your clothes last night. You probably want to throw those in the wash before they get up and run away to avoid their own smell."

She slung her purse over her shoulder. Silas followed her into the hall where she headed for the door, Maggie trailing behind her. Abruptly, she paused at the entrance to the kitchen and scooped a cup of kibble into Maggie's bowl, rubbing the dog's brown head. "There you go, princess."

Then she fished out her keys before opening the front door.

"Hey, thanks for driving me home."

"You're welcome." She flashed him a wry grin. "Oh, and don't worry, I didn't see anything. Except for your genitals."

The door closed behind her.

Mickey Mouse stared up at Silas from the bottom of his favorite cereal bowl. Technically it was a small mixing bowl. The thing held half a box of Cocoa Krispies, which was necessary when you had a werewolf's metabolism. It was empty now aside from a smear of milk residue. He had no memory of eating the cereal. His mind was too busy replaying Meredith's naked body striding toward his house on an endless loop.

"I am so fucked," he said to Maggie. She panted up at him and wagged her tail.

It wasn't only that Meredith was beautiful. She was also smart, funny, brave as fuck, and compassionate. She was possibly the perfect woman. And he had made her watch his ex-girlfriend fuck a demon and then thrown up on himself. And to top it all off, he'd told her he never wanted to have sex with her.

He leaned back in his kitchen chair and stared at the

ceiling. He should call in sick today. He'd never taken a mental health day before. Maybe it was time.

The piercing ringtone of his phone made him grab his throbbing head. Jason. He tapped the screen. "Are you back in town, bro?"

"Back and already at the hospital with Laina. You better get down here. Grateful is preparing to wake her up."

MEREDITH FILLED HER FOR FOX SAKE COFFEE MUG WITH THE thin, coffee-flavored water the humans drank at the station. Damn. When was Silas getting in? After the night they'd had, he seriously needed to rectify the caffeine situation.

"Yo, Meredith," the captain called from his office. "Can you come in here for a minute?"

"What's up?" She joined him, closing the door behind her for privacy.

He handed her a folder. "I need you to check out a potential shifter disturbance at the city zoo. Seems an extra bear has appeared in the exhibit, and the zookeepers are flipping out. Go make sure the guy finds his way home and tell him to get his jollies with his own kind."

"Sure. Uh, should I take Silas with me?"

"Didn't he tell you? He called in."

She frowned. "Sick?"

"No. Something with his sister. The family is meeting

at the hospital today." The captain's face contorted with sympathy. "Between you and me, I think they're preparing themselves for the worst."

"I've gotta go." She waved the folder. "I'll take care of this."

"Go get 'em, tiger."

She walked out the door, breaking into a run once she was safely out of his sight.

After the welcome-home hugs and small talk, Silas stood at the end of Laina's hospital bed with Jason, Selene, and Kyle by his side. Jason had his arm protectively around Selene, Kyle cradled Laina's hand in both of his, and Silas... he crossed his arms and prayed to the goddess this would be over quickly. Sometimes it was hard being single in a family of doubles.

Grateful waddled into the room a moment later, carrying a large grocery bag from the store in Red Grove where she lived. She locked the door behind her.

"Are you saving my sister with weekly groceries?" Silas looked pointedly at the bag.

She shrugged. "No groceries. It was the right size for what I needed."

"Whatever works," Kyle said. "Thanks for doing this."

"Don't thank me yet. Thank me when your wife recovers." Grateful pulled the stethoscope from her neck and pressed it to Laina's chest.

"Is there a chance it won't work?" Jason asked, exchanging glances with Selene.

"I've never worked with sulfralite before." Grateful returned her stethoscope to her neck and tucked her hands into the pockets of her lab coat, her belly stretching her scrubs underneath. "I promise I'll do everything I can."

A knock came on the door. Everyone froze. Grateful narrowed her eyes. The knock came again. "I'm in the middle of a procedure," she called. "What do you need?"

"It's Meredith. Is Silas in there?"

Grateful raised an eyebrow in Silas's direction. He sighed and crossed the room to open the door. An unexpected swell of warmth filled his chest at Meredith's smile on the other side.

"When you didn't show up at the station, I started to worry. Manahan said you'd be here. I thought you might... need someone." She searched his face. A slight blush colored her cheeks, and didn't that make him feel like the king of the world? She stepped in closer. "What's going on with Laina?"

"Who are you?" Grateful interrupted.

"Meredith." She glanced at the other faces in the room and then at Silas.

He should introduce her. He cleared his throat to speak, but when he opened his mouth, nothing came out.

"I'm Silas's new partner," Meredith said for him.

He didn't correct her. What was the point? "This is a family occasion, Meredith. And it's not safe."

She locked eyes with him, rubbing her palms together in tiny nervous circles. "I just thought you could use some moral support."

Goddess, she was beautiful, and it was kind of her to come. Thoughtful.

"Silas?" Grateful asked.

Inevitably, it came down to him. He should tell her to leave. They hadn't known each other long, and she didn't owe him anything. But when he looked at her, he couldn't find the strength. If she was willing to stay, he needed her. Closing the door, he ushered her deeper into the room and pulled her back against his chest. The full-body contact made his stomach flip and his pulse pound. "Give Grateful room," he whispered in her ear.

She smiled up at him over her shoulder, those warm brown eyes wrinkling at the corners. "Sure. Okay." She didn't pull away.

"You all might want to stand back for this," Grateful said.

Everyone but Kyle took a step away from Laina's bed. When Grateful gave Kyle a questioning look, he shook his head. "If she can survive it, I can too."

With an acquiescent nod, Grateful reached into her bag and retrieved a mass of bones and feathers held together with wooden rings and decorated with rough-hewn stone beads. Silas had never seen anything like it.

"What is that?" Selene asked, shivering in Jason's arms.

Silas felt it too, a cold rush coming off the thing.

"It's a juju—a magical charm. I've jerry-rigged this

one to draw out the substance emitting negative energy in Laina. Angel feathers—that's the key." She placed the juju on Laina's chest, where it rested like a spread hand.

"Angel feathers? Like from an actual angel?" Meredith's eyes popped.

"All we have to do is activate it, and this thing is going to become the world's strongest sulfralite magnet." Reaching behind her head, Grateful retrieved Nightshade from under her lab coat.

The sheath on her back was enchanted to conceal the blade, and Silas enjoyed the feeling of Meredith pressing against him at the sight of its purple glow. Grateful lowered the tip of the sword to the juju, energy writhing off the thing like an awakened serpent.

"Trezitae locul de muncati. Trezitae locul de muncieti."

The energy flowed into the grisly mass on Laina's chest. Silas gasped in time with Meredith as the juju rose up on bony legs, becoming a wicked-looking spider. It scampered across Laina's chest, its faceless head sniffing her torso. The thing stopped near her belly button, the site of one of her stab wounds. It lowered its feathered belly to her skin.

Slowly, almost imperceptibly at first, a faint vibration rattled the bones. The juju glowed pink, then red. Laina's body quivered.

"What's happening to her?" Kyle asked.

Grateful didn't answer.

The shaking grew more violent.

"I don't like this," Kyle protested. "She's seizing."

Before the witch could say anything, Selene doubled over, groaning and holding her stomach.

"What's wrong?" Jason gripped her shoulders.

"It hurts," Selene cried. "Stop it! Someone stop it!"

"Turn it off," Jason yelled to Grateful.

The witch shook her head, her eyes narrowing on Selene. "I couldn't even if I wanted to."

With a growl, Jason grabbed for the juju, but its power blew him backward, his body slamming into the radiator. Silas released Meredith and rushed to his brother's side.

Selene moaned, gripping her stomach. Jason struggled to rise, even with Silas's help. Behind him, Meredith hurried to Selene, rubbing her back and whispering comforting words.

The juju turned from red to purple, and Laina's body torqued off the bed. She parted her lips, and a fountain of black sprayed forth like something out of a horror movie. Grateful was there, ready with a deep plastic bag, which she pressed to Laina's mouth to catch the emission. Selene gave one last scream, and then black poured out of her mouth too. Powdery and copious, it fogged around her when it hit the floor.

"Don't breathe it in," Grateful commanded.

Silas held his breath and watched as Meredith cupped a hand over her nose and mouth. With a flick of Nightshade's blade, Grateful muttered a series of unintelligible syllables and a bubble of magic floated toward the black powder, consuming and containing it. Selene continued to purge whatever the black stuff was from her body. When she was finished, Grateful gave the all clear and everyone in the room drew in a deep breath.

"It's going to be okay. Breathe," Meredith whispered to Selene.

Something in Silas's chest tightened at the small kindness.

On Laina's stomach, the juju turned black. The bones and feathers toppled over and became inanimate once more. Silas finally got Jason off the floor, and his brother pulled Selene into his arms.

Meredith moved to Silas's side, blinking like the entire experience had left her shell-shocked. He let out a breath as he met her dark brown gaze, tension bleeding from his shoulders. Without a word, he threaded his fingers with hers. When she didn't protest, he pulled her to his side.

"Why was that inside me?" Selene asked, wiping her mouth on her sleeve. Tears flowed down her cheeks. She searched every face in the room, but no one had any answers, not even Grateful.

In the bed, Laina sputtered, her eyes fluttering open.

Kyle gathered her into his arms. "You're okay. You're going to be okay." He brushed her hair back from her face.

Her mouth worked.

"Water. She needs water," Kyle said.

Grateful obliged, bringing an oversized cup with a straw to Laina's lips. She drank greedily. Jason got the hint and pulled a half-empty bottle of water from Selene's purse, opening it and offering it to his fiancée.

Laina's gaze left Kyle and sought out Silas, her hand twitching by her side. "Siiiilas," she rasped.

"She wants you," Kyle said, glaring at Silas.

He left Meredith's side and crossed to Laina, taking her opposite hand in his.

Laina pulled him closer, her arm shaking with the effort. When her lips were near his ear, she rasped one word: "Dragon."

"What did she say?" Kyle asked as Laina collapsed in his arms, the machine she was attached to going haywire. "Laina? Laina?" Kyle shook her gently.

"She'll be okay. These things are meant for humans," Grateful said, her fingers finding Laina's pulse. "But she needs rest. Don't push her." She silenced the alarm and whispered to Laina to try to relax.

"She said *dragon*." Silas looked at his brother.

Jason, who had helped Selene into a chair, looked up in alarm. "Dragon? Did you say dragon?"

Silas nodded.

"She's free." Selene fisted Jason's shirt. "Ryker must have returned Nickelova's heart."

Jason shook his head. "He would never have given up that heart."

"Then how did the toxin get inside me?" Selene pointed to the black dust swirling inside Grateful's containment spell.

Silas rested his hands on his hips. "You two have been out of the country. It seems unlikely that the same person who infected Laina infected you."

"Unless she was already infected," Meredith said. "Who knows how long that was inside her?"

Grateful slid on a pair of rubber gloves and scooped the juju into a toxic-waste bag. "Meredith is right. Laina was stabbed. It's possible that a different mode of infection would have a different reaction in the host. When you were Nickelova's prisoner, did she give you anything to eat or drink?"

"Yes," Selene answered. "Not much. Water and an awful-tasting cake."

"My guess is she infected you then," Grateful said. "It's possible Nickelova simply didn't have a chance to use the power the sulfralite had over you."

Jason stroked the hair back from Selene's face, whispering to her, comforting her.

"What power is that? What does sulfralite do?" Meredith asked.

Silas frowned and gave her a quick rundown of the theory that Alex was using the stuff for mind control. "Sulfralite is a rare mineral only found in the underworld, which means—"

"It was brought here by a demon." Meredith turned her face toward Silas. "Do you think that's what was used to make that vampire stake himself?"

Silas nodded. "Yes."

"Can I speak to you alone?" Meredith gestured with her head toward the door.

"I'll be right back," Silas announced.

Every eye stared at him in various levels of shock as he followed Meredith from the room. Down the hall, she ducked inside a small visitors' room with couches and vending machines. Thankfully, there was no one else in it.

Meredith whirled on him as soon as the door closed. "Do you think the demon Soleil was with last night had something to do with Laina's injuries? How else would Alex get sulfralite?"

"Anything is possible."

"You have to talk to Soleil. You have to find out who that demon is. What if he had a hand in this?"

Silas nodded. "You're right. I'll confront her and find out the truth."

She nodded. "Can you tell if she's lying? What if she's in on it?"

"Soleil is a lot of things, but she's not a killer. Plus I'll know if she's hiding something from me. It'll be awkward to interrogate her, but it has to be done."

"It's the only way." Meredith nodded a few times, then licked her lips and rubbed her palms together. For a moment he took her in: warm brown eyes, fox-red hair, the way the shape of her face reminded him of Wonder Woman, how she was strong and kind.

"Thank you for taking care of me last night," he said.

"I didn't mind."

"I should have kept it together."

"It was a traumatic night. I don't blame you for going a little crazy."

He stepped in closer, close enough that he brushed the front of her blouse. She didn't back away. "Thanks for coming today. I needed someone, and you were there for me."

"Anytime." Her voice was thready.

He could hear her pulse pick up. Her lips parted on a deep inhale, as if she intended to say something. But then she turned like she might leave.

He raised a hand to gently block her shoulders. She looked up at him, her eyes wide, her expression open, expectant.

"You came here for me," he said matter-of-factly.

Her cheeks reddened and she shrugged. "I'm your partner. Isn't that what partners do?"

"You're not my partner."

"Why do you keep saying that?"

"Because the thing about partners..." He licked his lips. "Partners aren't supposed to do this."

He kissed her then. The kind of kiss you remember, not because of its carnal dexterity but because it percolates deep inside your soul long after it ends. He dug one hand into her hair and swept her against the wall, his other working under the hem of her blouse and feasting on the warmth of her skin.

Meredith stiffened at first, either shocked or confused by the passion behind his kiss. But soon her nails dug into the back of his shirt and she pulled him tighter against her, widening her stance to bring him even closer. She opened for him, and his tongue explored her mouth, his hips grinding into her lower belly. The move elicited a soft moan. A hard, aching need overcame him, his wolf begging him for more.

He recoiled when the door opened abruptly, trying his best to look casual and hide the raging hard-on he had for her. Exchanging awkward glances with Meredith, he waited as one of the doctors used a vending machine and then left as quickly as he'd come.

She exhaled deeply when the door closed again. "I guess I'm not your partner then."

"I think we better take this non-partnership somewhere more private. Go out with me tonight?"

"Valentine's?"

"Six thirty?"

She tipped her face up to give him an exaggerated wink. "I better say yes. Goddess knows you need a designated driver."

TWELVE

Silas wanted to ask Laina about the "dragon" comment, but Grateful wouldn't allow him near her room. If she didn't rest, there could be complications, and apparently that went for Selene as well. Grateful set her up in a room for observation.

After agreeing to meet him that night, Meredith excused herself to follow up on an assignment the captain had given her. Silas walked her to her car, then caught up with Jason and invited him to lunch. After what happened to Selene, they needed to talk.

"Two weeks in Italy and I come back to this," Jason said, straightening the cuff of his dress shirt. Damn, the guy still looked polished. Silas looked down at his wrinkled shirt and khakis and wondered how they could be related. "I'm not sure what I'll do if anything happens to Selene, Silas. I can't live without her. Not anymore."

"You won't have to. Grateful pulled that shit out of

her body. All she needs to do is rest and she's going to be fine. Nice ring by the way. So you made it official."

"I asked her on a beach in Positano. She's my mate. I can't wait to marry her."

"Congratulations, man." Silas grinned, genuinely happy for his brother. He looked happy and like he'd gained weight.

"What's going on with the redhead?"

He fumbled with a fry. "Meredith? She works with me. She's a detective."

Jason chuckled. "Right."

"What?"

"Only that the sexual tension between you was almost enough to distract me from what was going on with Laina today. Almost."

"That obvious, huh?"

"Yeah."

"It's irresponsible." He rubbed his jaw. "Shouldn't get involved with a partner."

Jason growled. "Goddess, Silas. Where you there today? Our lives could be over tomorrow. Do not fuck this up out of some desire to be *responsible*."

He took a bite of his burger to keep from arguing.

Thankfully, Jason changed the subject. "Besides Nickelova, what dragon would stab Laina? Dragon fae are rare. You haven't heard anything from the rest of her family, have you? They haven't waged war against us while I was away?" Jason asked over his pasta dish. He'd barely touched the stuff.

"No. The Siberian Dragon Fae distanced themselves

from Nickelova once she stole the amulet. Official word is that they will not interfere with the course of events. They've known she's hibernating in her mountain, but her brother sent word that the family wouldn't help her."

"Then if it was a dragon, it had to be her. But how?"

"I can think of three possibilities when it comes to Nickelova," Silas said. "One: she's here helping Alex without her heart. Two: she's here helping Alex and has somehow obtained her heart again. Or three: it wasn't a dragon at all. After the sulfralite infected Laina's system, the person who stabbed her could have suggested he or she was a dragon. The only theory we can potentially disprove is number two."

"Ryker," Jason said.

"Selene's right. We have to find out if he still has her heart."

They finished their lunch and then took the unmarked van into the vampire district. He parked under an old-fashioned tin-plate sign that read Lost Things with an illustration of a runaway boy smiling down on them. The thing always crept Silas out.

"Why do I have a feeling this is not going to go well?" Jason mumbled.

"Because demons don't like questions. Especially demons who make their living reselling dark magical artifacts," Silas said.

Jason had no argument with that. It was barely twilight, but Lost Things was brimming with shady-looking customers. A bald warlock in purple-and-black robes was levitating three silver balls in front of a shelf of weapons. Near the checkout counter, a woman who looked to be half-goblin dug through a basket of dehydrated mice. Across the store, a vampire in a heavy, hooded cloak stood motionless in front of a rack of carved figurines. It was too early for him to be up. Silas wondered if he might be ill.

The two navigated to the back of the store and rang the bell on the counter. After several minutes passed, Silas grew annoyed, shifting from foot to foot. Ryker was here. No way would he leave the store unattended with this many customers in it.

"I'm going in there," Silas said, gesturing toward the door to the back room.

"Are you insane?" Jason said in a stage whisper. "For all you know, he could have it rigged to steal your soul. You do not touch anything in Lost Things without permission. Trust me."

"Then how do you propose we get him out here?"

"Ryker!" Jason yelled toward the door. "I need to talk to you. It's about my friend, Grateful Knight. You know, the Hecate? I'm not sure if you know this, but she has the power to sentence practitioners of the dark arts to her hellmouth—"

There was a thump, and a black fog filtered under the door and formed into a dark and exotic-looking man. "Lower your voice, Mr. Flynn. Have you no respect for a man's business?"

"We need to talk to you. It's important." Jason paused, eyeing the dark man behind the counter. "Hey, you look great. Have you been working out or something?"

"Eating well." Ryker glanced toward Silas. "Perhaps we should take this conversation to the back room." He held the door open for them.

If the front of the store looked like a cursed rummage sale, the back room was even less organized. There was only one chair, parked unevenly in front of a desk heaped with papers and shipping boxes. Ryker promptly sat down in it.

"Now, what brings you two gentlemen into my humble establishment?" His voice held a gritty quality, not unlike Clint Eastwood in those old *Dirty Harry* movies.

Silas felt the weight of Ryker's gaze settle on him again. Was Ryker more fidgety than usual tonight? He didn't know the demon well, but his gut told him he was onto something here.

"I won't beat around the bush, Ryker," Silas began. "My sister was stabbed four days ago. There was sulfralite residue in the wound."

Ryker stilled, his face showing the slightest lines of worry. "Sulfralite? Are you quite certain? That is a substance even I have trouble obtaining."

"Quite certain," Silas said. "Grateful was able to negate the effects, but when our sister woke up, she said it was a dragon who stabbed her."

Ryker picked up a pen and tapped it rhythmically on his thigh. "I haven't felt a dragon's presence in this city for some time. Not since Nickelova."

"Exactly. That's why we're here," Jason said. "Do you still have her heart?"

"You're afraid her heart was reunited with her body and that she is the one who stabbed your sister?"

Silas spread his hands. "Do you have the heart or not?"

"Nickelova's heart is in a safe place. A safer place than this and nowhere near Nickelova."

"Where is it?"

"In. A. Safe. Place." He enunciated each word, blinking slowly. "That is the only explanation you need. If I told everyone who asked where it was, the place would no longer be safe now, would it?"

"You're sure though?" Jason asked.

"I held it in my hands as recently as yesterday. The heart is safe." Ryker tapped the pen harder against his leg. "It has not been returned to Nickelova's chest."

Silas lurched forward and grabbed Ryker by the collar. "You're lying. Tell me where the heart is."

Ryker's eyes blazed with internal fire.

"Knock it off, Silas," Jason said, tugging at his shoulder. "This isn't necessary."

Ryker wrapped his hand around Silas's wrist. "Unhand me," he said in a steady, calm tone. "I am not your enemy."

There was something other than resistance burning in Ryker's eyes. It was almost like... pity. Yes, pity. A chill rippled through Silas's body. He released Ryker and backed away. "It was you, last night."

"What was him?" Jason asked, looking between the two.

Ryker tilted his head to the side but said nothing.

Silas's gaze roved around the room, coming to rest on a bit of red sticking out from one of the shelves. He pushed the clutter aside. A mask. A silky red mask, splattered with blood. It didn't make sense. Soleil hated Ryker. She'd mentioned on multiple occasions how draining she found the incubus.

There was so much he wanted to say, but only one word came out of the fog of his befuddled brain. "Why?"

Ryker stood and opened the door to his office. "The heart is safe. Any other information you wish to know, you'll have to find out somewhere else. As for last night..." He leveled a knowing look on Silas. "It is not my story to tell."

Feeling dazed and confused, Silas allowed Jason to usher him from the office, past the line that had formed at the counter.

"What the hell was that all about?" Jason asked. "What happened last night?"

"Can you go check on Laina?" Silas asked Jason, handing him the keys. "Take the van. I need to follow up on something."

"Seriously? You're not going to tell me what's going on?"

"Please."

Jason nodded. "Fine. I'll see you back at the hospital."

Silas split from his brother in the darkening twilight and headed in the direction of the bordello.

Silas arrived at Maison des Étoilles without any idea of what he intended to say. He only knew that he needed to confront Soleil. He needed to hear from her own lips why she'd come to him, trying to reconcile, only to do what she did with Ryker immediately afterward. He didn't want her back. He had crossed that bridge and burned it behind him months ago. But there was more to this. Something was off about the situation. He felt it down to his soul.

"Mr. Flynn! Is Madam Soleil expecting you?" The fae holding the door wore a twinkling, gauzy black gown that looked like it was constructed out of the night itself. Her name was Astrial. Silas knew her well.

"No. Is she available?"

Astrial smiled sweetly. "We have strict instructions to show you back at any time." She turned her body and gestured toward the hall. "I trust you remember where to find her."

"I remember," Silas murmured.

He strode down the dimly lit hall to Soleil's room, remembering the many times he'd been here before. The door opened before he had a chance to knock, revealing the bright decor that seemed to magnify Soleil's glow: a white marble floor, a bubbling fountain, walls of windows. The room was crowded with plants that thrived from the light she put off.

"Silas!" she said excitedly. She tossed her arms

around his neck and pulled him into the warmth of the room. "Come in. I'm so glad you came. I was going to call you."

He staggered forward, blinded by her bright glow. She was overwhelming—the heat, the intensity, the fresh smell of her skin. The door closed behind them. He pushed her away.

"Soleil, we need to talk."

"Sounds serious." She smiled and backed toward a padded bench near the fountain. Her white dress fluttered against her golden skin. It was impossible to think of her as the same woman who'd done the things he'd seen her do. She looked sweet, innocent. But he knew better.

"I saw you," he murmured.

"What?" She sat down, crossing her legs and patting the seat beside her.

"I saw you last night. With Ryker."

Soleil's face fell, her eyebrows sinking in confusion. "What are you talking about?"

"I followed you to the club and watched what you did from the observation area. I saw you with Ryker."

"Wh-why? Why would you do that? Why did you follow me?" She pressed her hands to her heart.

"They found a substance in Laina's wound—one only a demon could obtain. I'd heard you were dating a demon. I knew he couldn't use the substance on you, but I wanted to make sure he wasn't manipulating you in another way."

"Ryker didn't use any substance on me." She tucked

her chin and looked up at him with an expression of betrayal. "I went of my own free will. I wasn't manipulated. Is that what you want to know?"

"You don't owe me an explanation. You can do what you want. But after all the times you complained about Ryker, I wondered why. Does he have something over you?"

"He isn't holding anything over me." Soleil's voice wavered with her words. Tears like liquid fire carved bright paths down her cheeks. "You stupid bastard. You have no idea what you saw."

"Enlighten me then." Silas sat down beside her.

"Ever since you told me Alex was back, I've been working to find him for you. I've sent you every scrap of information that comes through these walls."

"Thank you," he said. "But I have to be honest. The names haven't panned out. It's always like Alex is two steps ahead of me. Do you share the names with anyone other than me?"

"No," she said firmly. "It became clear to me that we were missing a key factor. The type of help Alex is getting isn't only from one healer or one vampire. There's something else going on here. Something much bigger."

"I have the same sense. Alex is acting strangely, running when he could fight. And now Laina and the sulfralite—"

"Sulfralite?"

"That's what they found in her body. That's why I suspected the demon."

"Ryker had nothing to do with the sulfralite."

"So he says."

She brushed a blond tress from her face. "Listen to me, Silas. I want to help you, but it's clear to me that there's only one person who has the power to find Alex before he's completely healed and it's too late."

"Who?"

Soleil sighed and strode to a particular square in the marble floor. "The one person who knew Alex best. The one who planned and schemed with him. The one creature strong enough to fight him and knowledgeable enough about his power to make a difference for us."

She waved a hand over the tile, and the heavy marble popped from the floor. She slid it aside. Her delicate, long-fingered hands dipped into the opening and retrieved a purple velvet sack.

"No," Silas muttered.

"It's been perfectly safe here. The floor is impenetrable as long as I'm alive."

"Is that what I think it is?"

"I cannot help you find Alex. He's too careful. The only one who can track him is the one from whom his power comes. Nickelova." She reached into the bag and pulled out a giant ruby the size of a large fist. It throbbed with an inner light from the cradle of her palm.

"Ryker gave that to you? I thought you said that a demon wouldn't give up a dragon's heart for anything?"

She snorted. "No, Ryker did not *give* it to me." Her face grew quite serious. "An incubus feeds on sex and sexual energy. I traded him what you saw last night for a few weeks with the heart. It's a loan, not a gift. He thinks

I'm using it to bolster the energy here. He thinks it will remain locked in my floor."

Silas wrapped his hands around the dragon's heart. "You had public sex with Ryker to get this for me?"

"Yes."

A deep, hostile anger flared behind Silas's breastbone. "You shouldn't have done that," he said through his teeth. "It's not fair for you to put that on my shoulders."

"I'm not blaming you. It was nothing for me to do it. I am what I am. And it needed to be done." She stood, stepping in close to the dragon heart cradled in his hands. "I had the currency Ryker wanted. I used it to buy you what you needed... because I care about you."

"Soleil, I'd never want you to do that." He scowled at her, bile rising in his throat.

"Why? Why do you care what I do?"

"I care for you as a friend. You know I care. It's not what it used to be, but I still care."

She backed away. "But only if I play by your rules, right?"

"No. I'll always be your friend. Even though we're not together anymore, I still want what's best for you. And Ryker is not what's best for you."

She stopped, her hands balling into fists. "Can't you see I did this for you?"

"I can, but you shouldn't have. I don't know what you expected would come of this—"

"I wanted you!" she said. "I wanted to prove to you that I still love you." She blinked her blue eyes at him.

He shook his head. "It's not like that anymore for me. We were at a crossroads, and we both went in opposite directions. There's no going back."

She wept in earnest. He reached out a hand to comfort her, but she shook her head. "Take the heart. Wake Nickelova. Find Alex. And then think long and hard if you are willing to lose me forever."

"Soleil..." Silas slipped the heart back into the purple bag and backed toward the door. He didn't feel good about this. It was like she was hanging on to some hope that wasn't there. "Goodbye, Soleil."

She turned away from him, her eyes fixating on her fountain. He left before she could say another word.

B y the time Silas reached his brick bungalow, Logan was waiting on the porch.

"You could have let yourself in."

"After last time, I thought I'd play it safe." He rubbed his chest where Silas had stabbed him. "Actually, I just got here. What's in the bag?"

Silas looked both ways and let him in the front door before answering. "Nickelova's heart."

"You're kidding. How did you manage to pry that from Ryker's demon fingers?"

"I didn't. Soleil did. She traded herself for the heart."

Logan whistled through his teeth. "Ryker was the demon she was seeing."

"Yeah." Silas rubbed Maggie's ears. "So I need you to protect the heart while it's here. Do you think Polina can put a stronger enchantment around the house?"

"I'll make sure of it."

Silas scratched behind one ear. "No exception for Soleil this time, okay?"

"Afraid she's going to change her mind?"

"Or he will." He sighed. "We're obviously not on the same page anymore."

"I'll take care of it."

With a nod of his head, Silas handed Logan the heart and moved into the kitchen to feed Maggie.

"About that protective enchantment..." Logan leaned against the doorjamb. "Do you want an exception for Meredith?"

Silas glanced at the clock. "Oh fuck, Meredith! I gotta go." Silas ran his hand through his hair. "I was supposed to meet her."

"At Valentine's?" Logan gave him a pitying look. "She was in earlier. Hate to tell you, but she was pretty upset when she left."

"Fuck!"

"I would have called, but I had no idea it was about you."

"I need to go to her. Can you watch the heart?"

Logan held up the bag. "I'm on it. What else do I have to do? Just run a restaurant and help Polina with her duties as an immortal witch. Babysitting your heart is exactly what I wanted to do with my night. "

"You're the best." Silas slapped his friend on the shoulder and jogged for the car.

MEREDITH BLOTTED UNDER HER EYES WITH A TISSUE. "STUPID. I'm so stupid. Why did I think this would work out?" She poured herself a glass of wine and tried to forget how beautiful Silas's ex-girlfriend was. He was probably there now, laughing at how dumb she was to believe she might have a date with the alpha.

She dialed her mother and was relieved when she picked up on the first ring. "Mom, it's Meredith. You won't believe what I did tonight. Total foolishness on my part."

"This isn't a good time, honey." Her mother's voice sounded subdued, depressed even.

Meredith had hoped she'd have snapped out of her funk by now, but instead, the depression she'd suffered since Alex murdered her father only seemed to grow deeper by the day.

"Mom, did you eat today?"

"Of course I ate."

"Oh good. And you got out of bed, right?"

"Seriously, Meredith, I don't have time for this. I simply have other things I need to do."

"Okay." She frowned. It sounded like her mother wanted her off the phone. Maybe she did have somewhere to be. "I was thinking of coming home to shift this month during the full moon. I don't want to shift at Rivergate."

Her mother blew out a deep breath. "I won't be here."

"What?"

"I'm taking a trip. You know, it's time for me to move on. Maybe I'll visit the ocean."

"A trip? With who? When did this happen?"

"Oh, just some friends. Don't worry if you can't contact me. We may be out of reach for a few days." She sucked in a deep breath. "It's time for me to do this."

"Mom, I'm so happy. I think this will be good for you."

"I certainly hope so. Now I really have to go."

After a hasty goodbye, Meredith hung up the phone. Great. Even her mother had better things to do than talk to her.

Still weeping, she undressed and wrapped herself in her fluffy pink bathrobe. Why couldn't she stop crying? Was it because she was thirty-four, never married, and desperately wanted to be? Was it the fact that her dreams of having a family were drifting away on the tide of estrogen that flowed daily from her body, leaving her with one more wrinkle, one more potential gray hair? She didn't have any yet, but she could feel them, right below the surface of her scalp, ready to burst forth and transform her from Spider-Man's Mary Jane to Aunt May overnight.

Or was it because she liked Silas? He was strong, sometimes gruff, but ultimately kind. His loyalty to the pack and his family was something any woman would want to be part of. He was honorable and intelligent, all wrapped up in a tight ass and broad chest. Goddess, he was attractive. The kiss they'd shared had seemed so authentic. But then, why had he stood her up?

She tucked a box of tissues under her arm, grabbed her wineglass and the bottle, and headed for the bathroom. A long soak in the tub and a few glasses of chardonnay and she'd be as good as new. She turned on the water in the bathtub, then rested her wine on the sink while she blew her nose. Finished the wine. Refilled her glass.

Maybe she'd get a cat. She'd been thinking about getting a cat. A rescue. One that no one else wanted—like her. She drank again. Blew her nose again.

She was about to pour herself another when a strange sound made her turn the water off and listen. The sound came again. Doorbell.

Oh fuck. Someone was at the door.

FOURTEEN

When Silas pulled up to the tiny yellow house that matched the address Manahan had given him, he had to smile. For all of Meredith's hardheaded attitude, her home was ultrafeminine. Freshly planted pansies lined both sides of the walk, and a wreath of grapevine and huckleberry graced her door. The front porch was tastefully decorated with potted plants and trees. He pressed the doorbell next to the cherry-red door.

He heard shuffling, and then the lace curtains moved aside. A muffled curse came from somewhere behind the peephole. The door didn't open. He imagined her standing there, hoping he'd go away.

"Meredith, I'm so sorry," he said through the door. "I should have called, but I was distracted. I had a break in the case today. Let me in and I'll tell you about it."

After a short beat, her voice called back, "Just a

minute." There were running footsteps, scrapes, and a loud thunk. She cursed.

"Are you okay?"

A few seconds later, the dead bolt gave way.

The puffy pink bathrobe she wore was stained at the collar with the remnants of what he thought was mascara, but Meredith must have washed her face, because she wasn't wearing a stitch of makeup. Only her red-rimmed eyes gave away the truth that she'd been crying. Her hair was pulled into a messy ponytail, the ends still curled as if it had been done earlier. And her shoulders were slumped.

Mine. The word came quick and firm and with the overwhelming urge to care for the woman in front of him. It was a possessive thought, uninvited, but it barreled into him nonetheless. Goddess, what could he say to her? He stared at her for an uncomfortable amount of time, then cleared his throat with a good hard cough.

"Can I make you something to eat?" he asked.

She laughed.

"If you don't have anything to cook, I could order something. You need to eat. *We* need to eat... and talk."

"I waited for you."

"I went to see Ryker about the heart. It turns out he was the demon who was with Soleil last night."

Her mouth popped open, and a tight inhale lifted her chest. "Shit on a shingle."

He nodded. "With a vomit burrito on the side."

Her countenance changed immediately, and she

reached for his shoulder, guiding him toward the kitchen. "Come on. Let's see what we've got."

"You sit down," he said. "After the ass I was to you tonight, let me make you something."

As it turned out, Meredith's homey decor extended right into her refrigerator. Silas found the barely touched remains of a roast chicken that he slipped into the oven, and a good selection of fresh vegetables. He pulled out some asparagus to sauté and put a few potatoes on the stove to boil.

"Nothing says home like a roast chicken," she said absently.

When he closed the fridge, he noticed a picture held to the door with a chili pepper magnet. "This is your family?" Silas remembered her father. His bright red hair was something you didn't soon forget. Grayson. He was a high-ranking member of Crescent Star. He'd never met Meredith's mother, who stood on her other side. What was her name again? He didn't remember. She had sleek black hair, peppered with gray, soulful brown eyes, and dark olive skin that signaled Mediterranean ancestry. Remembering her parents, he could see the resemblance in Meredith's brown eyes and red waves.

"Yeah. I keep it there to remind me to call Mom. She hasn't been herself since Dad's death."

Silas turned back to the stove and changed the subject. He was supposed to be cheering her up. "How long have you lived here?"

While she told him about the house and her neighbors, he finished heating the food, relieved when she slowly started smiling again. He pulled the chicken and asparagus from the stove, then brought the whipped potatoes to the table. "I can't really cook. Not like my friend Logan anyway. But I survive on the basics."

Meredith spooned a heap onto her plate and licked some off her thumb. "I'm barely proficient at cooking in general, but I can bake. You should taste my pie."

"I'd love to taste your pie." The words tumbled out of his mouth, latent sexual energy charging every word. *Easy, Silas.*

A slight blush stained her cheeks. "Would you like some wine?" Her voice chimed high and tight. She bent slightly as she rose from the chair and her robe buckled, giving him a delicious view of the inside curve of her breast. The lower half of his anatomy kicked in appreciation, and he placed a napkin over the evidence. *Fuck*, he wanted to be inside her, to bury his face in the coconut scent of her hair. Which made no sense because she wasn't exactly inviting his attention. Her fuzzy pink bathrobe could have been a prop on *Golden Girls*. Why then was the wolf inside him begging him to take his attraction to the next level? The thought of being with her made his body ache and his head swim. But that was the thing. He wasn't attracted to her clothes or even her appearance. It was the whole package: her smell, her smile, the fact that she'd cried over their missed date.

"Please. Wine would be great," he rumbled. Why was his voice trashed?

She returned to the table and filled two glasses.

"So did you dismantle Ryker or what?"

"No."

"No? After what we saw last night, I'm amazed you could show any restraint at all."

"It's none of my business. Soleil's a big girl. She can make her own choices. But I did go to see her, to question her about Ryker, make sure he wasn't responsible for the sulfralite."

"And?"

"She gave me Nickelova's heart."

Meredith froze. *"What?"*

"She told me last night's activities were her way of bartering with the demon for the heart. He's an incubus. Sex is his currency."

He left out the petty details. Meredith didn't need to know how Soleil had basically asked him to come back to her on her terms. It wasn't going to happen.

Meredith paused, her glass of wine halfway to her lips. "She still loves you."

Silas snorted derisively. "No."

"Yes. She allowed that demon to do those things to her for you. With that heart, you can control Nickelova. Ryker would never have given it to you without her intervention."

"You don't know that." Silas sipped his wine. "And I think we can agree Soleil seemed to enjoy every minute of the process."

Meredith swirled her wine in the bottom of her glass.

Silas pumped his knee, anxious he might have upset her. "I'll use the heart, but I hate what she did to get it. I can't respect someone who does something like that.

And the thought that she did what she did in some twisted way for me? It makes me sick. I don't want to be responsible for what we saw. If anything, it makes it worse."

"You're not responsible." She met his gaze and held it. "You're not."

"I know." He shrugged. "Besides, what Soleil does or does not do is not my problem. In fact, at the moment I'd rather not think of her at all." He reached across the table and covered her hand with his own. "I don't love her anymore."

"No?"

"I find myself smitten with someone else." He eyed her intently.

"Smitten?" She raised an eyebrow, her gaze dropping to where he stroked her skin with his thumb. Her bottom lip tucked between her teeth. Did she feel the electric charge building between them? Sense the tension like smoke in the air, growing thicker until he could hardly breathe?

"I enjoyed kissing you today," he said, locking eyes with her. "I think you enjoyed it too."

"I did, but…"

"But?"

"We work together," she said softly. "A physical relationship between us would be inappropriate. It's against department policy." She blinked rapidly, leaning back in her chair although keeping her hand exactly where it was, under his.

Silas nodded. "You're right."

He traced the veins along the underside of her fore-arm. She shifted in her seat. He could imagine her thighs pressing together under the table, and his erection throbbed to ease the cause of that particular affliction. He circled her wrist with his thumb and forefinger. If he didn't take her right now, he'd never forgive himself.

"The problem is, Meredith, I don't give a fuck about department policy."

MEREDITH HADN'T EXPECTED THINGS TO GET PHYSICAL THIS fast. An hour ago, she'd thought he'd stood her up. But as Silas rose from his seat and rounded the table to stand in front of her, the evidence of his desire was impossible to ignore. Her eyes widened and her cheeks warmed. But it was what was going on inside her that made her heart race. A dull ache blossomed deep within her core, a vigorous storm of heat that made her squirm.

He tugged her wrist hard and fast, lifting her from her seat. The front of her robe brushed against his chest.

"Oh," she said. Goddess, she was still wearing the dreadful pink robe. Without a stitch of makeup and with her hair pulled into a careless ponytail, her appearance was hardly flattering. But the fire in Silas's eyes only burned for her. By some miracle of the goddess, she'd bewitched him.

Her lips parted as she searched his face for any sign of insincerity or uncertainty. There was none. "It seems I don't care much about department policy either."

He threaded his fingers into her hair, cradling her neck. His lips grazed her pulse, working their way up to her ear. "I want to be inside you, Meredith. I want to make you scream."

"Maybe we should wait." *Was that her voice?* She did not want to wait.

He ran his nose along her neck, inhaling deeply. "I don't think we should wait."

"As alpha, I suppose you're used to getting what you want," she whispered, his arousal a sweet spice in her nose.

"I am." His mouth hovered over hers. "But what I want is for you to want me too. I want more than a fling. If you're not ready for that, you're worth waiting for."

He took half a step back. The gap that formed between them left her cold. The small distance was almost painful.

Her resolve toppled like a house of cards. "I don't want to wait."

Sweeping forward, she rose on her tiptoes and pressed her lips to his. Meredith wasn't a virgin. She'd been kissed plenty of times. But this kiss was different. As he responded to her advance, his mouth raided hers in a territorial battle for lips and tongue. His kiss was desperate and wanting, testing her boundaries, his tongue staking claim to every corner of her mouth, his massive body bending her backward in his arms. She melted. Hot, wet heat bloomed between her thighs. Whatever he wanted tonight, she was all in, unconditionally.

She needed this. If she were honest with herself, she'd pined for Silas since they'd met. His intense attention made her feel like a queen, like someone had pulled back the shades on her life and let in the sun. She moaned.

His fingers skimmed the neckline of her robe, between the soft pink and her skin.

"I could change into something more... something else," she whispered. She leaned back as he worked his way down her neck to the sensitive skin between her breasts.

"Are you kidding? I love you in pink," he murmured into her skin. He untied the belt of her robe, spreading the sides wide.

He pulled back to look at her, a growl rumbling in his chest. "You are incredible. The most beautiful thing I've ever seen."

She laughed, her eyes rolling toward the ceiling. "Well, not the most beautiful. I've seen your ex-girlfriend naked."

His growl grew louder, more intense, and his hands gripped her waist, spanning the area from hip to lower rib. "The *most* beautiful, Meredith." He didn't break eye contact. "There is no one I'd rather be with than you. No one."

His gaze traced her flesh, her face, her collarbones, her belly button. She could feel him look at her, the heat of his stare a palpable thing. His perusal finally abated at the red mound that marked her sex.

From her waist, he skimmed up her sides to cup her

breasts, his thumbs flicking her nipples. The hard pearls responded to his touch, and she tilted her head back, knees going weak with every electric pulse he sent through her.

"Do you like this?" He lowered his lips to her flesh. Goddess, his tongue was an instrument. He fondled one breast while his mouth toyed with the other, coaxing her nipple out even farther. He made sure to give the opposite its due.

"Silas, by the goddess," she whispered, her eyes closed, her face tilted toward the ceiling. "I'm on fire."

He skimmed his hands down her sides to rest on her hips, then lowered himself to his knees in front of her. His nose traced the porcelain flesh of her lower abdomen. "Let me help you with that."

He spread her with his fingers and licked up her center. Meredith moaned and arched, bracing herself on his shoulders. It wasn't only the pleasure of the act itself that drove her wild. This was Silas, the First Alpha, subjugating himself before her. The idea that he wanted her, wanted her enough to do this, was an intense thrill. She felt worshipped.

Her body rocked against his mouth, her moans growing in intensity. He didn't let up. He licked and sucked while she writhed above him. Like a pot boiling over, she swelled above the edge, her entire body stiffening, then spasming as her orgasm overflowed the sides of her being, too much to contain. Her knees buckled. Thank the goddess he was there to catch her.

He swept her into his arms. "Bedroom," he demanded.

"Down the hall and to the left."

Content in his arms, she leaned her face against the soft cotton of his shirt. He found her bedroom and lowered her onto her comforter, pushing her robe off her shoulders. She tossed it aside, completely exposed.

"This is hardly fair," she said, eyeing his clothed state with reproach. She sat up, legs spread and bent at the knee, and reached for his belt.

"You are a sight, Meredith. By the goddess, I have to be inside you."

She freed his cock and pulled his pants down over his hips. He was big, long, and thick. On impulse, she leaned forward and licked up his shaft, enjoying the growl she provoked. Everything about the way he looked at her made her feel like a goddess, like she could undo him with a wink of her eye. She wrapped her lips around his cock, sucking him deep into the back of her throat.

With a rumble that might have been a purr, he unfastened a few buttons of his shirt, enough to pull it over his head. She held eye contact while she worked. Goddess, he tasted good, the masculine scent of his skin arousing her once more. She stroked the heavy weights between his thighs while he shimmied out of his pants.

"Meredith, you don't know what you do to me."

"Please," she whispered, "show me."

Lying back she held her arms out for him. He crawled between her legs, pulled her hips off the bed. She was no delicate flower, but the sheer size of him was intimidating. She spread her legs wider.

He pressed against her opening, then worked his cock into her with small circles of his hips. She gasped and tensed around him, each thrust stretching her to the limit. At last, when he was completely inside her, he stopped and closed his eyes.

"What's wrong?" she asked.

"When I take what's mine," he whispered, "I take it slowly. I savor every minute." He kissed her in a languid, teasing way. "Being with you feels right, like you've always been mine and I've always been yours. Does it bother you that I say you're mine?"

Her gaze met his, and her arms and legs wrapped tighter around him. "No," she answered genuinely. "I feel the same way."

He thrust into her hard and quick. All she wanted was for him to be deeper. She raised her hips, breaking a sweat as she moved beneath him. Hips rising and falling like a machine, she became more animal than human, working with his movements to meet him thrust for thrust. Everything was sharper, more real.

He reached behind her knees and hooked her legs on his shoulders. In this position, deep and exposed, she lost all control. She gave herself over to the rhythm, screaming his name as another orgasm ripped through her.

The room rippled with light and heat that seemed to radiate from their connection. His body pulsed above her. Slowly, he lowered her trembling legs. Tucking her face into the spot where his neck met his shoulder, she rode out the aftershocks while her fingers stroked along his spine. All her worries about Alex, Nickelova's heart, and her new job were gone, replaced by this man in her arms.

"I'm glad you became my partner," he whispered.

"I'm not your partner, remember?" she said breathlessly, a wry smile turning the corner of her lips. "But I'd like to be your girlfriend."

He answered with a hard laugh. "Done. What a beautiful way to start a relationship."

FIFTEEN

They're awake. The text from Jason had come in the middle of the night, but Silas didn't see it until early morning. Not that he'd been asleep. He'd turned off his phone to focus on making his little fox whimper with pleasure. She had the sexiest bark, a deep, throaty noise she made at the brink of ecstasy that drove Silas crazy. And as strong as she was and as sure of herself, he reveled in his ability to reduce her to a puddle of need between the sheets.

It had been a long time since he'd been with a woman, and it was never like this. Soleil was too hard to read, and her level of experience always intimidated him, as if he were competing with hundreds of unknown suitors. For a while it was a thrill, an accomplishment to conquer the unconquerable. But then he learned that she'd never truly been his, and the act lost all meaning for him.

Meredith was a different story. In many ways, she

was his equal, a shifter and a detective, and she was open to a real relationship. He only hoped that from where they began, they had somewhere to go.

"You look serious," she said, running her nails along his stomach.

"Jason says my sister and Selene are up. I need to go to the hospital. Laina might be ready to talk."

"They're recovered? I'll get dressed and come with you."

"You should go into the office. With the shift coming, I'll need you to be there in case the city needs a supernatural detective in my absence."

She propped herself on one elbow. "We have this thing called cell phones, Silas. Captain Manahan can call me if he needs me."

"This is family stuff. No need to involve yourself."

She sat up, the blanket pooling around her waist. "You're going to talk to your siblings about the dragon heart, and I'm going to be standing right next to you when you do. As I recall, I was okay helping with family stuff when Grateful extracted the sulfralite from your sister. I think I can handle visiting her."

"Meredith..."

"You want to raise a dragon from her magically induced sleep. I know you, Silas. You're already making up your mind not to include me in this quest. You think you need to keep me safe. One night in bed with you and you've moved me from the category of coworker to someone you need to protect. But I'm not made of glass."

"Why shouldn't I protect you? I thought we established you're my girlfriend?"

"I'll be your girlfriend, but I won't be your damsel in distress. I'm not helpless, and you need me."

He needed her, but not for this. This was too dangerous. But he knew the look. The hard, cool look that said he was flirting with disaster if he pushed the issue. He didn't want to start his new relationship in the doghouse. It wouldn't hurt for her to accompany him to the hospital, although there was no way in hell he'd allow her anywhere near Nickelova.

"Okay. Get ready. We'll go together."

She stood up, allowing the covers to fall from her body and giving him an unobstructed view of her lithe figure. Although his body was sore from last night's activities, he hardened again at the sight of her, the round curve of her ass and sway of her hips. His wolf growled, and his skin rippled with a desire to own her, to mark her, to claim her.

When she saw the look in his eyes, she squealed and ran for the shower. He caught up to her in three long strides, snagging her around the waist. His hands explored her body, her hair, her perfectly round ass. His wolf surged inside him. Pressing his lips to the soft skin behind her ear, he growled, "*Mine.*" His eyes flashed yellow in the bathroom mirror, that part of his soul that was the wolf joining the party. He was done fighting this.

"Yours." She panted, her pulse hammering against his lips.

Without a word, he wrapped his hand in her hair and tugged, watching her reflection as she braced herself on the pedestal sink, arched her back, and spread her legs wider. She was ready for him, the scent of her arousal a sharp tang in his nose. He entered her from behind in one slick thrust, a growl rending from his throat.

She gasped, her eyes fluttering closed. Holding back was torture, but he forced himself to wait for her grip on the sink to relax. The hungry look she cast over her shoulder at him then was all the encouragement he needed. He pulled out, almost to the tip, and then thrust into her hard and fast. She moaned and arched, lifting her ass so he could get a better angle and moving against him. Quickening the pace. Fuck, she was wet and needy. He wasn't going to last long with her bucking against him like this.

Reaching between her legs, he stroked circles around her clit, his thrusts becoming more and more urgent, the sound of flesh slapping flesh bouncing off the tile. The feel of her inner walls tight around his cock, her flushed face in the mirror, drawn from pleasure, eyes hooded and breath coming in pants, it was everything he'd wanted from the first time he'd touched her.

His wolf surged.

Shoving her head to the side, he folded over her and bit down on the place her shoulder met her neck, unleashing himself and claiming her with a possessive growl that was purely animal.

"Silas!" Her body convulsed, her inner walls pulsing

around his cock, Breathlessly, he gave in to his own orgasm. Goddess, she was a drug, pure ambrosia. Precious. His vice. His mate. How had he refused this for so long?

When he finally came down from the high, he pulled back and licked the mark he'd left in her flesh. Still deep within her, he brought his lips to her ear. "I'll protect you if I want to, Meredith. It's my prerogative. A wolf protects his *mate*."

Goddess help him if she had a problem with that label. The deed was done. As far as he was concerned, she was his. But he needn't have worried. She turned in his arms and kissed him like there was no tomorrow.

When Silas reached Laina's room, Meredith at his side, he was relieved to find his sister sitting up and eating lunch and Selene tucked into Jason's side, completely recovered. The color was back in both their cheeks. If he hadn't known better, he wouldn't have guessed his sister had been in a coma less than twenty-four hours ago or that Selene had coughed up a frightening amount of cursed powder.

"It's about time," Jason said. "For a detective, it took you long enough to catch on to what was happening here."

Silas ignored him, crossing the room to give Laina a kiss on the cheek. "Welcome back, sister."

Laina pulled him into a hug before glancing behind him. "Is this the legendary Meredith? I don't remember meeting you, but Jason and Selene told me you were here before."

"I'm glad you're feeling better." Meredith shook her hand.

"I'm glad my brother finally has a partner," Laina said. "I've always worried he didn't have enough backup."

Silas was tempted to protest the partner remark out of habit but stopped himself. Meredith *was* his partner and more. "Laina, I hate to pressure you, but we need to know what happened. You said something about a dragon."

She nodded. "I was coming out of Four Paws, still in the parking lot. It wasn't even fully dark. Nickelova appeared out of nowhere and stabbed me three times with a dark black blade. She was gone before my head hit the pavement."

Silas furrowed his brow. "It wasn't Nickelova."

"It was!" Laina scoffed. "I think I know what she looks like by now. We were face-to-face when she stabbed me. I was close enough to smell her hair."

"She doesn't have a heart," Selene said. "Jason and I watched her seal herself into a cocoon at the top of her mountain. She was mortal and miles away from any help in one of the most brutal environments on the planet."

Laina met his gaze. "I know what I saw. She's here, in Carlton City, and she stabbed me."

Meredith gripped the bedrail beside him and squinted at Jason and Selene. "Isn't it possible? You said she put herself in the cocoon. She might have taken herself out. She's more vulnerable without a heart, but if she's willing to take the risk, she could be the one helping Alex."

"He ripped her heart out of her chest," Jason said. "Why would she help the man who tore out her heart?"

Meredith shrugged. "I don't know. But I believe your sister."

"Why would I lie?" Laina said.

"No one thinks you're lying. I believe you think you saw Nickelova. It just doesn't seem probable," Jason said.

"There's only one way to know for sure," Silas said. "We go back to the mountain and see if she's still there. And if she is, we wake her up."

"Ryker gave you the heart," Jason said incredulously.

Silas shook his head. "Ryker gave Soleil the heart. Soleil gave it to me."

"You have Nickelova's heart?" Laina's mouth popped open. "By the goddess, Silas."

"Did you forget the portal is gone? How do you plan to get to her mountain?"

"That is a job for one of our witchy friends, and in this case, I think the Smuggler's Notch witch, Polina, is the one for the job." He trusted Polina as much as he trusted Logan, and considering he'd recently embraced accepting the help of others, now was the time to ask for this favor.

"After the shift, right?" Laina said. "You're going to wait until after the shift when I'm stronger."

Silas looked at her sympathetically. "You're pregnant. You and your baby barely made it through this stabbing ordeal. Don't you think you should keep yourself safe? Think of the baby."

"I'm going," she said. "Believe me, if Kyle can't keep me in this bed, you won't either."

Silas snorted. "Where is the doting husband?"

"Sleeping for the first time since I was stabbed. I had to threaten his life to get him to go home." Laina sat up straighter in bed. "So we're in agreement then? We go after the shift."

Silas darted a glance between Jason and Meredith. "After the shift."

"There's something I need to talk to you about," Meredith said to Silas as they made their way back to the car.

"Sounds serious. Is this about my overprotective nature or something else?"

"No." Meredith snorted. "You are way overprotective, but that's not what this is about."

"Then what is it?"

"I don't want to shift with you at Rivergate."

He turned to her. "Is it because you shifted at my place the other night?"

"No. I can shift more than once a month. I can shift

whenever I want, although too many times a day is dangerous. No. I'm simply not comfortable going there. The last time I was at Rivergate, my father was with me."

Silas gave an understanding grunt. "Does it hold bad memories for you?"

"That and I'm not ready for what it might mean for us to be seen together. You're pack royalty, and I'm a pack orphan. I don't want sympathy. I don't want sideways glances. And when push comes to shove, I am different. I change into a fox, not a wolf."

"No one cares about that."

"You don't care about that. Others will care, especially if said fox is dating their alpha. I'm not ready to open myself up to formal pack society. You know how it is. You know how people treat anyone who dates royalty. I'll be front-page news."

Silas's face said it all. He knew she was right.

"Out of curiosity, did you ever tell the Lycanthropic Society about Soleil when you were dating?"

"No," he said quickly. "They would never have accepted her."

Meredith nodded. Perhaps his relationship with Soleil was less serious than she'd assumed.

"If she had changed, I would have," Silas said. "I wouldn't have let tradition stop me from being with her."

"But your plan was to wait until things were serious. Together forever serious."

He nodded. "Yes."

"So let's wait for that with us. This is pretty new. Let's give it time to breathe."

He pulled her into his arms and kissed her gently on the lips. "Deal. But since you won't be shifting…"

"Yeah?"

"I wonder if I can ask a favor."

SIXTEEN

Organizing the monthly shift was one of the hardest aspects of being alpha. On top of his full-time job, Silas was charged with ensuring the safety of the roughly two hundred wolves who chose to shift at Rivergate Manor. Shifting there wasn't mandatory. Wolves could choose to risk managing their own transitions. But if a wolf signed up to be at Rivergate, Silas was responsible for making sure they left in the same condition as they arrived.

That took magic. Grateful had used her power to add an enchantment around the property to keep supernaturals and humans out, and recently, following Selene's abduction, to keep wolves in. It also took enough food to feed an army and an intimate knowledge of the needs of the pack. Teenagers shifting for the first time needed mentors. Older wolves needed added protection. A few wolves with medical backgrounds volunteered in a first aid tent to treat those who woke up with wolf-induced injuries.

All of that required time and leadership, and although Silas didn't do it all himself, it was amazing how many things bubbled to the top. Which meant that the dragon heart waited in the safe under his bed, his new relationship with Meredith was relegated to the back burner, and Alex's whereabouts remained a mystery. But before he could give himself over to the moon and the wild, there was one thing he needed to do.

"It's taken care of," Logan said. "The new enchantment around your house is in place. No one is getting their hands on that heart."

Silas paced Logan's office at Valentine's, feeling restless.

"I need you to give Meredith access."

Logan gave a slow, lopsided smile. "Oh?"

"She's going to feed Maggie while I'm managing the shift."

"When she was here before, I got the sense she wasn't your everyday werewolf."

"Half werewolf. Half skinwalker. She shifts into a fox."

"Skinwalker? I thought they could shift into anything?"

"Normally. Must be something about the werewolf blood."

Logan nodded. "So she doesn't have to shift with the moon."

"Nope. Anytime she wants. She goes home regularly

to shift though. Her mother's been depressed since Alex murdered her father. Meredith looks out for her. But this month she's staying, so she agreed to watch Maggie."

"Enough said. I'll ask Polina to alter the enchantment to allow her in."

"Thanks, Logan." Silas took a seat across the desk from him.

"Meredith must be pretty special. You wouldn't give just anyone access to your place or Maggie, especially with the heart there."

"She is." Silas leaned his elbows on the desk. "I think she might be the one."

Eyes widening, Logan chuckled long and low. "The sly fox has stolen your heart? I thought I saw a spark when you were here last, but it was hard to tell if it was love or the fumes off all the vodka and tonics."

"Ugh. Don't remind me."

"She must love you. Anyone else would have left your drunk ass on my couch."

Silas hoped Logan was right. He caught himself smiling like an idiot and changed the subject. "What about the portal to Nickelova's mountain? Can Polina do it?"

Logan nodded. "Not a portal exactly, but she can get you there. She travels by gold dust."

"Hey, whatever works. I knew I could count on you."

Logan stood and rounded the desk. "Can you spare a few minutes for a beer with an old friend before you go? I want to hear more about you and Meredith."

Silas scratched his stubble. "Only if you tell me what it's like being Polina's caretaker."

"For that you'll have to commit to two beers." Logan gave a low chuckle.

With a thump on his friend's back, Silas opened the door. "It's a hard job, but I'll make the sacrifice for you, my friend."

"You know, between Grateful and your sister both being pregnant, Polina has been talking about babies in her sleep."

"Does that bother you?"

"Not at all." Logan bobbed an eyebrow. "I'm willing to practice as long as she wants me to though."

Organizing the monthly shift was never easy, but neither was maintaining a decade-long friendship. Silas followed Logan from his office, eager to fulfill his two-beer promise.

SEVENTEEN

Days later, with Silas performing his duties at Rivergate, Meredith let herself into his small brick home to take care of Maggie. She was happy to do this for him, to allow him to stay with his pack for the three days of the full moon. She liked how it made her feel. Like she'd become an important part of his life. She hoped it was the beginning of something more.

"Hey, girl." She rubbed Maggie's floppy ears and filled the mutt's bowls. She'd take her out back for a run when she was done eating. Maggie had a doggie door, so technically all she needed was feeding, but Meredith didn't think it was proper to leave the dog alone so much. She'd decided to stay a few hours to play with the pup.

A rattle came from the front door, as if someone was trying the knob. She hadn't locked it when she came in and wondered what was stopping whoever it was from entering. Unless it was someone supernatural who couldn't get past the enchantment. Her fingers grazed the butt of the gun tucked into the small of her back. Still there. She strode across the room and opened the door.

"Soleil?" She almost didn't recognize the blonde, her sunny glow masked by the bright day behind her.

"Excuse me? Do I know you?" Soleil smoothed the fabric of her fitted, plum-colored dress.

"Uh, no, I guess we haven't met. I'm Silas's partner, Meredith." She wasn't sure why she didn't say she was his girlfriend. A gut feeling. A remnant of awkwardness still clung to the word, especially under Soleil's scrutiny.

"Is Silas here? I need to ask him something before he leaves for Rivergate."

"I'm sorry, he decided to spend the day at the mansion with his pack. I can give him a message for you."

"If Silas isn't here, why are you in his house?"

She smiled at Soleil, the type of smile she used on families of victims or criminals who came into the station. It was a soothing, everything-is-okay smile. But the strange clenching in her gut told her it was necessary. No explanation was owed the woman, but she offered the simplest one. "I'm helping with Maggie."

The fae mirrored her smile, her hands folding elegantly in front of her hips. "Would you please invite me in? I believe I've left something important in Silas's bedroom."

Meredith shifted back slightly. "You left something in his bedroom? When?"

"A few nights ago. He did tell you we've been seeing

each other? For years actually. I've never had any problems entering the house before, but..." Soleil flourished one hand toward the door, then used it to smooth a stray hair back into her chignon.

"Strange, I was under the impression you broke up some time ago." Meredith's heart quickened with unease, but she did her best to maintain a calm demeanor. Her time as a detective had taught her a person's words were a jewel that must be examined under a microscope and from multiple angles to determine their worth. Her heart might throw itself on the floor in a tantrum at the thought of Soleil with Silas only a few nights ago, but her brain was counting backward, finding no evidence that the conjecture held any truth. How could Silas have spent the night with Soleil when he'd stayed with her every night since they'd made love the first time?

Soleil placed a hand on her chest. "Technically, I guess, our relationship is on hiatus while we each explore our goals for our future. Mind you, it's only because he wants more than I'm willing to give at the moment. But he made it clear his invitation is always open. And I have to admit, every day we are apart, I'm more tempted to say yes." She bit her lip gingerly.

Meredith fought the urge to roll her eyes. Her stomach hurt. Was it possible Silas had continued his relationship with Soleil at the same time he dated her? *No*, she thought. Not after the way he'd reacted to watching Soleil in the club. Even after learning of Soleil's motivation to do what she did, he'd made it crystal clear that he wasn't in love with her anymore.

"I'm sorry for your trouble, but Silas won't be back until Tuesday. I can let him know you stopped by."

"Don't be silly. Simply invite me in, and I'll obtain what I'm after." She trailed her fingertips along the invisible barrier between them.

"I... I'm not sure that would be for the best, Soleil," Meredith said. "Silas had the enchantment changed for a reason. If I invite you in, I'd be betraying his trust. Like I said before, I can give him a message for you."

Agitated, Soleil shifted uneasily on the stoop, her formfitting dress out of place in the suburban setting. Tiny sparks of energy danced across her buttery skin. "I know what you are," she said, sizing up Meredith. "You're not like him. You're not what you say you are."

"I think you should go," Meredith said.

Maggie had finished eating and was by her side, a low growl curling the dog's lips.

Soleil lowered her chin. "Be careful, Meredith. You may think you know Silas, but you don't. He's damaged in ways you couldn't possibly imagine."

"You should know. You inflicted some of that damage. Why are you here anyway? Did your demon lover catch on to what you were doing and want his trinket back?" Her words lashed out with the snap of a fist.

Soleil's face fell. "Excuse me?"

"I saw your show the other night." Meredith stared her down. Internally, she chastised herself for letting on that she knew about the heart or Ryker. It was a stupid thing to do, showing all her cards. It fanned the flames of her ego but did nothing to improve the situation. She was better than that. Smarter than that.

Soleil narrowed her eyes but didn't engage. "Tell Silas I was here," she said steadily. Backing into the bright sunlight, she washed away, her golden skin melding into a yellow flash that carried her from the street.

"You better believe I'll tell him." She reached for her phone and dialed his number.

Silas needed to wake Nickelova, and he needed to do it fast. He knew Soleil. For her to come for the heart was a sign of fear. She'd never renege on a gift if she wasn't terribly afraid. Ryker must have put the heat on her, asked for the heart back. After learning what happened between her and Meredith, Silas had avoided Soleil's attempts to contact him, but he couldn't do so forever. He planned to address it *after* he used the heart to raise Nickelova.

"I can only take two," Polina said. The redheaded witch stood in Silas's living room, her gaze darting between Jason, Laina, Selene, and Meredith as if she was overwhelmed by their presence. Logan had said it was possible for her to transport him to Nickelova's mountain using gold dust. He never promised it would be easy.

"Me and Jason," Silas said. "I have the heart, and Jason has the memory to get us there."

"Wait, what about us?" Meredith glanced at Laina, who seemed equally disappointed at being excluded.

Polina's poofy green dress made her look like the good witch from *The Wizard of Oz*. She tucked her red hair behind her ear and shook her head. "Traveling by gold dust is not as easy as it sounds. In a few minutes, I will use Jason's memory to drag him and his brother halfway around the world through the veins of metal between my mountain and Nickelova's. This is not a simple task." She spread her hands. "Impossible with more than two."

"There's no other way?" Laina asked.

Polina shook her head.

Selene said nothing, but Silas had the distinct impression she wasn't disappointed. She'd be happy never to see Nickelova or her mountain again.

Silas loaded the heart into his leather backpack and strapped it onto his shoulders. Traveling by metal was a tricky business. He'd heard it compared to being forced through a straw one molecule at a time. But he had to take the risk.

"Remember, Silas," Selene said, "the ancient texts say Nickelova must obey you as long as you possess the heart. But she can lie to you. She'll try to manipulate you. Don't fall for it. You must keep the heart from her at all costs."

"I plan on it."

"There's always the chance she's not there," Laina said. "I know what I saw. Nickelova was in Carlton City."

"We'll find out soon enough," Jason said.

Selene kissed Jason and pulled him into a tight embrace. "Don't be long. I expect to see you tonight. We have a date." She backed away toward Laina and Meredith.

Silas considered Meredith. The relationship was still new enough that he wasn't sure what to expect. Would she kiss him goodbye? Shed tears in fear for his life? React angrily to him going without her?

Her jaw tightened, and her eyes narrowed on his face. "Silas, get back here in one piece, or I'll kick your ass."

"Duly noted," he drawled. "What will you do to my ass if I do make it back in one piece?"

"I guess you'll have to wait and see." Meredith waggled her eyebrows at him.

After a moment of silence as Jason, Selene, and Laina exchanged awkward glances, Polina cleared her throat. "Shall we?"

Silas took Jason's hand and then Polina's. The corners of the witch's mouth twitched. "This may hurt a little." She scooped a handful of gold dust from the bag at her waist and sprinkled it over their heads.

Jason came apart first, dissolving into a swirl of glittery pieces. Silas followed, feeling his cells scatter to the wind, his arms and legs breaking apart. He was swept away until nothing made sense anymore. There was no up or down, awake or asleep... Only the flow of liquid metal.

When he finally came together again, he inhaled long and deep. His cheek was pressed against cold stone, and his body felt rubbery, boneless. He blinked rapidly as Polina's slippered feet came into focus.

"We're here," she said. "Thank the goddess. You two were heavier than I imagined."

Silas had been wrong. Traveling by gold dust was not like being filtered through a straw. It was worse. Much, much worse.

"Here, drink this." Polina brought a bottle to Silas's lips.

He drank greedily, sputtering when his initial thirst gave way enough for him to taste what he was swallowing. Whatever it was, it wasn't water.

"What is that?" He stuck his tongue out, hoping the frigid cold would numb his taste buds.

"A potion of water lily root, orchid worm, and spirulina to speed recovery and combat altitude sickness." She crossed the cave to Jason and brought the tonic to his lips.

Silas double-checked that his backpack was still on his shoulders, then pushed himself up on his hands and knees. He pulled his parka tighter around him. They were right inside the mouth of the cave, where blowing snow made the outdoors look like a winter wonderland.

"Come on," Jason said, coughing. He regarded the bottle in Polina's hand as if it were rat poison.

He led them deeper into the cave, the cavern becoming darker and darker as they descended into the mountain until even Silas's supernatural sight failed him.

"Allow me," Polina said. The tip of her wand glowed to life.

"There's a fireplace against that far wall," Jason said. "If you hocus-pocus that thing, it will make it easier for us to see."

Polina circled her wand, and a large fire ignited in a *Citizen Kane*-sized alcove in the stone, bathing the cave in warm light. A carpet and sofa in the main chamber were covered in a thick layer of soot, although a frayed corner suggested it was once patterned red. Behind the furniture, there was a coffin-sized silver egg.

"She's here," Silas said.

But Jason clearly already knew as much. He was standing next to the metallic pod, running his fingers along its shell. The thing was eerily lustrous, like an alien artifact, with plate-sized overlapping scales that reflected the flickering light of the fire.

Jason knocked on the shell. It sounded solid. Something was in there. "She's got to be inside."

Approaching slowly, Polina raised her wand, her eyes wide with distrust of the foreign object.

Silas slid the backpack from his shoulders. Once he'd freed the heart from its purple velvet bag, the egg vibrated, emitting a low hum.

"Did you see that?" Jason held his hands over the egg, grinning excitedly. "I'd say she knows we're here."

"Are you suggesting the dragon fae has been inside this thing all this time?" Polina paced the periphery, inspecting the scales.

"As far as we know," Jason said.

She touched the egg, her face straining against some invisible force. "It looks like metal, but it isn't. I'm a metal witch; I have no power over this. It's biological, not elemental."

"Selene told me Nickelova might react to the proximity of the heart," Jason said. "Try it, Silas."

Cupping the large, throbbing ruby in both hands, Silas passed it over the cocoon, stopping where he'd expect Nickelova's chest to be. Loud and clear, he said, "Come out, Nickelova. I have something for you."

The egg vibrated again, and the giant plates began to shift. With a sound like grinding gears, the scales slid and stacked, one on top of the other like some giant puzzle box. As the hard, metallic shell folded away, a leathery snakeskin was exposed. It writhed as if the serpent within had swallowed a giant rat.

Silas squeezed the heart. "Come on, you bitch, come and get it."

The snakeskin split down the middle, the sound of tearing leather making Silas feel queasy. A puff of foul-smelling steam rose from the broken flesh.

"Ugh!" Silas covered his nose and mouth with the back of his arm.

The skin shriveled and rolled, the cocoon opening like some gigantic fleshy baked potato. Polina crept forward, wand pointed menacingly toward the opening. The steam was too thick to see inside. Jason waved his hands in a ridiculous effort to fan the haze away while Silas squinted his eyes in the hopes of confirming a visual of Nickelova. The heart tight within his grip, he leaned over the opening.

A pale round sphere broke through the fog. No, not a sphere. A head. The bald head of a corpse with shriveled skin and receding lips. Skeletal arms splayed over the sides of the cocoon, one bony hand reaching for Silas and the heart.

"Miiine," the thing rasped, its dried tongue protruding between its teeth.

"Is that Nickelova?" Jason stepped back in revulsion.

Polina grimaced. "She is mortal. Suspending herself may have prolonged her life, but without food or water, she has fed on herself these months. She will die here if we don't get her help."

"Heeaaart." The skeletal fingers clawed at Silas.

"Sorry. No." Silas lifted the heart out of her reach.

Jason shook his head. "The fae hospital will never take her, not after what she's done."

"Then we bring her to Saint John's. Grateful will help us," Silas said.

"I must warn you, I'm not at all sure she'll survive the journey." Polina shrugged.

"Take her separately. Then come back for the two of us," Silas said.

Polina scowled. "Me? Take her alone? Sure, send the witch along with the dragon woman. Make the witch do it. She won't mind. It's not as if the dragon is a killer or anything. Oh wait, she is, and the past lover of the man who almost murdered my husband *and* my familiar—"

"Polina!" Silas raised his voice to stop her rambling.

"She won't hurt you. She's... decimated. Besides, she can't do magic as long as I have this." He held up the heart. "And she's not strong enough to do anything else."

Nickelova's distended eyes locked on the heart cradled in Silas's hand.

"Fine," Polina said bitterly. "Help me lift her out of this thing."

Because Silas had the heart, Jason took the lead, lifting Nickelova from the silver scales. Even from a distance, Silas could see she was too light. She looked like a mummy, barely more than a skeleton. Nothing like the woman Silas had known. Nickelova's body had once contained a dragon. Now it seemed barely capable of containing her life.

Polina wrapped an arm around Nickelova's chest and glanced between the two brothers. "Don't get comfortable. I don't plan on staying with this one any longer than I have to." She released a handful of gold dust over their heads. The two came apart and melded into the mountain.

"You know what this means?" Jason crossed his arms over his chest and blew out a deep breath.

"Huh?"

"Whoever attacked Laina wasn't Nickelova. Which means our sister was duped and someone else is helping Alex. Someone who's not even on our radar."

By the time Silas arrived in Carlton City with Polina, the others had transported Nickelova to the hospital. Grateful had her in isolation, hooked up to so many wires and tubes Silas wouldn't have recognized her if he hadn't known who she was.

"It doesn't even look like her," he said.

"It's her." Grateful hooked her finger inside the cuff of one of her rubber gloves and stripped both from her hands. "I'm disappointed Bojingles Fae Hospital wouldn't take her. The woman doesn't have a heartbeat. You have no idea the steps I had to take to keep her identity a secret."

"Can I interrogate her?"

"You can try, but keep in mind she's fragile. I've got magic and medicine propping her up. I'm not at all sure she'll live through this."

He quirked an eyebrow. "She could still die? You've got her pumped full of everything under the sun, and we still might lose her?"

"She put her mortal body in a magically induced coma meant for a supernatural creature. With no food or water, her body has fed on itself and the remains of magic in the single dragon scale she saved these past months. My guess is she wouldn't have lasted much longer if you hadn't woken her up. It's touch and go."

"I have questions, and she's the only one with the answers."

Grateful sighed. "She's refusing to eat."

"What? Why?"

"Says she'd rather be dead than help you."

"Fan-fucking-tastic."

"But she's conscious and alive now. I'd make the most of it." Grateful patted his shoulder supportively. "Who knows how long she'll be with us." With a nod, she padded down the hall to her next patient.

Adjusting his backpack, Silas stepped into the sterile scent and incessant beeping of Nickelova's room. Only in movies had he seen a body as emaciated as hers. Death pressed up against her like a lover. A full tray of hospital food sat untouched on her bedside table—beef stew, Jell-O, a dinner roll, the works. It smelled appetizing enough. A bag of phosphorescent fluids dripped through an IV in her arm.

"I made the same mistake with Alex," she said, unprompted. "It's why he wasn't healing despite the fire lily juice and the magic of my presence. I never fed him. Your humanlike constitution makes you vulnerable to hunger. Now I'm vulnerable too."

"Where is Alex?"

She snorted softly. "I have no idea."

"You must be able to sense when he uses your amulet."

"I could if he was using it. He's not. I haven't felt the ripple of the amulet's use in some time. Of course, I'm weaker without my heart. If you gave it back to me, I might be able to help you."

"Find him first, and then we'll talk about your heart."

"I have no magic without it. I had one dragon scale, and I used all its magic to preserve myself. I am useless to you now." She turned her head away.

"I highly doubt that." He strode to the end of the bed. "My sister was stabbed by someone who looked exactly like you. How is that possible? Do you have a twin?"

"No." Her gaze darted in his direction. "Perhaps it was Alex with a camouflage charm."

"There was a protective enchantment against him around the property."

She adjusted in the bed as if she was in pain. "You're fucked. You are so fucked," she said through a forced smile.

"Why?"

"Because if someone else is helping Alex and using my identity to do so, your sister is only the beginning. Let me guess, there have been other incidences, other strange occurrences. Unexplained phenomena?"

"Maybe." Silas pictured the vampire stabbing himself in the chest.

"This isn't about Alex anymore." She paused, breaking into a fit of coughing. "This is bigger. Much bigger." She closed her eyes and sank into her pillow.

"Don't fall asleep. Tell me. Tell me what you know, or I swear to the goddess, I'll crush your heart with my bare hands."

That made her entire body vibrate with laughter. "You're going to kill me, Detective? As if I'm afraid to die. As if I didn't imagine my death a thousand times in that tomb I made in my mountain. You idiot. I welcome death. Death is far preferable to what's coming."

"And that is?"

"War. The underworld is rising. Panaal has been suppressed for far too long."

"Panaal?"

"The horned god of the underworld." She gave him a smug look. "You don't even know who he is."

"The devil. You're blaming this on the devil?"

"Panaal is not the devil. He's the balance, the equal and opposite of Hecate. The goddess has abused her position for far too long, intervened on behalf of the witches, fae, and shifters who do her bidding. But demons, some fae, and vampires are gathering in numbers, coming together to advance the cause of their forgotten cultures and traditions. They will avenge their ancestors. They will take back this world for their progeny."

"This again? When are you going to drop this idea that you can unite the supernatural communities under common rulership? It can't be done."

"Look at me, wolf. Do I look like I'm in any condition to unite supernaturals? Oh no. You should wish it were still my goal to do so. Our friend Alex has found an advocate in Panaal, and the forces he is engaging are far more powerful than I ever was."

"But still focused on the subjugation of humans?"

She jutted her chin toward him. "The suppression of supernatural power is a trend whose heyday is over. Panaal knows this and is ready to turn the tides."

"And Alex is his tool for making it happen?"

The corners of her mouth curled in smug satisfaction.

"But how? I can't imagine Hecate would be keen on this idea."

She pressed her lips together and closed her eyes.

"Now is not the time to clam up." He reached into his backpack and squeezed the heart inside.

Every machine in the room went haywire as Nickelova's body bucked off the bed, her eyes rolling back in her head. He released the heart, and she flopped onto the sheets, fragile limbs splayed like a fallen bird.

Although her eyes were closed, she laughed softly. "Go ahead and kill me. Get it over with."

Staring at her as she lay there like a heap of skin and bones, he was tempted to do as she asked. She'd hurt his pack, almost killed his family, and helped Alex, his mortal enemy. It would feel good to watch her die. But she was useless to him dead.

There was more she was keeping from him. A key piece of information. Namely how Alex planned to raise the underworld, why he brainwashed a vampire into committing suicide, and most importantly, why he was waiting to attack. Alex must have healed by now. He obviously had help and power. So why hadn't the other shoe dropped?

Silas examined the dragon heart in his hands. The ancient tomes Selene had found on the subject of using it were hazy and lacking. But his gut told him that Nickelova had more to fear than death from the thing in his hands. For her to beg for death, it must be more powerful than she was letting on.

"Sit up, Nickelova." The sharp command emanated from deep within him, deeper than his lungs or his voice.

There was a moment of hesitation, and then her body shook violently. She jackknifed off the mattress. "Fuck you," she said through her teeth.

Silas squinted at her. "Interesting. You were hoping to die. Hoping I wouldn't figure this out. It's not pain you respond to; it's intent. It takes more than a simple request. You have to know what you want before you ask. I'm an alpha werewolf. I have loads of experience with intent. Every alpha command requires it. Now pick up your fork and eat everything on that tray."

Her hand slapped the bedside table as if she were a marionette and someone was pulling her strings. She awkwardly fisted her fork and brought a trembling bite to her lips. Sheer horror flitted through her expression, her throat swallowing as if the motion was involuntary.

Silas grinned. "You will take care of yourself, Nick-elova. You will remain safe and eat and drink your fill. And you will grow healthier. You're no good to me dead."

"You bastard," she said between bites. A piece of meat tumbled from her lips onto her lap.

"Careful. You wouldn't want to have to eat that off the floor." He backed toward the door. "I'll see you in a few days. I bet by then you'll be feeling much better." He slipped into the corridor, her screams of anguish following him.

EIGHTEEN

Any serious investigation started with an effective crime map. Fortunately for Silas, Meredith was already on it. While he'd been dealing with Nickelova, she'd set up a corkboard along half his office wall and covered it with every contact Silas, Jason, or Laina had had with Alex or one of his cronies. The apartment building in the vampire district, the crime scene outside Carlton City, Copper Herald Health & Wellness, and ZeroHour.

"Don't forget the Four Paws parking lot." Laina rubbed her stomach as if she was already guarding the baby inside. Her hand circled the small mound of her lower abdomen. Was it only his imagination, or did she already look pregnant? Kyle massaged her shoulders, hovering protectively.

"Whoever stabbed Laina could change his or her appearance to look like Nickelova," Kyle said. "That's a clue, isn't it?"

"Did Nickelova actually say Alex was going to raise Panaal?" Selene asked.

"More or less. She said Alex was his tool. That his goal is to overthrow Hecate as the master of this world and turn the tables, unleashing the underworld."

"Who else thinks it would be a bad idea to allow that to happen?" Jason raised one hand.

"Bad is the understatement of the year. It would be chaos," Selene said. "War. Violent, bloody carnage until there was nothing left to eat or be eaten."

"So... bad," Jason said.

Selene tilted her head and squinted at her mate, her mouth twitching with a suppressed smile.

"What is he waiting for?" Meredith asked no one in particular. She'd taken a seat in Silas's chair and rested her boots on the desk.

"I know enough from my study of the goddess to presume Alex is working out some kind of ritual," Selene said. Every eye in the room snapped to her. "Crossing dimensions takes magic and energy. Lots of energy. If he's opening a pathway to the underworld, literally raising Panaal, physically and permanently, he'll have to complete a ritual powerful enough to merge this dimension with the next."

"Blood magic?" Silas asked, thinking of the dark sorcery he'd heard Grateful talk about.

"Yes and no. Most likely it will require blood," Selene answered, "but Alex is a werewolf. Even with the dragon fae amulet, his body can't wield elemental magic like a witch. He'll have to use ritual, not sorcery. Only, all werewolf rituals are pleas to the goddess. Whatever ritual he's trying to perform must turn everything I know on its head. Something like that would require a major source of metaphysical power… Like… like… a celestial event."

"An exploding star or something?" Meredith asked.

Selene rose and crossed the room to Silas's wall calendar. Her finger skimmed the page and landed on a square. "Holy shit."

"What is it?" Silas strode to her side to get a better look.

"A full eclipse of the moon."

"Goddess, why didn't I think of that? I knew it was coming. We've been preparing at Rivergate for weeks."

"Fill in your newest werewolf," Kyle said. As a hybrid, he'd only been shifting since he'd met Laina, and even then not as regularly as a full-blood. Some months he simply helped with the tent. "What happens to werewolves during a lunar eclipse?"

"The shift is irregular. Some wolves will shift back to human when the light of the moon is blocked."

"Wolves like Alex?"

"With the added power of the amulet, I'd count on it."

Jason leaned against the desk, crossing his legs at the ankle. "So theoretically, Alex hasn't attacked us yet because he's storing up power and collecting ingredients to perform a massive ritual to open a gate between dimensions. And we have evidence of this."

"He took bones from that crime scene," Meredith said.

"Bones from an unconsecrated grave," Silas added. "I don't know what it means, but it sure sounds like an ingredient for a spell."

A collective groan rose between them.

"Selene, do you think you can find the ritual?" Jason asked. "Maybe we can stop him from obtaining all the components to perform the spell effectively before the lunar eclipse."

She shook her head. "This is dark magic, Jason. Artemis isn't going to have anything like this in the sanctuary texts, not even from a theoretical perspective."

Laina sighed. "Of course not. This is black magic."

"There *is* one place we can find books on rituals like this," Selene said, glancing over her shoulder at Jason. "But I doubt you're going to like it, Silas."

"Ryker," Jason said.

"Ryker," Selene confirmed.

"Ryker! Who's to say he wasn't the one to provide Alex with the ritual in the first place?" Silas asked. He didn't trust Ryker. How could they be sure Ryker wasn't responsible for the sulfralite they'd found in Laina's wound? "Can demons disguise themselves as other people? How do we know it wasn't Ryker who stabbed Laina?"

"Whoa, whoa, whoa," Jason said. "Ryker's not a Sunday school teacher, but he lives based on one very basic principle: he acts in his own best interest. He has no motivation to change the status quo. Why would he compromise his business? More money? The guy is rich.

Power? He doesn't need it. He's very persuasive. He gets what he wants."

"Besides, demons can't look like someone else," Meredith said softly.

Silas turned around to face her. She'd removed her feet from the desk and was studying the crime map as if she couldn't quite put her thoughts together. "A demon can possess someone, make them do something they don't want to do, but a demon can't change their appearance to look like another person. Well, no more than you or I could disguise ourselves. There are charms of course. Costumes. Illusion. Camouflage."

"The enchantment around the property would null an illusion or camouflage charm, and it wasn't a costume." Laina's voice was firm.

"A demon could have possessed Nickelova and forced her to stab Laina, but that demon could not transform into a Nickelova look-alike without strong illusionary magic," Meredith said.

"How do you know?" Silas asked.

"Because the only creatures who can change their appearance without charms, spells, or enchantments are skinwalkers. It's the pride of my mother's people."

"So do you think a skinwalker did this?" Jason asked.

"No. That's the thing. Skinwalkers hate Alex and everything he stands for. He killed my father. No way would any of my mother's people help him. There are other communities, but they are notoriously neutral. What motivation could they possibly have?"

"What if magic *was* involved?" Kyle chimed in. "Gerty's and Grateful's wards are strong but probably not impervious. Maybe a witch or fae deconstructed the enchantment and simply used magic to convince Laina they looked like Nickelova after they stabbed her. That stuff she was infected with could have changed her memories."

Laina shrugged. "It seemed real, but I'll admit it's possible."

"I could check with Gerty. See if she's heard any rumblings from the dark fae," Kyle said.

Silas scratched the stubble on his jaw. "It's worth a shot."

"And I can check with Grateful about the witches," Laina said. At Jason's quizzical look, she added, "She is my neighbor. I'll pop over for a visit."

Jason put his hand on Selene's shoulder. "We'll check out Lost Things and see if Ryker can help us figure out where Alex might have obtained this ritual."

"And I'll see what I can learn from Nickelova." Silas reached for his coffee. When was the last time he'd slept? When was the last time he'd eaten?

Meredith stood from behind the desk. "And I'll make sure Silas eats something and lies down before he falls over."

Laina and Jason exchanged glances. "Thank you, Meredith."

He was tempted to protest, to tell her all he needed was a cup of coffee and he was good to go, but he knew it was a lie. He was on the verge of collapse, and he hadn't even realized it until now.

She slid her fingers into his, her red hair swinging over one shoulder as she met his gaze. "Come on, hero. I'm taking you home."

NINETEEN

Silas sank into Meredith's sofa, oddly drained. The thing wasn't much to look at, but its gray cushions were remarkably cozy. The padding swaddled him. Usually he could manage fatigue like this. Maybe the stress was finally getting to him.

With one hand on the backpack holding Nickelova's heart, he propped his feet on the upholstered coffee table and rested his eyes. "Twenty minutes and then I have to get back to the case."

Meredith covered him with a crocheted blanket. "We just theorized that Alex wouldn't strike until the lunar eclipse. Nickelova isn't recovered enough to help you yet. She needs time. Selene hasn't found the ritual yet. She needs time. And Laina and Kyle need time to talk to Grateful and Gerty. That means you, Silas, have time." She kissed him gently. "You need to take care of yourself so that you can be strong for everyone else when the time comes."

He tipped his head back and closed his eyes. "Twenty minutes."

"You know the beauty of our relationship?"

"Hmm?"

"Because I'm a mixed breed, I don't have to do what you say." The corner of her mouth twitched. "I'm going to go make us sandwiches and my favorite apricot tea. When I come back, you're going to eat and then you're going to bed."

Once she left the room, Silas laughed softly. Meredith's hardheaded nature was one of the things he loved best about her, but this time she was wrong. Twenty minutes and he'd be good to go.

He leaned his head back again, eyes closing. He'd just slipped into sleep, or at least he thought he had, when a bright light burned through the cracks in his eyelids. Was he dreaming? He'd fallen asleep on the beach or inside a tanning bed. He'd forgotten his sunglasses.

"Silas?"

He blinked rapidly. "Soleil? What are *you* doing here?"

"This is the only way I could talk to you." When he sat up with a start, she pressed a finger to his lips. "You sealed me out of your place. I can't get through the enchantment anymore. I was hoping I'd find you here eventually."

"What's going on?"

"I came to warn you. What you're doing will end in disaster."

His face tightened. "Could you be any more cryptic? What are you talking about?"

"I made a terrible mistake." Her face twisted. "You need to return the heart to me before it's too late."

"Not likely." He snorted derisively. He hooked an arm through the backpack.

She eyed the bag, obviously deducing its contents. "You don't understand. It's a trap." Noise from the kitchen made her glance in that direction. She lowered her voice. "She's not who you think she is."

"You're not who I thought you were."

Soleil pulled back as if he'd slapped her. "I am exactly who you thought I was," she snapped. "I gave you the heart, and I'm sorry I have to ask for it back. But it's for your own good. If you ever loved me—"

"Don't go there, Soleil. That ship has long since sailed. I respect what we had, but it's over. People's lives are depending on this. I'm sorry, but no."

"You don't understand. If you don't return the heart, everyone you think you're saving will be destroyed."

"How?"

"I'm... not sure. I don't know." She shook her head, looking confused and disoriented. Or was it guilt he saw in the way her mouth tightened? Someone had put her up to this. He was sure of it.

"You need to go," he said. "Now."

Soleil stared at him for a long moment. "It's over, isn't it? Permanently over. Even if I gave up what I do and did everything your way, it would be too late." Slowly she shook her head. "You're in love with Meredith. And you are a one-woman man." Her eyes opened wide with the realization, and she blinked several times as though she found it difficult to fathom that he'd moved on.

Silas had to consciously force himself to hold eye contact, although he desperately wanted to look away. He didn't want to see the hurt in her eyes. "Yes. I'm in love with Meredith." It was the first time he'd said it aloud. Why hadn't he said it to Meredith?

"I'll never understand how limited your love is, to only be capable of one lover at a time." Soleil tilted her head as she examined him. "It's more than that though. You don't trust me like you once did. Not since Ryker."

Light beaded in the corner of her eye, and it took Silas a moment to realize she was crying, literally shedding sunlight.

"I'm sorry if I hurt you. I think you have reasons for doing what you're doing, but I can't trust you on this. I need the heart a little while longer."

She brushed a tear away. "I'm happy to hear you've moved on. It gives me closure."

"Is that the real reason you're here? Closure?"

"No." She shook her head vehemently. "I'm here to save your life. You have no idea what you're dealing with."

"Then tell me. Tell me the truth. Do you know something about what Alex is planning?"

She turned, rubbing her temples. "I can't. I don't know the details. All I know is I was tricked into giving you that heart, and I was tricked for a reason." She grabbed one strap of the backpack and tried to pull it from his grip. "You must give it back."

Silas held firm. "There is no way I'm giving this to you. Not without a better explanation. Hell, even *with* a better explanation." A bad feeling was gathering in his chest. "Does this have to do with the lunar eclipse?"

She pulled harder on the backpack until they were engaged in a full-out tug-of-war. When it was clear Silas had her outmuscled, Soleil's usual sunny glow morphed. "This is for your own good!"

The heat she was putting off increased from a gentle ray of sunshine to what Silas imagined the inside of an oven might feel like. His skin reddened. His hands started to blister. The smell of burning hair tinged the air. He had no choice but to close his eyes and turn his face away. He released the backpack, shaking with pain as he flipped over the back of the couch to escape her scalding heat.

"I'm sorry," she cried.

"Not as sorry as I am." Meredith stood in the kitchen doorway, her gun drawn.

Soleil turned toward the light of the window, her form dulling at the edges as she blended and faded into her preferred mode of travel.

Pop. Pop. Pop. The bullets plowed into Soleil's chest, sending showers of sunlight that left cigarette-sized burns in the couch and rug before fizzling out. And then her light faded and she stared, shivering, toward the ceiling.

"Bet you weren't expecting me to have iron bullets,

bitch." Meredith marched to Soleil's side and yanked the scorched backpack from her hands. Then, with one look at Silas, she pulled her phone from her back pocket. "I need an ambulance… Two victims… Fae and werewolf… Yes. 336 Maple Grove…"

Why was she looking at him like that? And why couldn't Silas feel his hands? His charred, skinless hands. He leaned his head back against the carpet and closed his eyes.

TWENTY

"I want her guarded around the clock," Meredith shouted into the phone. "She almost killed one of our detectives."

Silas watched her pace the room, the dull ache of his body as he came out of sleep growing more intense. And he was thirsty. Very thirsty.

"Thank you. Okay. Got it. I'll be here until then." Meredith slid the phone back into her pocket. "How ya feeling, Alpha?"

"Like burnt toast," he rasped.

"Exactly how you look then." She nabbed a plastic cup from the bedside table and brought a straw to his lips. He sucked greedily, expecting water but getting a delicious, sweet liquid instead. With raised eyebrows, he pinned the cup between two bandaged hands and drained it dry.

"Peony nectar," she said. "It's supposed to speed healing. They covered your burns in fire lily balm, but the doctor said it would take at least twenty-four hours for your skin to grow back. And it's not going to feel good when it does."

"Heart?"

"I have it. It's fine. Your backpack is ruined, but dragon hearts are remarkably heat resistant." She laughed.

"She said it was a trap."

"Really? The person trying to steal the heart told you the heart was leading you down a road to doom. You don't say?"

He licked his lips. "She said someone tricked her into giving me the heart. What if she wasn't lying? What if someone manipulated Soleil?"

The corners of Meredith's mouth pulled back in contemplation. "I think she gave you the heart to win you back. Her demon lover got angry, demanded its return. She sensed it was over with you anyway and regretted her earlier generosity."

"It is the simplest explanation," he mumbled.

"Occam's razor—the simplest hypothesis is the most likely to be true."

He shook his head slightly. "She said... there was something she couldn't tell me. A reason she'd changed her mind."

"Hmm. That's convenient."

"I think one of us should interrogate her."

"Well, when she wakes up, that might be an option. Right now a bunch of fae doctors are trying to pick the iron out of her chest without setting themselves on fire."

With a moan, he sought to scratch his shoulder, the movement causing pain to radiate through his entire body. Meredith carefully scratched the spot for him.

"I can ask them to give you something for the pain." She refilled his drink from a pitcher on the bedside table. "But Jason and Selene are on their way to give you an update. You might want to stay sharp."

As promised, a knock came on the door a few minutes later, and Jason and Selene entered. "We came as soon as we heard."

Meredith welcomed them in. Kissing a small space above Silas's right eyebrow that didn't hurt as much as the rest of him, she gathered her things. "While you three talk, I'm going to go take care of a few things. I'll be back later." She swept from the room.

"How's it going, brother?" Jason said, scanning his bandages with a look of pity.

"Hurts," Silas said. He didn't expand on the statement. Even his lips hurt.

"We're about to make you feel a hell of a lot better." Jason took a seat in the chair near the bed. "Ryker wasn't happy when he heard you had the heart. Soleil had promised to keep it in her possession while Alex was on the move, and Ryker was worried it wasn't safe enough in his shop anyway. Apparently celestial fae are known to have hiding places that are impervious to outsiders. He acted rather hoodwinked and regretted taking Soleil up on her offer, although the sex was, in his words, delectable."

Silas scowled. So it wasn't Ryker who'd pressured

Soleil to get the heart back. He didn't even know she'd given it to him until Jason had said something.

"Sorry. That last part was probably an unnecessary detail." Jason crossed his arms. "Maybe you should take this, Selene."

With a conciliatory nod, Selene said, "When we asked Ryker about the ritual, he became extremely agitated. After a cursory inspection of his inventory, he admitted he'd only ever heard of one book with magic dark enough to mingle dimensions. It's a text called *The Book of Flesh and Bone*. It's like Panaal's own grimoire or something. It's written in blood on dried human skin with spells that Ryker said are powerful enough to raise the dead. There's only one copy, and he says it's been missing for years."

"No. He did not say that," Silas mumbled. "*The Book of Flesh and Bone*? Are you sure?"

"Yes. He said it used to belong to a clan of shifters."

"Nekomata," Silas said.

"How did you know that?"

"Because I helped Grateful Knight defeat the last group of supernatural baddies that tried to use that book to change the natural law." Too many words. Silas pressed the side of his cold cup against his sore lips. He needed to talk to Grateful. He tried to sit up, but the pain was too great. He fell back onto the pillow with a groan.

Looking worried, Selene reached for the call button. "I'll get the nurse."

Shaking his head, Silas breathed through the pain and tried to speak without moving his lips. "A few years ago, a group of vampires attempted to use *The Book of Flesh and Bone* to make themselves daywalkers. Grateful defeated them and took possession of the book. As far as I know, she still has it."

"That's good news. If she has it, then Alex doesn't," Selene said.

Jason glanced at her. "But Alex has a spell. We know he's working toward a major event."

"Ask Grateful," Silas mumbled.

"Laina was going there anyway. I'll text her," Jason said.

"If she'll let us see it, if we know what the spell is, it might not matter how Alex got a copy. We might be able to stop him," Selene said.

Silas nodded, then pointed at the call button. "Nurse." He needed medication for the pain and anything that might help him heal faster. If Alex had a spell from *The Book of Flesh and Bone*, things had gone from bad to much, much worse.

"We have a problem."

Silas woke to a worried-looking Grateful Knight standing over his bed. The drugs the fae nurse had given him were still raging in his system, and his vision wavered like he was viewing her in a fun house mirror. "Whassup, homegirl?"

"By the goddess. Seriously, Silas? Sober up. We've got trouble. Big fucking trouble." Grateful rubbed her lower back with both hands, her belly looking even larger than the last time he'd seen her.

He tried to sit up, shaking his head to clear it. "You heard 'bout the book?"

"Yeah… I heard. Laina stopped by to ask me about the ritual. Jason texted her about the book while she was still at my place."

"Do you think it could be the source of the ritual Alex is attempting?"

"*The Book of Flesh and Bone* is the same cursed text that opened up the hellmouth in the cemetery behind my house. It has the power to raise the dead, to build a bridge between hell and our world. And the spells and rituals inside can be wielded by anyone, even humans."

"And werewolves," he babbled.

"Yes. Even werewolves. If Alex has a spell from that book, we're in trouble. This isn't about your pack anymore. This concerns all of us."

"But you have the book. How could he have a spell if you have the book?"

"After I battled the Nekomata for that book, I knew there was no place I could hide it that would be safe. I was a new witch. My magic wasn't strong enough to protect it at the time."

"So where is the book now?"

"Luckily, a very powerful supernatural being owed me a favor. See, I'd saved this person and her friend from certain death at the hands of a mountain troll." Grateful's eyes widened.

"Mountain troll? Wait, you don't mean…"

"I gave it to Soleil to protect for me. She sealed it inside the marble floor of her bedroom. Celestial fae have hiding places that are impenetrable. It was the vampires who wanted it, and I knew it would be safe there because they can't touch her."

"But it's not only the vampires who want it anymore."

"No."

"Is the book still sealed within Soleil's floor?"

"I assume so, but given that she's still unconscious and barely clinging to life in a room down the hall, this isn't the right time to ask her."

"Fuck. If she gave Alex that book… She told me someone tricked her."

"She can't give it to anyone. Soleil offered me a fae favor. A fae favor is not like a favor between humans or even you and me. It's a binding magical contract. I asked her to seal the book within her protective walls for her lifetime. She did so. It can't be undone. A fae favor is as good as gold, and it lasts their entire life."

"Which means the book can only be accessed if and when Soleil dies," Silas said, suddenly sobering.

"Yes." Grateful's face fell. "So you see the problem. Celestial fae usually live thousands of years unless they're shot with iron bullets. Seems too coincidental that Soleil gets shot exactly when Alex needs the book most."

"Meredith shot Soleil to stop her from stealing the heart. It had nothing to do with Alex." He frowned. "We need to find out if that book is still in her room at the bordello."

Grateful frowned. "Soleil alone can access her hiding place."

Silas sighed heavily, the pain creeping up on him like a bad cold. He closed his eyes. "Then we wait until she's awake and we ask her."

TWENTY-ONE

Nightmares plagued Silas that night. He dreamed he was holding the heart, its red pulse beating between his fingers. Soleil was on her knees in front of him.

"You stole my heart, Silas Flynn!" she cried, her face contorted in anguish. The walls around him burst into flames, and as they burned, Soleil shot him a look of desperation. "She's not what she seems."

Then the dream shifted to Meredith's face as she pulled the trigger. Once, twice, three times. Iron bullets. When had she loaded iron bullets?

She's not what she seems.

"Hey, sleepyhead." Silas woke to Meredith hovering over him. "It's almost noon. Is the balm working? How do you feel?" She kissed him on the forehead.

He rubbed his bandaged hands together, grabbed a loose edge and started unraveling. His skin was pink but whole. He bent and straightened his fingers, testing the new skin. "Doesn't hurt anymore."

"Good."

Silas stared at her for a moment, still shaken by his nightmare. "Can I ask you something?"

"Sure. What's on your mind?"

"Why did you shoot her?"

Her eyebrows dipped in confusion. "Soleil? She was trying to steal the heart and was about to burn you alive. Why do you think? I was saving your life."

"But you shot her with iron bullets. Three times, even though the first seemed pretty effective. When did you load iron bullets? We've been using silver."

"I heard her talking to you, and I had a bad feeling." She tapped his bed rail with her pinky. "I'm a supernatural detective, same as you. I loaded the iron bullets because I thought I might need them. And as for shooting her three times—you were a burned, bloody mess. I got a little overexcited to save your life." She stroked her fingers through the side of his hair.

"Why have I never met you before? I mean, I knew your father. You say you've been to Rivergate, but I can't remember ever seeing you or your mother."

She shrugged. "I don't know. We never ran into each other. And I never shifted there because I'm a fox, not a wolf. It's only my mother and me, and she's been in a depression since my dad was murdered. She's traveling now, which is why I didn't introduce you." She squinted. "What is this about, Silas?"

"I feel like you're hiding something from me. Like I don't really know you."

She huffed. "Don't know me? We've stayed up talking every night since we met. You know me better than my therapist."

"What are you keeping from me?"

A shadow crossed her features, gone as swiftly as it came. If he hadn't been a detective, he doubted he'd have noticed it at all. But he *was* a detective, and Meredith was definitely hiding something.

Meredith parted her lips to respond when an alarm blared. The lights in the hall began to flash, and a crowd of doctors and nurses stomped past the open door. *Code blue. Code blue. Room 213*, blared a voice over the loud-speaker.

"That's Soleil's room." Meredith rushed into the hall.

"Wait!" Still sore, Silas pushed his aching body out of bed, hobbling into the throng of doctors and nurses. It wasn't hard to find the room. A crowd had gathered outside the door. A curtain of blue and green uniforms worn by equally colorful fae blocked the wall of windows along 213.

By the time Silas reached the hubbub, it was clear something had gone terribly wrong. A uniformed officer he recognized from the CCPD, Brighton was his name, hovered near the door as a tiny blue man stood on a stool and pressed an octagonal panel to Soleil's chest. There was a flash of light. The heart rate monitor pinged, a jagged peak forming on the display, and the doctors turned their faces toward the machine, frowning when the peak flattened once again.

"More fire lily, Doctor?" a green nurse with gossamer wings asked.

"It won't help. The iron levels in her blood are too far advanced." He placed two tapered fingers below her right collarbone, where Silas understood her second heart to be. And then he waited.

Soleil's normally sunny complexion was ashen, her blond hair turned black at the roots. Her eyes had sunk into her skull in a way that looked fake, almost as if she were wearing Halloween makeup.

The blue doctor wiped tears from his eyes. "I must ask everyone to evacuate the room." The staff scattered, their arms laden with equipment. They seemed to be stripping the area of everything that wasn't nailed down.

"What's going on?" Silas pushed through the crowd, a salmon swimming upstream, and forced his way into the glass chamber that was room 213.

"I'm sorry, sir. It isn't safe here. You must leave the room." The doctor placed a gentle hand on his elbow. "She's dying."

A painful lump formed in Silas's throat, and his next words came out as unintelligible squeaks. "No. She can't be."

"She is dying." The doctor touched his elbow. "I am sorry, sir, but you can't be with her when she goes. Celestial fae, like the stars they are from, do not go gently."

"Let me say goodbye." Silas's shoulders slumped.

"Quickly."

Silas approached Soleil. He tried to take her hand, but the skin of her extremities had turned black and burned as if liquid magma surged beneath her skin. "I wanted things to be different," he said. "I loved you once. You didn't deserve this."

Tears pricked the corners of his eyes, but he didn't cry, couldn't, whether by the heat in the room or his pride. He leaned over and pressed his lips to hers.

The kiss burned. Even though he did it quickly, only a peck, he might as well have kissed a hot iron.

"We must leave now, Mr. Flynn." The blue doctor tugged at his hand. "We have to seal the door!" His small size was no match for Silas's stature or strength, but it didn't matter. Silas followed willingly, the heat driving him from the room.

Once he was in the hall, the blue doctor closed the glass door and turned a giant wheel, steam venting above their heads. There was a suctioning sound, and a light above the door blinked from red to green.

"Vacuum seal is complete, Doctor," a bright pink nurse said.

Through the glass, Silas watched as fiery black magma swallowed Soleil's face and then her hands. The blanket over her burst into flames as her flesh expanded, inflating like a balloon. With a whoosh of flames, the bed incinerated, but although it turned to ash beneath her, her body did not fall to the floor. Instead, it hovered like a planet at the center of a void. Anything that resembled the Soleil Silas had known was gone, replaced by a sphere of liquid fire.

He swallowed around the lump in his throat, waiting and wondering what would happen next. A minute passed, then two, until finally what was left of her exploded, pushing out against the glass. The containment gave a menacing groan. Red light and bits of rock tapped the windows like storming hail, then collapsed in on itself, compressing into something dark and dense and completely devoid of life.

"I'm sorry for your loss," the doctor said, avoiding eye contact as he hurried toward his next patient.

Silas wiped under his eyes and searched the gathered crowd for Meredith, but she was gone. His phone rang.

"Is it true?" Grateful asked.

"Yes. She's dead."

"We've got to get the book."

Silas turned in a circle, searching the crowd. No Meredith. "I'll meet you at the bordello."

As soon as Silas saw the door of Maison des Étoilles hanging open, he knew something was way off. The door was never left open, not even in perfect weather. Breaking into a run, he climbed the steps, drawing his gun as he entered the bordello. No one was at the reception desk, but as he passed into the hall, he heard a moan. Backing up, he crept toward the sound and found Astrial collapsed behind the desk, a bloody gash near her temple.

"Astrial!" Silas knelt beside her and placed a hand on

her shoulder.

Her eyes fluttered. "I'm okay. By the goddess, Silas, something is wrong with Soleil."

He sucked in a breath. Of course there was something wrong with Soleil. She was dead. But he couldn't bring himself to say so. Instead, he stared blankly at the celestial fae.

"She came through the door a few minutes ago and pushed me so hard I banged my head on the corner of the desk. It happened so fast. She seemed really angry. Do you know what happened?"

Silas stiffened, his jaw tightening to the point of pain. "Soleil was here?"

"Is here, I think. She pushed me down and stormed to her room."

Helping Astrial to a seated position, Silas stood and turned toward Soleil's room. "Wait here."

He strode forward, drawing his gun. Soleil's door was closed, but light filtered through the crack under it. A shadow passed. Someone was in there.

Silently he released a slow, even breath through pursed lips, double-checked that the safety was off on his weapon, and reached for the doorknob, Glock steady in his right hand. With a kick, he flung the door open, ready for anything.

"Silas, thank the goddess you're here." Meredith stood by a gaping hole in the marble floor. An empty hole. "There's something we need to talk about. Look at this." She pointed toward a puddle of goo like a smear of blood-tinged petroleum jelly on the floor near her feet.

"What are you doing here?" Silas holstered his gun. "Astrial said someone pushed her down on the way back here. Was that you?"

Meredith shook her head. "No. But Silas, someone stole the book. We have to figure out who—"

"How did you know about the book?"

Her face etched with confusion. "We talked about it with Jason and Selene."

"No. *We* didn't talk about it. I talked about it with Jason and Selene. You weren't in the room."

"Yes, I was. Don't you remember?"

He studied her, his brain throbbing with the events of the day. "Are you a skinwalker?"

"My mother is a skinwalker. I'm a shifter. I told you—"

"So you can *only* turn into a fox?" He narrowed his eyes, his voice rising in volume.

"Yes. You know that. Why are you yelling at me?"

"Why did Astrial think Soleil pushed her down and came back here when Soleil is dead, and the only person standing here is you?"

"That's what I'm trying to tell you." The words caught in her throat. "Silas, if someone disguised themselves as Soleil, it must have been the same person who disguised themselves as Nickelova and stabbed Laina. Someone working for Alex." She looked back down at the hole in the floor, the hole where the book once was.

"How would Alex know Soleil was dead?"

"How should I know?" She raised her hands slightly.

"You knew Soleil was dying. You left the hospital to

come here without speaking with me first. Why didn't you wait for me?"

"Because I knew that Alex wouldn't wait." Meredith frowned. "We don't have time for this. I think—"

"The day we met, what did we fight about," he snapped, his hand resting on the handle of his gun.

She scoffed, spreading her hands in a way that looked genuine. "First the coffee. Then my position. You hate flavored coffee, and you have a mug with a wiener dog on it. Silas, it's me."

It looked like her. It smelled like her. *She isn't what she seems.* "Did you kill Soleil in order to get the book?"

Meredith shook her head. "You *know* it wasn't me. Look at me, do I have the book?"

She didn't. He wanted to believe her. God, he loved her. But his gut instinct told him something was off.

She took a step toward the door. "We have to go, Silas. We have to find him and stop this."

He shook his head. "Soleil is dead. We need to regroup. Make a plan."

Meredith took another step toward him. "There isn't time for that. You don't understand. I need to—"

He blinked, his head throbbing. "How is it you made it back here before me but didn't see whoever took the book, Meredith?"

"I came as soon as I could," Grateful called from the hallway.

Silas glanced at the witch for a fraction of a second. It was a fraction of a second too long.

A red blur bolted between his legs and past Grateful,

who leaped back and flattened herself against the wall. Meredith, in her fox form, raced down the hall. Silas ran after her.

"Meredith, wait!" He skidded around the corner toward the exit, but she was already gone.

"What the hell?" Grateful yelled, catching up to him in the foyer.

"Was that a fox?" Astrial asked, pressing a rag to her bleeding head.

He stared out the open door, a heavy feeling growing in his chest.

"Why did she bolt like that?"

"I have no idea." He ran a hand down his face. He didn't want to think that Meredith was somehow helping Alex, but why would she run? Still, it was Meredith. There had to be an explanation.

When Grateful didn't say anything, he turned to her. Shit, she was crying. He wiped a stray tear from the witch's cheek. For the first time, it hit him that Soleil was really dead. Gone.

"I can't believe this has happened," Grateful whispered. "Soleil was a bridesmaid at my wedding. She gave me a hand-embroidered baby blanket at my baby shower not two weeks ago. She was one of my best friends." The powerful witch rubbed circles over her belly, suddenly looking vulnerable and unbelievably sad.

"Mine too," he said. "Mine too." He pulled Grateful into a hug, then prepared himself to break the news to Astrial.

TWENTY-TWO

S ilas braced himself as he met his captain for a debrief at the CCPD. He'd had a bad feeling ever since he left the bordello, and not just because the book was gone and Soleil was dead. Something was up with Meredith. Case in point, she wasn't here.

"Soleil was murdered"—Captain Manahan kept his voice low, his eyes darting toward his office door—"by Meredith."

"Meredith shot her, but she was defending me," Silas insisted. There was no way the love of his life had murdered Soleil on purpose.

Manahan rubbed his head as if he was fighting an intense headache. "She didn't just shoot her. Silas, I'm sorry to be the one to tell you this, but she finished the job at Bojingles."

"What?" Silas balked. "Impossible. She was in my room with me when Soleil died."

"Officer Brighton said Meredith visited Soleil

moments before she died, and he thinks he saw her put something into her IV. We're pulling the video, but it tracks with the events leading to her death."

Silas scrubbed his face with his hands. He'd been on so many painkillers everything was a blur. Had she done it while he was sleeping, before she'd come to see him?

"Don't beat yourself up over it, Silas. You trusted her. I trusted her. Impeccable references." Manahan frowned, looking like he'd been up all night, trying to process the news about the detective he'd hired. "Of course I've got my people on this. We'll find her."

"She might not have been acting of her own free will," Silas said. It couldn't be true. It just couldn't. "Alex has ways of controlling people." If it had been Meredith, he wanted to think she was under the influence of sulfralite, but she'd been in the room when Grateful had drawn the black powder out of Laina and Selene. As of then, she hadn't been infected. And he'd spent most of the days since in her company.

"Yeah, well, we can figure that out when she's behind bars."

Silas rubbed his palms on his thighs. "I'll need to search her place."

"You still have a key?"

"Yeah."

"No sense bothering with a warrant then."

"Right."

"What about the book?"

"Grateful Knight says she knows someone who's seen *The Book of Flesh and Bone* in person. He might remember something about the spell. She's taking me to see him tonight."

"A vampire." Manahan spat out the word out like it tasted bad.

"How'd you guess?"

"Anyone who was alive long enough to read that book is either ancient or a friend of the last vampire who had it. Ancient or evil. Or both."

"She's worked with this guy before. He might be able to help. After seeing that vampire stake himself in the chest at ZeroHour, it's time we spoke with someone from his coven anyway."

Silas's skin tingled with a sudden rush of air in the closed room. Manahan. He was on to something, his wide eyes and sparked intuition making the air vibrate.

"You ever think that vamp stabbed himself because he knew Meredith would shoot him anyway?" Manahan asked.

Was it possible she'd been playing him the entire time? No. He refused to believe it. Goddess, he needed a shower. "I'll let you know what I find out."

"Be careful out there... but not too careful." Manahan picked up his coffee and took a long swig.

Silas stood to leave. "You know better than to think I would be."

AT TIMES LIKE THIS, SILAS WISHED HE STILL HAD A ZAFKA. After Alex murdered his last decoy and hospitalized

Laina's, Silas decided to leave the position unfilled temporarily. He didn't want anyone else's blood on his hands. But as he followed Grateful through an abandoned garage to a door with a conspicuous smear of red across the chipped paint, he longed for a body double. Vampires were dangerous. Always.

"You'd better let me go first. As a rule, vampires don't love werewolves. You know, on account of your bite being fatal to them," Grateful said.

"Only when we've shifted into wolf form. The rest of the time, vamps are stronger and faster." Silas eyed the dark doorway. "Is this the only way?"

"There are other passageways to Club Cabal, but they take longer. Believe me, once we're down there, you'll thank me for choosing the shortest route." Her sword, Nightshade, ignited, its purple glow illuminating a cobwebbed staircase that spiraled toward the gates of hell.

"You were saying something about going first?" He swallowed hard and moved aside to allow her to pass.

"These passageways connect businesses all over the city," Grateful said as she descended. "They were built by humans during Prohibition to smuggle moonshine. The vampires learned to feed on the smugglers. Bootleggers were less likely to complain to the authorities when one or two of their kind went missing. Doing so would give away their illicit activities."

"Great. So basically that rusty, fetid scent is, in fact, dried human blood."

"Do yourself a favor and don't look too closely at the walls."

"Too late." Silas turned his gaze away from the scratch marks in the stone. At some point in the past, someone had wanted out of this tunnel bad enough to try to claw their way through solid rock.

"So how's Lucas?" Silas asked, trying to distract himself from their surroundings.

"He's walking now. That's normal for a one-year-old. The floating, not so much."

"Floating?"

"Right out of his crib. We've had to pad his room."

"That bad, huh?"

"You know how human babies are using a spoon at this age? Maybe saying dada?"

"Yeah…"

"Imagine if, instead, they could set the walls on fire or make a million roaches pour from the pipes."

"No."

"Yes. He has quite the temper and an ever-growing grasp of his power. Rick and I are trying to teach him control, but I think he's too young to understand what he's doing. If he uses his magic without permission, he gets a time-out."

"Has to sit in the corner, huh?"

She glanced sheepishly in his direction. "In my attic. It's the only place that's safe."

Silas grunted. "You don't leave him up there?"

"No! Not alone. One of us is always with him, and he likes to play with Poe. But I'm not gonna lie. The kid spends a lot of time up there. I don't know how I'm going to do it with two." She sighed heavily.

"You'll do fine. You're a great mom. And hey, about the attic, ya gotta do what ya gotta do. Can't have the little tyke raising the dead or anything." He laughed.

She chuckled briefly before her smile melted into a more concerned expression.

"I hear music," Silas said.

"We're almost there."

They reached a set of stairs that led to another door, this one newly painted. A much different series of scents tickled Silas's nose: the spicy tang of cologne, the oaky scent of barrel-aged cognac and bourbon, the rich scent of tobacco, the musk of desire. The smooth crooning sound of a cool jazz tune grew louder as Grateful opened a door at the end of the corridor.

They entered a speakeasy lifted straight out of the 1920s. Waitresses milled through the crowd in flapper dresses and bobbed hairstyles. Red velvet fabric contrasted with dark wood furniture and mirrored walls. A dance floor was surrounded by a few dozen tightly spaced cocktail tables, each laden with guests dressed to the fang in jewels and couture. One face turned toward them, then another, until the entire establishment was staring at Grateful.

The music stopped, appalled expressions on the band members' faces. Fangs dropped. A female ran for the back exit.

"What are they staring at?" Silas whispered. "Is it because you're pregnant?"

"No. It's because I could end them in a heartbeat." Grateful sheathed Nightshade and held up her hands. "I'm looking for Julius," she said in a loud, clear voice.

The bartender pointed to a staircase at the back of the establishment. "He's in his bedroom."

"Please, as you were!" Grateful said, hands still in the air. Gradually, as she led the way to the back staircase, the music started up again and the place came back to life. "Being a Hecate does not always mean a warm welcome."

"I guess not."

The second floor was enormous. Grateful stopped at one of twelve doors along a lengthy hallway that looked like something out of a modern-day castle.

"How do you know which one is his bedroom?" Silas asked.

"That's a story for another time." Grateful raised an eyebrow before rapping three times on the six-paneled mahogany door. There was no answer. "Hold on to your ass. This could get ugly."

She whispered a spell, and the knob turned a bright shade of purple. It opened easily at the turn of her wrist.

Inside, Silas gaped at a room that belonged in a movie. Two stories high, the walls were lined with floor-to-ceiling bookshelves filled with leather-bound volumes from an age gone by. A massive four-poster bed wrapped in red velvet stood at the center of the room, oddly out of place among what otherwise could be a library. A fireplace blazed near a pair of Louis XVI-style chairs. And between those two chairs, a tall, dark vampire drank from the neck of a twentysomething human. She wore a medieval-style dress, the bodice of which had been pulled down to reveal her breasts. Silas averted his eyes.

Julius came off the girl's throat with a pop and whispered something in her ear. She covered herself and staggered from the room. Silas assumed her drunken swagger was more likely due to blood loss than alcohol. The vampire wiped blood from the sides of his mouth with his thumb.

"Grateful Knight, to what do I owe the pleasure?" His eyes flicked to her enormous belly and he grimaced.

"Is she going to be okay?" Silas interrupted, gesturing in the direction the human girl had hobbled. "She could barely stand up."

Julius leaned an elbow against the mantel. "Not that I owe you an explanation, wolf, but Stephanie is a professional blood donor. Believe me, she can take care of herself."

"Since when do you hire out for blood?" Grateful asked.

"Are you here to talk about my love life, or would you care to explain why you've brought a werewolf into my home?"

"This is Silas. I think you've met before, at my wedding. No? He's a detective for the CCPD."

Julius ran a hand through his longish, dark brown hair. He reminded Silas of a petulant rock star, good-looking in a cologne model sort of way with a perpetually brooding air. "I'm hungry, Grateful. Get to the point."

"Soleil is dead. *The Book of Flesh and Bone* was taken from her room. It's out there again, and we think Alex Bloodright has it."

Julius stilled. Silas hadn't spent much time with vampires, but he found his lack of movement unsettling. He didn't even breathe. But then, vampires didn't need to breathe, did they?

"Would you like a drink?" the vampire said. "I suddenly feel I need one." He paced to a bar behind the giant bed. "Silas, can I get you a brandy? I take you for a brandy man."

"Brandy would be fine."

"Water," Grateful said. "While you're pouring, what do you think Alex is doing with the book? I take it from your reaction that you know who he is."

Brandy gurgled from the decanter, Julius intent on its dark flow into the snifter in his hand. "I know who Alex is. Everyone in the vampire district knows of Alex."

"Where is he?" Silas growled.

Julius returned to where they waited by the fire and handed them their drinks. "Down, doggie. If I knew, I'd tell you. Alex and I are hardly besties. I know of him, that is all."

"I found sulfralite in one of his victims," Grateful said.

"Sulfralite?" Julius tipped his head skeptically. "Are you sure?"

"Positive." Grateful sniffed the water in her glass before taking a long drink.

"One of your kind staked himself right in front of me," Silas said. "That's not usual behavior for a vamp, is it?"

Julius stilled. "Did, by chance, the vampire in question have a tattoo of an ankh symbol on this area of his neck?" He ran a finger along his throat.

"Yeah. How did you know?" Silas asked.

"It's worse than I thought," Julius murmured. He tossed back his scotch and poured another. "I think Alex is up to something. Something dark."

A chill traveled Silas's spine. "We came to the same conclusion. We think he's trying to raise Panaal."

The vampire stiffened, his body going still as marble, eyes cold, dark. "Perhaps we should take a seat and discuss this further." He pointed his long, tapered fingers toward the chairs near the fire.

The entire situation made Silas jumpy. He turned too quickly, bumping into Grateful and accidentally dropping his glass. It shattered near his toes. He bent down to pick up the pieces, but Grateful grabbed his arm.

"Don't bother. I'll get it." She took a deep breath and blew. The pieces of glass whisked off the floor, binding together and re-forming in his hand. The remaining brandy poured itself back inside. When it was whole again, she took another deep breath and licked her lips. "I wouldn't drink that." She glanced knowingly toward the floor and shook her head. With a sigh, Silas followed her to the chairs, handing the repaired glass to Julius on the way.

"What do you know about the spell Alex might be using?" Silas sat down, crossing his arms against the less-than-magical feeling going on within his chest. It wasn't comfortable knowing you were sitting between a vampire who could drain you dry and a witch who could blow you to bits with a whistle.

"I've seen this before," Julius began, lowering into one of the antique chairs. "A thousand years ago, there was a witch..."

"A thousand years ago?" Silas chuckled, but Julius and Grateful stared at him without a hint of levity in their expressions. "Sorry. I forgot you, uh, live that long."

"As I was saying"—Julius sipped his scotch—"around a thousand years ago, there was a witch, a dark sorceress who wanted to raise Panaal—"

"Seems like that's a popular goal of you darky-dark types," Silas said.

"You might believe such a thing, wolf, but in fact, only a creation of the goddess can complete the spell."

"Huh?" Silas glanced at Grateful for an explanation, but it was Julius who gave it.

"Witches, shifters, and the light fae, in all their forms, are the goddess's creation. Dark fae, vampires, and demons were created by the horned god, Panaal."

"What about ogres? Leprechauns? Trolls?" Silas asked.

"Leprechauns are a type of dark fae. The others evolved over time from mixing species."

"Primordial boom-chicka-wow-wow. Got it."

Julius turned to Grateful, a look of annoyance on his face as if Silas were an oversized and inconvenient dolt. Grateful refused eye contact and sipped her water.

What a pretentious asshole. Silas stretched his legs out and crossed them at the ankle.

"As I was saying, Alex is only capable of completing this specific ritual because he is a werewolf. Legend has it that every supernatural being has strengths and weaknesses that were won or lost based on a game of chance between Hecate and Panaal."

"I'm guessing it wasn't Parcheesi." Silas laughed and shifted in his chair as Julius stared down his perfectly straight nose at him. "Just trying to lighten the mood." He quieted, wishing he had another brandy.

"No one knows the games of the gods. It is assumed it had something to do with a labyrinth as both Hecate and Panaal live in one. But I digress. Hecate won the game and chose to rule over the day, and Panaal received the night by default, and that is how we have existed to this day. Humans were another matter entirely. They have their own creator, their own gods. We've lived in balance with them based on ancient magic and natural law."

"Sooo I take it Panaal isn't a fan of the status quo?" Grateful asked.

"Existing as a creature of the night is not the paradise you might think it is." Julius stared into the fire, swirling his scotch. "My kind would have performed the ritual centuries ago if it was possible, but the old magic doesn't allow it. Only a creation of the goddess can undo what has been done."

"No offense, but since you admit you're in the 'raise Panaal' camp, how can we trust anything you say?" Silas asked.

Julius exchanged a long, wistful look with Grateful. "If you couldn't trust me, you'd be drained and fed to the ogres downstairs by now. No one would ever find your remains, wolf. Ogres ingest everything, even the bones."

"Is that a threat?"

"A reality. I have made my peace with this existence of mine. There are things... people... I would hate to see come to an untimely end. Suffice it to say, I'm on your side. Although my patience wears thin with your discourtesy."

"You were saying," Grateful interrupted, giving Silas the side-eye. "One thousand years ago..."

"I was close to a dark witch who wanted to break the natural law. It is said that if a son or daughter of Hecate sacrifices a representative of each of the primary sons and daughters of Panaal, that Panaal will rise, all the prior rules of order will end, and the game will be played again, most likely with a much different end."

"Why would you assume a different end?"

"Because while the original game was played by the gods, with their new creations waiting in the shadows, the book says that the new game will feature all of us playing against each other. It will be an all-out war between creatures of the night and those of the day, and humans will be our pawns in the game."

Silas shrugged. "Doesn't mean your kind will win."

"Yes, it does," Grateful said. "Because not only will our kind be battling the creatures of the night, our nature will require us to protect the humans from slaughter. We'll have to fight twice as hard, and we won't have the protections we do today. Vampires will be able to walk in daylight. Demons will possess humans at will."

"Exactly." Julius finished his scotch. "Chaos. Disorder. Thousands of years of war."

Silas leaned forward, bracing his elbows against his knees. "So how did you stop this witch?"

Only Julius's eyes shifted toward Silas, the rest of him unnaturally still. "I seduced her and tore her heart from her chest with my bare hands. Sorry, but I doubt that will work on Alex. From what I hear, he doesn't swing that way."

"So then, we have to stop him from getting the ingredients for the spell," Grateful said. "He'll need a demon, a dark fae, and a vampire. We have the only dark fae I know of locked in a room in Saint Johns."

"What would he want with unconsecrated bones?" Silas asked.

"If they are a demon's human bones, they can be used to summon a demon," Julius said.

"A demon's human bones? I didn't think demons had bones, let alone human ones."

"If a human allows a demon to possess him or her and then dies, the demon will live on but will maintain a connection to the human's bones. Control the bones and you control the demon."

"Fuck," Silas said. "So he has access to a demon."

"And he also has a vampire," Julius seethed.

"He does? How do you know?"

"Because two of my coven went missing recently. A couple. Both with ankh tattoos. The vampire Silas saw stab himself in the chest is undoubtedly one of our missing brethren, the male. His mate is still missing."

"Which means Alex has her."

Julius nodded slowly.

"He still needs a dark fae," Grateful said. "And we have Nickelova locked down tight. We can still stop this. It's not like her kind is common."

"Fuck!" Silas grabbed his head as he bounded from the frilly chair and paced the space in front of the fire.

"What is it?" Grateful asked.

Silas turned toward the witch and the vampire. "I no longer have Nickelova's heart."

TWENTY-THREE

The last person to have Nickelova's heart was Meredith. He'd had it with him when Soleil had almost burned him alive and Meredith had shot her. Meredith had told him she'd put it somewhere safe, but was that before or after she aligned herself with Alex? Or had she always been helping Alex? He still hoped there was another explanation for her strange behavior, but if there was, he couldn't guess it.

Intuition was the lifeblood of good detective work. You could have all the facts, all the witnesses, but to know the truth took a sixth sense, the ability to ask all the right questions and fit all the pieces together. Silas's intuition was humming. There was something off about this Meredith thing.

It wasn't only that she was his fated mate. He loved her—he was sure of that now. He'd never told her as much, but he supposed his heart had leaped out of his chest and ran to her the moment she'd walked into the station and announced she was his partner. Regardless of his feelings though, how could she be helping Alex of her own free will after knowing the man killed her father? No. The more he thought about it, the more certain he was that she was infected with sulfralite and under Alex's control.

He jiggled her key in her lock and let himself into her small home. The stench of melted fabric burned in his throat. Damn. The couch was scorched like a campfire marshmallow. *Had* Soleil meant to kill him? Would she have stopped if Meredith hadn't shot her? Maybe. But only because he'd relinquished Nickelova's heart.

"Meredith? Are you here? We need to talk." Silently he drew his gun. He had no intention of shooting her if he saw her, but if she was under Alex's influence, he might have to defend himself. That was the only explanation for what the captain had said. Meredith wasn't a killer. At least, he believed she wasn't.

He crept forward, moving past the kitchen to sweep into the bathroom and then the two bedrooms. When he was sure the place was deserted, he reholstered his weapon.

Damn, the place smelled like burnt coffee. He followed the scent to the kitchen where he found the warmer on the ancient Mr. Coffee had burned the remains of a pot to a thick sludge. He turned the machine off, snorting the scent from his nose.

She wasn't there. And by the looks of things, she hadn't been since the incident with Soleil. The box of apricot tea she'd said she was going to make him was still on the counter next to two dried-out sandwiches with congealing mayonnaise.

"Shit, where did you go? Does he have you too?"

His head began to pound. He was supposed to keep her safe. If Alex got to her, he'd never forgive himself.

Defeated, he picked up the phone and called Grateful, updating her on what Manahan had told him.

"I don't know what to tell you, Silas. Nickelova is here, safely behind my enchantment," Grateful said. "If Meredith has the heart or the book and gave it to Alex, he hasn't tried to use it yet."

He ended the call, noticing the photo of her parents he'd seen before on the fridge. Should he call Meredith's mother? It was possible she'd go to her to hide. He chided himself for not insisting he meet Mrs. Turner when Grayson was still alive. He didn't even know her first name. He'd have to check with the Lycanthropic Society secretary for her contact information. Resolved that this was a dead end, he turned off all the lights and left for home.

"Be careful."

Silas jumped at the whisper, turning from his car to find Grateful standing behind him in his driveway. "When did you get here?"

"Just now. Hey, didn't you give Meredith a free pass through the enchantment around your house?"

Silas frowned. "Fuck."

"Yeah. So I say again, be careful."

He crept up the stairs to the front stoop. He could hear Maggie run to the door, her nails clicking on the hardwood. If Meredith had been there recently, he couldn't tell. What traces of her scent he could pick up could have been from before. He entered the house with one hand on his gun.

"Looks okay," he said.

Grateful nodded in agreement but didn't lower her sword as she entered his living room. Silas scratched Maggie's head, sniffing the air.

"What the hell?" He turned the corner into his kitchen, shaking his head.

"What do you smell?"

"She was here."

Grateful raised her sword higher.

"She's not here now. Hours ago. Maybe yesterday. Her scent has faded. But she fed Maggie. She left the kibble out."

"Why would she come here to feed your dog?"

"I have no idea." He moved deeper into the room. "The door to my bedroom is closed. I know I left it open."

"What if it's a trap? There could be a bomb under the house for all we know, just waiting to be tripped by opening the door."

"Wouldn't Nightshade alert you if there was?"

"Nightshade detects supernatural threats, not physical ones."

"I don't think there's a bomb. Why would she feed Maggie and then blow her up?"

"Why would she call an ambulance for Soleil and then inject her with something to kill her?"

"Touché."

Grateful crowded up behind him with her sword, her pregnant belly bumping into his back. She murmured something, and a wave of purple wrapped around both of them. "Protection spell. Stay close to me."

"What about Maggie?"

She called the dog, and Silas lifted the pooch into his arms. "She's covered."

"Okay, I'm going in." He turned the knob and slowly opened the door with his free hand. What he saw inside made his chest feel heavy. A wave of exhaustion overcame him. The horizon had flipped upside down. Nothing made sense anymore.

"It's not a bomb," he said.

Grateful peered around him toward the bed. "Holy crow! That is the one thing I did not expect to see here."

There, on top of his comforter, was Nickelova's heart.

TWENTY-FOUR

"If Meredith is helping Alex, why would she return the heart?" Silas lifted the fist-sized ruby from the bed, staring at the throbbing, internal glow with stark curiosity.

"If she's *not* helping Alex, why would she kill Soleil?"

Silas glanced at Grateful. "I have no idea." He turned the events over in his head, but none of it made sense.

"Maybe she was magically compelled to do what she did, but then when the spell wore off, she returned this to me. Or she returned this to me before she was compelled, but that would mean Meredith purposefully shot Soleil."

Grateful snorted. "Alex isn't stupid. If he had Meredith under his influence for five minutes, he'd be sure to get that heart in four."

Silas sighed. What was he missing that he couldn't draw a line from point A to point B? What did this mean? And how should he proceed with the case?

Grateful groaned and sheathed her sword. "I just thought of a reason."

"Hit me."

"She returned the heart to you because she wants you to use it."

"Huh?"

"Nickelova will lead you to Alex. Alex probably needs Nickelova for the spell. She's the dark fae sacrifice. It's a trap. He needs her, and this is a way to make sure she's delivered."

Silas set the heart down and backed up a step.

"What's wrong? You don't look so hot." Grateful placed a hand on his shoulder.

"How could I be so stupid?" He stared at Grateful in horror. "Soleil tried to warn me. She said the heart was a trap. She wanted the heart back so that I couldn't use it to get to Alex. She was trying to protect me. Alex doesn't only need the heart; he needs Nickelova too. Everything that's happened has driven us to bring Nickelova and her heart here. We've done his dirty work for him."

"And Meredith killed her. She must have known Soleil figured out the plan."

The pit was back in Silas's chest. *Why, Meredith? Why?* "So what do we do? We've got to do something to stop Alex." Silas's pulse pounded like a bass drum against his sternum.

"Simple. You won't play into his hands. You won't use Nickelova to find Alex."

His back pocket vibrated. With a deep breath, he answered his phone.

"Silas?" Kyle's voice sounded annoyed.

"Yeah?"

"Can I talk to Laina for a minute? She's not answering her phone."

"Laina's not here." Why would he think Laina was with him?

"What are you talking about? You came by the cottage and picked her up. She left with you not five minutes ago. You said it was an emergency."

Silas grabbed Grateful's arm, fear draining all the warmth from his body. "Kyle, that *wasn't* me."

Hours later, it was evident Laina was gone. Silas, Jason, and Selene had searched the city for her while Polina attempted a locator spell. Gerty and Kyle enlisted the trees, sending word out through the forest fae to report any sight of Laina. And Rick and Grateful flew over rural Red Grove in shifts, searching for any clue to where Alex had taken her. But when they all met at Rivergate to discuss the results of their quest, Laina was nowhere to be found.

"He wants Nickelova and the heart. Alex will trade Laina for the fae he needs," Grateful said. She'd arrived alone, Rick returning home to watch Lucas.

"If I bring Alex his dragon fae, he'll be able to complete the spell." Silas rubbed the back of his neck. He had to do something. He refused to allow Alex to hurt Laina, but he wasn't going to cave to his demands either.

"I don't care what he does with Nickelova. I want my wife back!" Kyle yelled.

Gerty and Selene tried to comfort him.

Jason cracked his neck, a deep furrow appearing in his brow. "What if we turn the tables on his plan?"

"What are you suggesting?" Grateful asked.

"If Silas uses Nickelova to find Alex, maybe the rest of us can follow him in secret. Once we know where Alex is, we can act."

Silas nodded slowly. "Polina, Logan said you couldn't see Alex's future, but you can see mine, right?" He gestured at his chest.

Polina was a metal witch. Not only could she travel by gold dust, she could see the future in the stretch of silver she had in her magic room. It didn't work on Alex, but it would work on Silas.

Grateful held up a finger. "We can use Polina's magic mirror to follow you. We'll come to you as soon as we have a location."

Polina nodded eagerly. "It will work. Logan can reach you in an instant."

"Rick and I can follow from a distance," Logan added. "We can cloak ourselves."

"Build a trap out of Alex's trap," Kyle said. "It could work. It has to work."

"I'll go with Silas," Jason said.

"It's too risky, brother."

"No. It's too risky for you to go alone. Nickelova might try something funny. If I'm there, I can have your back." One thing about Jason, the guy knew how to play the hand he was dealt.

"It's a plan," Silas said. "Jason and I will use Nickelova and the heart to find Alex. Grateful and Polina will observe us using magic. Once we lock onto Alex's location, either Logan or Rick will come to our aid."

"What about me?" Kyle asked.

"I need you and Gerty to stay at the cottage in case Laina comes back without us or the forest fae learn where she is. Selene needs to help here, managing preparations for the shift tomorrow. No one can know the royal family is at risk. It would cause a panic. We don't know where he's holding Laina. If something goes wrong, all of you are our backup."

After a brief conversation with Gerty, Kyle reluctantly agreed. "Do this for me, Silas. Bring my wife and my baby back alive."

"I will," Silas said, and he meant it.

"I'll make preparations," Grateful said.

Polina shrugged. "My silver is ready. No preparations are needed."

"I need to find a babysitter," Grateful mumbled.

Silas exchanged glances with the rest of the group. "We go first thing in the morning."

TWENTY-FIVE

When Silas arrived at the hospital, he was surprised to find that Nickelova had fully recovered. Her skin was plump, her complexion vigorous. Even her platinum bob was back in place. Considering she'd been bald less than a week ago, he took her full head of hair as certain evidence that magic was involved in her healing. He'd have to thank Grateful for her help after this was over. Come to think of it, he'd owe Grateful a debt of gratitude for a few things if they all came out of this alive.

"You're looking better," Silas said to Nickelova, the heart firmly in his hand. "You've gained weight."

"That will happen when you're forced to eat sixteen hours a day." She refused to look at him, choosing to focus intently on a spot on the hospital wall instead. The room was a pit, covered in stacks of trays and strewn clothing. There were only two people who could tend to Nickelova: Grateful and her trusted friend Michelle. No one else could see, hear, or clean up after her, and by the looks of it, Nickelova didn't feel the need to pick up after herself.

"It's time to go. We need to find Alex."

"Tomorrow night is the lunar eclipse. Trying to nip his plan in the bud?" She stage-whispered the last as if she were speaking to a small child. "I'm sorry to tell you, this plan is far beyond the bud stage."

"Get dressed."

"You can't stop him, you know. No one has ever been able to stop Alex. Not even me. He thinks three steps ahead."

Silas elevated the heart. "You will get dressed," he said with intention. "And then you will take me to Alex."

She bounded from the bed like it was on fire and reached for a pair of jeans hanging over the arm of the only chair in the room. "Are you going to stand there and watch me?"

"I'll wait outside. Don't dally. We have work to do." He slid into the hall, tucking the heart back into the new satchel he'd purchased to replace the backpack Soleil had barbecued.

Jason approached from the direction of the parking garage. "Is she cooperating?"

"You could call it that. How is Kyle doing?"

"Selene is keeping him calm. He didn't sleep last night. Gerty has her eye on the place. I didn't emphasize the fact that Kyle might be Fireborn Pack's first hybrid alpha if something happens to all of us."

"He knows."

"This plan," Jason said, "you're sure your witchy friends are up to the task?"

"Positive. Polina and Grateful are a powerful duo. We're covered."

"Hey, you're friends with Logan. Have you ever seen Polina's magic mirror?" Jason asked.

"No. But he's told me about it. Apparently it's this giant stretch of silver that tells the future. It's ancient and practically foolproof. If they see us in trouble, they'll send help."

"Right. In the form of Rick and Logan, their caretakers."

"Both of them can shift into beasts big enough to hold off a T. rex. That I have seen," Silas said. "Believe me, we're in good hands."

"And Alex won't see them coming." Jason rubbed his hands together. "This has to work."

"It's going to work."

Jason leaned against the wall and fidgeted with his tie. He was too dressed up for this type of work, but Silas rarely saw Jason in jeans and a T-shirt. It wasn't his style.

"You nervous, brother?" Silas asked.

"Actually, I was wondering…"

"Yeah?"

The lines in Jason's face etched a more serious expression than was strictly at home there. "How are you handling this? You lost a woman you once loved and the woman you were in love with all on the same day. And now this thing with Laina."

"You're wondering why I'm not collapsed on the floor in a puddle of my own tears."

"It has crossed my mind."

"Soleil and I were close once. I loved Meredith. I still love her, despite everything. But there's something I love more." He adjusted the satchel on his shoulder. "Our family, Jason. What would Dad say if I crumbled and left our sister in danger? And what kind of alpha would I be if I let the pack down?"

"He'd say you were human."

Silas swatted a hand between them. "I'm not human. I'm a werewolf, and I'm the alpha. I'm not going to give Alex the satisfaction of knowing he got the best of me even for a minute."

"But shit, you're only one wolf. Anyone else would be crushed. Sometimes we don't choose these things."

He paused, blinking at his brother. "It hurts. It does. Meredith is my mate." There, he'd said it.

Jason inhaled through his teeth. "You're sure."

He nodded once. "I planned to seal the deal before this happened. I still can't believe she'd betray us."

His brother's hand landed on his shoulder and squeezed. "Are you sure you can do this? What if you have to face her? What if you have to end her?"

"I'll do what I have to do."

Jason shook his head. "I'll back you up, and then I'll be there for you... after."

The water was getting a little deep for Silas, his mood drifting toward self-pity, so he was relieved when the door opened and Nickelova stood fully dressed at the threshold.

"We'll need a car," she said. "I feel the amulet from a distance."

"It's not in the city?"

"No."

"Let's go." Silas began to walk away.

"I can't leave the room, Einstein," Nickelova said.

Jason laughed. "Oh, that's my fault. Grateful told me to…" He removed a red cloth from his pocket and scrubbed the threshold near her feet. He'd barely cleared a six-inch patch when she leaped over his head and bolted down the hall.

Silas squeezed the heart inside his bag.

"Ahhh." Nickelova froze, arching her back as if she was in pain. Reluctantly, she limped back to his side.

"You will stay close to us, Nickelova," Silas commanded. "You will not try to escape or call attention to yourself."

Her eyes stared, empty and hateful, toward the window.

"Come on. We're wasting daylight."

Silas kept an eye on Nickelova while Jason drove. The dragon fae directed them onto the highway and out of the city. It was a good thing the Ford Transit had a full tank of gas.

"You're sure this is the way?" Silas asked from the passenger's seat, the dark fae's heart securely in his lap.

"The dragon-scale amulet calls to me. I'm sure."

Nickelova's tightly crossed arms didn't fill him with confidence in her, but she had no other choice than to tell him the truth. He'd made sure of that.

"There's only one town in this direction—Red Grove." They'd already searched every inch around Laina's cabin.

She shrugged and stared aimlessly out her window. "This is where I sense it."

Silas scanned the horizon for anything unusual. They passed Monk's Hill Cemetery and Grateful's house, continuing through the tiny town of Red Grove. Nothing. A few miles past Laina's cabin, they were officially in the middle of nowhere.

"It's here," Nickelova said.

"Here? There's nothing out here." Jason pumped the brakes and scanned the area.

"It's here. I can feel it." Nickelova stared at the field on the side of the road. A few trees grew in the expanse of space, but nothing dense enough to hide Alex.

"Why would he even be out here?" Silas said. None of this made sense. "Is Alex invisible?"

"I don't know if he's invisible," Nickelova snapped. "You ordered me to bring you to Alex by tracking the power of the amulet. I feel the amulet here, and Alex would never go anywhere without it. That's all I know."

Silas called Grateful.

"It's Polina, Silas. Grateful is, uh—"

He balked at the sound of Polina's voice. "You've got to be kidding me—"

"At the hospital with Rick, giving birth," Polina confirmed.

"We can't turn back. Alex has Laina." Silas exchanged a worried glance with Jason.

"Relax. I'm going to help you. I'm watching you in my mirror, and Logan is nearby."

"Nickelova says Alex is here, but I see nothing."

"I have a vision of you hugging Laina, but the image is fuzzy," Polina said. "I think the dragon fae magic is interfering with my divination."

"Well, there's a whole lotta nothing out here. Unless Alex has made himself a cloak of invisibility," Silas said.

"I can see it now. Laina is there, Silas. Somewhere. I'm sending Logan."

"Not too close. I don't want to alert Alex to our presence if he is here." Silas ended the call and climbed from the van, opening the back door for Nickelova. "You lead the way."

Nickelova hesitated for a moment, scanning the field.

Silas exchanged glances with Jason.

"It's this way." She strode toward two trees in the distance, Silas and Jason following close behind.

"Why do I feel like she's not telling us everything?" Jason said.

"Because she's a tyrannical killer who almost ate your fiancée."

"Yep. That's why."

Nickelova stopped short of the area between the two

trees.

"Why did you stop? Where's Alex?" Silas demanded.

She raised one hand, a look of confusion on her face.

"Did you see that?" Jason asked.

"What?"

"The air near Nickelova's hand kind of shimmered. I feel like I've seen this before." Jason tipped his head to the side and squinted.

"I can feel it." Nickelova stepped forward and extended her arm. Her hand perforated the misty afternoon light and disappeared to the elbow.

"Silas, stop her!" Logan yelled from behind him, where he'd just arrived.

Silas glimpsed his friend for only a moment, and then Nickelova's hands clamped on his and Jason's shoulders.

"It's a portal!" Jason yelled.

But it was too late. Silas winced as he and Jason pitched forward along with Nickelova, toppling into nothingness.

"Silas!" Logan yelled, but his friend's voice was cut off as all three of them landed inside what looked like an empty barn.

"Where are we, Nickelova?" Silas growled.

"I have no idea," she said snarkily. "But I did what you ordered me to do. It's here." She pointed across the barn.

Hanging from a tack hook on the wall was the dragon fae amulet. Silas crossed the large space and lifted the heavy talisman from the hook, draping the chain over his palm. It looked authentic. What was it doing here?

"What the hell is going on?" he murmured.

His phone rang.

"The amulet is here," he answered, registering that the number was Polina's. "But Alex and Laina aren't with it."

"Silas, where are you? I can't see you anymore," Polina yelled, a tinge of panic in her voice.

"I'm in some kind of barn."

"Silas? Silas? Are you there?"

"I'm here. Polina?"

The line went dead.

"What is this place?" Jason asked. He stared at Nickelova, who was turning a slow circle.

"He lured us here," she said ominously, shaking her head. "I told you. He's always three steps ahead. Always."

Silas pressed the GPS app on his phone. "I can't get any service. Nickelova, take us back the way we came." He rested his hand on the heart in his bag.

"I can't." She shrugged. "The portal is closed, and I have no power without my heart."

Silas searched the walls for any opening, but there were no doors or windows.

"We have the amulet. Can you use it to get us out of here?" Jason asked Nickelova.

"I can try." She held a hand out to Silas.

"You will use this amulet only to return us to Red Grove," Silas commanded with his hand inside his bag, gripping her heart. Although she rolled her eyes, he handed the amulet to her.

Draping it across both palms, she closed her eyes and

tried again. Although the amulet pulsed, nothing changed.

"I can't," she said. "There's magic, powerful magic, preventing me from creating a portal."

Silas removed the amulet from her grasp and stared at it hopelessly. He couldn't use it, and there were no doors or windows. *Fuck.*

"You could give me back my heart," she said again. "I'd be stronger."

"Fat chance," Jason said, trying his phone again.

"It won't help you anyway. Nothing can help you now." Alex materialized at the center of the barn, dark blond hair a wild mess around his head. His skin was even paler than before and waxy as a corpse, and his eyes were dark as the depths of hell. A familiar face appeared at his side.

"Laina?" Silas reached for his sister. "Are you okay? Did he hurt you?"

She strode to Silas and tossed her arms around his shoulders. He hugged her back, but the hug felt unfamiliar, almost as if he were hugging a stranger. He couldn't describe why, exactly, whether it was the pressure or the length of the hug. But Laina wasn't herself. Had he infected her with sulfralite again?

As Laina retreated from the hug, she swiped the amulet from his grip and tossed it to Alex.

"What are you doing?" Jason spread his hands, a look of betrayal on his face. Laina backed toward Alex, her eyes going dull and blank.

"What have you done to her?" Silas drew his gun and leveled it on Alex's head. "Let us out of here."

"That's not going to happen."

Silas pulled the trigger. Although the gun fired, the bullet never reached its target. The amulet pulsed and its magic wrenched the gun from his hand; the bullet rerouted into the ceiling. His Glock skimmed across the floor into the wall.

"Try to be civil, Silas. While you're still alive, it's the least you can do." Alex held out a hand to Nickelova and summoned her with his fingers.

She ran to his side. "I knew you'd come for me."

"Oh, Nickelova. Of course I would. I need you."

"I need you too," she said. "Give me my heart, and we'll pick up where we left off."

He gripped her by the lower jaw. "Not yet."

Nickelova's face fell. He pushed her aside and turned toward Silas. "The thing about you, Silas, is you are utterly predictable. Always brave. Always selfless. I knew if I stabbed Laina and made her believe it was Nickelova, you'd retrieve her from that mountain and use her to find me. Ryker would never have given me her heart. The demon could smell me a mile away. But I easily deceived and manipulated your ex-girlfriend into doing the dirty work for me, and believe me, from what I hear, Ryker was dirty work."

"Shut up. You shut the fuck up," Silas said.

"My heart, Alex," Nickelova whimpered. "Give it to me."

"Don't worry, darling. You won't need it until

tomorrow night. It only has to be inside your chest a moment before I sacrifice you."

Nickelova looked confused as she backed away from him. "Sacrifice me? What are you talking about?"

"The ritual I must perform requires a demon, a vampire, and a dark fae along with a whole lot of energy and a blood sacrifice. Raising Panaal isn't easy, but it will be worth it. At least for me. *You'll* be dead."

Nickelova gave a high-pitched sob, then pleaded with Alex in earnest.

Silas used the distraction to nudge his brother and gesture toward the gun behind them. He wasn't thick enough to believe he could successfully shoot Alex. But if he could get that gun and kill Nickelova, they might be able to stop the ritual. Jason slowly backed toward the weapon, and Silas thought of ways to distract Alex.

"How did you do it?" Silas interrupted. "How did you make Laina believe it was Nickelova who stabbed her when she was up in that mountain the entire time?"

"The same way I convinced Soleil you needed the heart and how I was able to obtain *The Book of Flesh and Bone*." Alex walked over to Laina, who stared at a spot on the floor as if not in her right mind. He touched her shoulder. "Show them."

Immediately Laina's body pitched forward, her scapula breaking, one arm wrapping unnaturally behind her head. There was a ripping sound and a splat as something gooey and slick hit the ground. When she stood up again, she was dark-haired, olive-skinned, and had brown eyes that carried the blank expression of someone who wasn't quite awake.

"No," Silas murmured.

"Who is that?" Jason asked.

"Have you met Olivia Turner of Crescent Star Pack?" Alex asked. "Skinwalkers are incredibly powerful, especially when her position as a Lycanthropic Society member gives her a free pass through any of your enchantments." Alex placed a hand on Olivia's shoulder.

"Where's our sister?" Silas demanded.

"Safe for now," Alex said.

"Leave Laina out of this," Jason said. "Can't we settle this like men?"

Alex snorted. "If you still think this is about settling a score, you haven't been paying attention."

Silas clenched his fists. In the place where Olivia had shifted, he noticed a smear of goop that looked like pink-tinged petroleum jelly. That's what he'd seen in Soleil's room when he confronted Meredith. It had been Olivia who had stolen *The Book of Flesh and Bone*. It was Olivia working for Alex. So then where was Meredith?

Just then, Jason reached the Glock and kicked the gun toward Silas. He dove for it, rolling and firing toward Nickelova's head. With one pulse of the amulet, Silas found himself flattened against the far wall of the barn. His bullet, once again, missed its mark.

"You two better get some rest," Alex said. "Tomorrow night, everything changes."

The amulet pulsed again, and Silas lost consciousness.

TWENTY-SIX

When Silas came to, the moss under him was wet and cold, but it was the ache of his pounding head that irked him the most. He pushed himself up and rubbed the back of his neck. Jason rested by his side, still blissfully asleep. The two of them were in a cage in the woods, although which woods, he had no idea. The trees didn't look familiar. The Spanish moss that dangled from the branches seemed to indicate they were south of the Mason-Dixon Line. He sniffed the air. Nothing smelled familiar.

"Aaargh." Jason rolled over and grabbed his head.

"Yeah, whatever that bastard hit us with wasn't soft and cuddly." Silas dabbed a sore spot on his temple, and his finger came away bloody.

"Where the hell are we?"

"I have no idea, but based on the foliage, I'd say somewhere in the southeast. Maybe the Carolinas? It's been years since I've been anywhere near here. I could be wrong." Silas looked up, searching for the sun. "What time do you think it is?"

"No idea. My phone's gone."

"Mine too."

"What do you want to bet that he moved us so that Grateful and Polina couldn't track our location?" Jason furrowed his brow. "They will be able to find us eventually though, right?"

"Oh, you missed the part where Polina told me that Grateful went into labor. It's just Polina and Logan helping us."

"Oookay. But Polina's a powerful Hecate too. She's got us covered, right? She can find us with that magic-mirror thing she has."

"I hope so, but we're out of her jurisdiction. If she's able to find us, she'll have to get the permission of the local Hecate to retrieve us. That'll take time." The sun was barely over the tops of the trees to his left. Assuming that was east, he'd guess it was nine or ten o'clock.

"Alex knew what he was doing," Jason said. "He rigged that entire situation to ensure we brought him exactly what he wanted."

"We should've killed Nickelova while we had the chance."

"And put Laina at risk? We didn't have a choice. He's been pulling our strings for weeks."

Cautiously, Silas placed a hand on one of the bars and hoisted himself to standing. "The cage doesn't appear to be enchanted. My hand isn't burned or anything."

"That's a relief," Jason said sarcastically. "Too bad it's

a cage built for an elephant. Geez, this is overkill even for Alex." He tugged at the bars to demonstrate they were unbendable.

"Maybe we can break the lock?" Silas inspected the periphery of the cage, looking for a door. There was none.

"No lock. No door." Jason tipped his head back. "We can try to climb, but the bars above us don't look any weaker."

"Dig?" Silas jammed a hand into the dirt.

The ground was rock-hard under the moss, and his attempts resulted in nothing more than a scraped hand. He kicked the dirt with the heel of his boot, but the packed earth might as well have been concrete. Jason wasn't faring any better.

Silas groaned. "Without a tool to power through this stuff, it might take us two days."

"We don't have two days."

"We shift tonight. Our wolves will be able to dig out in no time."

"At the same time Alex is here, performing his ritual? That seems convenient," Jason said.

"What are the chances he didn't think of the burrowing?"

"Zero. He's a wolf like us. He knows we can dig."

"There must be something about the dirt, an enchantment to keep us from going under," Silas said. "If there isn't, he's counting on us getting out somehow."

"Another trap," Jason said with a groan. He paced the length of the cage, looking more and more like an animal. "We need a plan. Think, Silas."

Silas searched the surrounding area, focusing on a clearing of trees behind the cage. "There's something here."

Jason crossed the cage to get a better look. In the center of the clearing were three intertwining circles of irregularly sized rocks. At the front of the rock formation stood a stone altar, overgrown with moss and vines. The entire scene looked like a horror-movie set.

"Three beings to sacrifice, three circles," Jason said.

"Nickelova, a demon, and a vampire." Silas leaned his forehead against the bars, willing his brain to come up with a solution.

"Where's he getting the demon?"

"The bones he stole from our crime scene. Plus Julius said he was missing a vampire from his coven."

"Fuck. What do you think the altar is for?"

"No idea. But the spells in *The Book of Flesh and Bone* always require a blood sacrifice. Maybe he intends to kill them one by one."

"On the upside, Laina isn't here. Maybe he let her go."

Silas gripped the bars until his knuckles turned white. He hoped what Jason said was possible, but nothing about his experience with Alex suggested he'd have any compassion for Laina.

"Do you think Meredith is helping her mother?" Jason asked.

Only his brother would know how to poke the sore spot in his soul with such precision. Silas shrugged his shoulders and let out a deep breath. "The last thing she said to me was that there was something she had to do, but I think she knew her mom was involved. That goop that happened when her mom shifted, that was in Soleil's room. Meredith was trying to show it to me, and then she was gone."

"So maybe she was just trying to save her mom."

"Maybe."

Jason paced the length of the cage again. "What would her motivation be to help Alex?"

Silas tipped his head slightly. "Maybe Meredith and her mother felt abandoned by the pack after what happened with Alex. Or maybe it's metaphysical. When Alex killed their alpha, it's possible they bonded to him in an irrevocable way."

"Possible but unlikely since Olivia isn't a werewolf. Olivia looked like she was drugged. Probably sulfralite. Maybe Meredith was too."

"Could be. I want to believe there's a logical explanation."

"Yeah. There is. If you love her, have faith in that."

"As a detective, I have to accept the possibility that she planned this the entire time and wanted to be involved in every step of this case because she was using me."

Jason punched his shoulder, hard.

"Oww! What was that for?"

"For swimming back out to the island of Silas without proof that your mate betrayed you. It's equally possible that there's been a horrible misunderstanding brought on by the orchestrations of a madman."

Silas gave Jason a reluctant nod. He wanted that to be true, wanted it with every fiber of his being. To think that the first person he'd let in since his parents were killed was someone working with their murderer was too painful to entertain. But no matter if she meant to hurt him or not, she'd chosen to run instead of telling him the truth. If she wasn't guilty of something, if she had nothing to hide, she would have stayed. But he couldn't be distracted with all that now. "Back to the problem at hand. How do we get out of here?"

"Help me try to bend the bars. Maybe we can do it if we work together." Jason used both hands to pull one bar while Silas pulled the other. He ground his heels in and grunted with the effort. But even with all their weight and strength behind the effort, the bars didn't budge. "What now?"

"I'm thinking." Silas sat down in the middle of the cage and rubbed his aching head.

"I can't believe this is happening. I finally get my life together, finally find true love with Selene, and what happens? Alex. It's always fucking Alex." Jason rested his head on his fists.

Silas could relate. He'd thought for sure Meredith was *the* one person he could trust. He also thought he'd easily be able to apprehend Alex in the rogue wolf's weakened state. But neither of those things panned out. Life was strange. There were things he could count on: himself, his family, the pack, the phases of the moon. Everything else was merely a shot in the dark. No matter how sure he was that he was aiming in the right direction, there was always the chance his shot would hit nothing at all.

He inspected the bars above their heads again. He'd climb up and test every one for weakness. He wasn't hopeful he'd find a way out, but it would give him something to do.

"I want you to promise me something," Jason said.

"What?"

"If you get a chance to kill Alex, promise me you will. No hesitation. No bringing him in for questioning or sending him to prison. Dead. He has to die."

"The ethical thing to do would be to have a trial. A lot of folks who lost family members to Alex want to feel the closure that would come with participating in the justice process."

"I know what people want. I am asking you, as family, as your brother. Promise me, Silas. You know as well as I do that we can't risk it. He's got to die."

Silas stood and started climbing the bars. "I promise. I promise as your brother. From here on out, I'm not a detective. I'm a prisoner of war. And POWs can't be blamed for killing their captors."

Jason closed his eyes. "Thank you."

"Now you have to promise me something."

"Anything."

"When it comes time to kill Alex, you need to let me do it."

A warm breeze blew through the cage, smelling of composting leaves and humid forest. Jason's face was at war with itself, his jaw twitching, his eyes narrowing. His lips twisted before seeming to come to some resolve. "Deal."

THE COOL MORNING GAVE WAY QUICKLY TO SWELTERING humidity and then to hours of overhead sun that baked them within the cage. Silas and Jason removed their jackets to use for shade and rolled up their sleeves and pant legs. Still, the heat made Silas feel ill. His head swam, and his tongue felt thick and dry as a stone.

His brain was so fried that he didn't trust his own ears when a rumble came from a distance.

"Do you hear that?" Silas rose, his throat too dry to speak louder than a whisper. The sun had begun to set, and long shadows stretched across his brother's face, distorting his features. But there was no hiding his sunken cheekbones and cracked lips. A werewolf's metabolism before the full moon required seven times the calories and hydration of a human. They might have only been in there for a day, but both of them were starving to death.

"Sounds like an engine," Jason rasped. He stood, pulling the suit jacket he'd been using for shade off his head.

A black Suburban rumbled up a two-rut lane through the woods, Alex behind the wheel and a Latino man Silas didn't recognize in the passenger's seat. Alex parked, climbed out, and stared down his nose at Silas.

"This is what you've come to, Alex?" Silas said. "Too

cowardly to fight us one-on-one, so you lock us in here to die of thirst?"

Alex reached into the Suburban and pulled out a bottle of water, handing it to Silas between the bars. "Drink up. I wouldn't want you to die before you had a chance to serve my purpose."

Silas only hesitated for a moment. He offed the cap and gulped down a third of the bottle, then handed the remainder to Jason.

"What exactly do you need us for?" he asked.

"To witness the dawn of a new age. Every revolution needs witnesses. You'll be the ones to tell the others what happens here. You'll tell them what's coming, what the future holds for your pack. And you'll know exactly what's in store for them if they don't comply."

The other man exited the vehicle and came to stand at Alex's side. His eyes were dull, lifeless. "Olivia, change back into yourself. Your appearance is disconcerting."

The man contorted, folding at the waist. He expelled the same slimy excrement Silas had seen before as he shifted back into Meredith's mother. "Would you like me to bring the book?" she asked once her transformation was complete.

"No. No one touches the book but me," Alex said. "Bring the fae."

Olivia opened the back door of the Suburban and pulled Nickelova from her seat. The dragon fae looked like death warmed over. Her hands were bound, her hair was matted, and her complexion was blotchy, as if she'd spent hours crying.

"Alex, please. You loved me once," she whined. Her mascara ran in long black trails from under her eyes to the delicate bones of her jaw. "I can help you. We could rule together, just as we always planned."

Alex retrieved Silas's bag from the vehicle, the one he'd carried Nickelova's heart in, and hooked it on his shoulder. Then he reached behind the seat and hoisted *The Book of Flesh and Bone* into his arms.

Silas's stomach turned at the atrocity in Alex's hands. It appeared to be made of human skin, the spine a series of bones as if a human backbone had been cracked and flattened to adorn the thick, leathery binding. As Alex passed, a cold breeze came off the thing, sending goose bumps up Silas's arms and across his chest. But the worst part was the smell. *The Book of Flesh and Bone* smelled like fetid death bound in misery.

Olivia thrust Nickelova into one of the three stone circles as Alex crossed to the altar and opened the book.

"Alex, please! Have mercy," she begged.

"Mercy?" Alex laughed. "Like you had mercy on me when you planned to replace me with Jason? You bet on the wrong pony, and now it's time to settle up."

He pulled the heart from the bag. Olivia released Nickelova and backed from the circle.

"*Ukta rho morbidae titan,*" Alex read from the book.

The stones around Nickelova glowed purple. She rushed toward the periphery, her body slapping the invisible force that had walled her in. "No. No. Alex, please! Let me out."

Alex approached her with the heart. "I think I've had

this long enough. Goddess knows when you give a man your heart, it's never for keeps."

His hand cut through the purple magic containing Nickelova and violently shoved the heart against her chest. Silas grimaced as her flesh parted to accommodate the organ, her body writhing with obvious pain. When it was done, Nickelova gasped like a baby taking her first breath and clutched at her chest.

Taking pleasure in her pain, Alex paced around the stones, a wicked grin on his face. Once she'd recovered, she raged against the walls of her cage, pounding and clawing at the boundary.

"I warn you, shifting into your dragon form in that circle won't help you escape, but it will be extremely painful," Alex said, then turned toward Olivia. "One down, two to go. Let's call our demon."

TWENTY-SEVEN

S ilas paced the cage, an almost comical opposite to Jason, who had become unnaturally still in Alex's presence. As much as he hated Nickelova, if there was a way to free her, he would. She was far less dangerous than Alex.

"Do you remember these?" Alex asked, pulling a bag of bones from the Suburban. Silas's forehead tightened to the point of pain, a muscle in his jaw tensing and releasing in time with his heart.

"The girl's bones from the human crime scene," Silas said.

"You wondered why I'd taken them, why I'd stripped the girl's flesh from them." Alex gave him a smug look, and the presumptuousness of the statement wasn't lost on Silas. "While there is no shortage of human-on-human crime, it seems the perpetrator of this particular murder had a secret. She was possessed by a demon. A new demon, birthed into this world by a young girl who played with the wrong Ouija board."

"A demon's human bones," Silas said, remembering Julius's theory.

"You're familiar? I'd not heard of it as a werewolf, but one learns things in one's travels. Shall we call this one? An interesting fact about demons is they can fold space and travel from one place to another in practically no time. This shouldn't take long." Alex dumped the bones into the second circle, eyeing the darkening sky. "Come out, come out, wherever you are." He pulled a lighter from the pocket of his cargo shorts and squatted down to run the flickering flame beneath the end of the femur.

A cold wind manifested in the trees, darkness gathering between the branches in the woods across from the cage. Shadows danced and expanded, stretching and poking toward the ritual site. Silas could swear he heard whispers in the rustling leaves. And then a woman was there, a dark woman with large upturned eyes and tattoos that glowed beneath the long sleeves of her shirt.

"Why have you summoned me, wolf," she hissed.

"Step into the circle."

"No."

Alex thrust the lighter under the bones, and the demon twisted in discomfort, a high-pitched keening escaping her throat. With jerky, tortured movements, she stepped into the circle despite herself.

"Ukta rho morbidae titan." Alex retracted the flame.

The demon turned into a dark mist, flying left, then right, but the ring was sealed. She bounced off the walls of the cell, shrieking in a way that forced Silas to cover his ears.

Alex seemed unruffled by the sound. He turned his face toward the darkening sky and the full moon, whose face was already visible in it. "We're running out of time. Bring the vampire."

A familiar tug rolled under Silas's skin, and he understood the urgency in Alex's voice. The shift was almost upon them. He winced as his spine elongated, pitching him forward, then eased off slightly. He'd be a wolf soon. So would Alex. But the coming lunar eclipse meant they wouldn't stay that way. He'd shift back at some point, and so would Alex. The perfect conditions for him to complete his ritual.

"Silas," Jason whispered. "We're both starving. What if our wolves—"

"Try to eat each other? They won't. We're pack. Just try to remember to dig." In fact, Silas wasn't sure how their intense hunger and thirst would manifest after the shift, but it was his job to remain positive for his brother. A leader never admitted defeat.

Alex groaned, fighting the shift, his hands pawing at the ends of his shirt. He pulled it over his head. Meanwhile, Olivia dragged the vampire from the truck—a woman with pale hair and an ankh tattoo on her neck, just below her ear. Normally a vampire could easily outmuscle and outmaneuver a shifter, but this female vamp looked like she hadn't fed in weeks. Her cheeks were sunken, and her eyes were dull. Drugged, Silas guessed, just like her mate, the vampire who'd staked himself at ZeroHour. She'd been fed sulfralite like her partner.

Beside him, Jason began madly stripping out of his suit, a red flush coloring his cheeks above his thickening beard. Silas's pulse pounded in his ears, his breath coming in huffs. He unbuttoned his jeans and lifted his T-shirt over his head.

Alex sealed the vampire within the third circle, then stumbled to the place where the circles of the triquetra overlapped. Directly outside their purple boundary, he started a bonfire, igniting the kindling beneath a teepee of firewood.

Silas groaned in chorus with Alex and Jason as the moon tugged at the wolf within. This was the ultimate betrayal. Despite hating Alex with every molecule of his being, this shift, this reaction to the moon, was a reminder that they were made from the same stuff, cut from the same primordial cloth. How he would have loved to think he was fundamentally different from Alex, that the man was a monster the likes of which had never been seen before nor would be seen again. But that wasn't the case. Alex was a werewolf, same as him. A werewolf who had turned himself into a monster by choice. Which meant there was a potential monster in everyone. The thought made Silas want to come out of his skin.

The wave of pain ebbed. As the pile of branches blazed to life, Alex backed to the altar at the front of the formation and braced himself on the stone table.

"Almost time." He madly flipped pages in the grotesque book.

Olivia strode, machinelike, to his side, the fine wrinkles around her mouth and eyes deepening in the light of the fire. Alex wrapped a length of chain around his torso and padlocked it to the base of the table.

"Keep me in this spot," he said to Olivia. "Do you understand?"

Olivia nodded robotically.

Alex pitched forward in time with the same wave of pain that sliced through Silas. Older wolves shifted faster. Because Alex and Silas were the same age, the shift was upon them both. Jason, on the other hand, might have a few minutes more.

There was a soft rustle in the bushes behind Silas.

"What is that?" Jason asked, squinting into the dark foliage.

Silas couldn't answer. He finished removing his clothes as his stomach hollowed out and his jaw jutted forward.

Two reflective amber eyes blinked at him from the darkness, low to the ground.

"A raccoon?" Jason whispered, creeping toward the back of the cage.

Silas didn't care what it was. His hands hit the dirt, his fingers bending under as claws sprouted from his first knuckle. Jet-black hair budded from his forearms and climbed toward his shoulders, bubbling under and bursting through his skin. He squatted on his haunches, his throat elongating with his ears.

In his altered state, he could hear the small animal breathing in the bushes outside the cage, smell the wild, musky scent of its coat. With sharp eyes, he blinked up at the full moon above and howled. Jason joined in, his throaty human moan morphing into a proper wolf call. Alex picked up on the song, instinct overriding animosity as he raised his nose to the moon.

The last thing Silas registered before the wolf completely took over was the steady sound of digging near the back of the cage. Whatever was in that bush was scratching at the dirt as if its life depended on it.

THE ALPHA'S PAWS WERE IN THE DIRT. NO, IT WAS HIS HANDS, and they weren't working as they had a minute ago. The wolf beside him was faring better, throwing dirt with fully functional front claws. Silas came into his head in a rush, his human body bent over a hole. His wolf had been digging, trying to get at something on the other side of the bars.

Jason's wolf stuck his head into the hole, snapping at the animal in the bushes behind them. He was still too big to fit through, and he retreated to dig again. Silas turned his face toward the full moon, now totally eclipsed, blacked out by the shadow of the earth. He'd shifted back faster. Jason would likely follow in a few minutes.

Jason's wolf whined as the creature from the bushes

emerged, a dainty red fox with upturned ears and a long, bushy tail.

"Meredith?" Silas whispered.

The fox's eyes blinked knowingly.

A sound behind him made her scamper into the bushes. He looked over his shoulder. The altar. Alex. The rogue wolf was shifting back, almost human again in the light of the fire. Olivia was still there, hovering over him like some kind of prison warden.

Silas looked back down at his hands, at the place where Jason was still digging. The hole was almost big enough. Almost. It would be a tight fit. Silas pushed Jason's wolf away, thankful when the beast obeyed. He must have still recognized Silas as alpha even in his human form. He grabbed Jason's suit jacket and tossed it into the hole, lining the jagged earth at the bottom. Silas tried to slide under, but his shoulders wouldn't fit. *Fuck.* Jason was slightly smaller; maybe he'd fit when he shifted back. Silas backed out of the hole.

"Alex. Please. There's still time to stop this," he heard Nickelova beg.

Quickly, Silas pooled his clothing to conceal the hole and crossed to the bars in time to see Alex stand, fully shifted, behind the stone table.

"Get the sacrifice," he ordered Olivia, leaning over the book.

Sacrifice. Another sacrifice? Something besides the three?

Olivia strode to the Suburban and opened the hatch. There was the thump of something heavy being repositioned, and then the woman emerged with another woman in her arms, one with mahogany hair and a curvy build.

Silas forced his eyes to focus in the dim light and tried to get a better look. He sucked air through his teeth. Even if he couldn't see her face, he could smell her. Laina.

"Let her go! I will kill you," Silas bellowed. "I will rip your heart out with my bare hands!"

Alex grinned over the pages of *The Book of Flesh and Bone*. He moved aside slightly in order to give Olivia room to arrange Laina on the massive stone table behind the book. What was wrong with her? She wasn't just unconscious. By the way her arm dangled lifelessly over the edge of the stone, Silas might have presumed she was dead.

"I gave you a chance to join me," Alex said, looking directly at him. "I gave you a chance to die. Now you will live with your sister's blood on your hands, as your parents' blood is on your hands."

"You fucking bastard. Don't you do it." Silas gripped the bars until his knuckles turned white. "Back away from her now!"

He gave Silas a patronizing look. "It's over. Laina's blood and that of her unborn child will be the ultimate sacrifice. Watch, Alpha," he spat out. "Learn what happens to those who cross Alex Ravien Bloodright."

Alex placed his hand on the open book and began to chant. The amulet around his neck ignited, glowing bright red. Sweat beaded across his forehead as his face tightened with concentration. Purple flames sparked near the bonfire, then spread along the stones, encircling the demon, the vampire, and Nickelova.

The dragon fae's screams rent the darkness. Ordinary fire couldn't hurt a dark fae, but this was far from ordinary. It blistered her flesh. Silas covered his ears at her pitiful cries. She was helpless against the flames that consumed her. The vampire, drugged and barely conscious, did not scream at all. She burned as if she were already dead. The demon's shrieks rivaled Nickelova's.

Silas had no personal attachment to the three creatures burning alive. Nickelova, at least, had earned her place in the flames. But no creature deserved the brutality of this ritual. The entire thing turned his stomach. Evil by any definition. And he knew Laina was next.

As Alex continued his chant, Silas noticed something change. The glow of the amulet faded with Nickelova's screams. Was it possible that once she was dead, its magic would die altogether?

And then it was over. Nickelova and the demon went abruptly silent. The three rings were swallowed entirely by fire, Nickelova's body now unrecognizable, a silhouette of ash. The demon was gone too, along with the bones that had called it there. The vampire had been reduced to a pile of dust.

Alex slumped over the book, his chant becoming weaker. The amulet was as dark as an ordinary piece of jewelry. Now was Silas's chance. Alex was drained, and Nickelova's death appeared to have rendered the amulet useless. If he could escape, he might be able to take Alex down.

A hand landed on his shoulder. Jason. His brother pointed toward the hole. Meredith, human Meredith, stood naked on the other side of the bars. She motioned to him, glancing back at Alex.

Silas approached her cautiously. "Can I trust you?" he whispered.

"It wasn't me," she said. "Whatever you think I did, it was my mother. She made herself look like me. Do you remember what I tried to show you in Soleil's room?"

"The pink-tinged jelly."

"Every time a skinwalker shifts, they leave behind an excretion. It's a thick mucus their body produces to protect them from the shift. When I saw it in Soleil's room, I knew my mother had been the one to steal the book."

"Why didn't you tell me? Why did you run?"

"I left you the heart, knowing the enchantment around your house would protect it," she babbled, not answering his question. "I thought you'd destroy Nickelova and end this. But then my mother lured your sister away."

"I hate to break up this little reunion, but we've got to hurry. Come on, brother. There's no time for this." Jason glanced over his shoulder.

Alex's chanting grew louder, the fire blazing toward the sky in great plumes.

Silas stared at Meredith, trying to fit all the pieces

together in his head. Had she been the one to shoot Soleil? Why had she run?

Jason shoved him aside. "Snap out of it! You can talk it out once we've saved Laina and are standing over Alex's body."

He tried his best to fit through the hole. It was too small, even for him. Meredith picked up a stick and started breaking off pieces of rocky soil, helping Jason fight his way through.

"Can you shift back? It will be faster if you dig," Jason said.

With tears in her eyes, Meredith took one more look at Silas and shifted into fox form. She dug frantically at the hole.

Jason succeeded in getting his head and one arm through but could go no farther.

"What now?" Silas murmured, his heart a lead weight in his chest.

As if in answer to his question, the ground began to shake. He bent his knees to avoid falling over. Jason backed out of the hole, and together, they turned around to face the ritual. The three interlocking circles crumbled and dropped as if a massive sinkhole had formed beneath it. Fire shot from the hole, sparks cascading into the night sky with a bloom of sulfur-scented air. In the center of it all, a dark figure rose, a huge beast, humanoid but for two massive horns growing from the sides of its head. The sight of the thing filled Silas's heart with the kind of dread he'd only known in nightmares.

"By the goddess," Jason murmured by his side. "What the hell is that thing?"

Silas took a deep breath before answering. "We've never been formally introduced, but I'm guessing that's Panaal."

Olivia held a dagger out to Alex, whose eyes focused on Laina's unconscious body.

Rage filled Silas, a deep, hot need for revenge that made his skin bubble as his wolf came to the surface. He hated Alex, and as the goddess was his witness, he would not let him win. Concentrating all his hateful energy on his right hand, Silas drew on the eclipsed moon above and willed the appendage to shift. His bones broke and his fingers melded into his palm.

"Silas… Holy shit." Jason stared in amazement at his shifted hand. "I didn't know that was possible!"

Silas glanced toward Meredith's fox, who was still digging frantically. "Neither did I." Plunging his shifted hand into the earth, Silas dug, giant claws ripping through the stone and packed earth. In no time, the hole was big enough for Jason to fit through. Meredith's fox backed away as Silas slid under and arose outside the cage with only one goal in mind. He was going to kill Alex Bloodright.

TWENTY-EIGHT

Through the fire and smoke, Silas tried to take in the horror that was Panaal. Aside from his size—he was at least eight feet tall and twice Silas's width—his horns and the reddish tinge of his skin were a ringer for the human concept of the devil. Panaal's terrible eyes absorbed the light of the fire, soulless pits of darkness that chilled Silas to the bone. The beast was here but not completely corporeal. His form flickered with the fire.

Alex's grin broadened as he viewed Panaal. "My lord, I free you from your ancient bindings!"

Panaal's presence caused the earth to quake, the fault line beginning under the immortal being's cloven hooves.

Flattening his hand atop the shaking book, Alex read again, the guttural series of syllables coming fast and frantic. As he accepted the diamond-shaped blade from Olivia, its obsidian color flashed in the firelight. A black blade. Laina had mentioned it was a black blade that had stabbed her at Four Paws. Alex had marked her as his sacrifice from the beginning!

Silas sprang into motion as the bastard centered the blade over Laina's abdomen.

"No!" Silas screamed.

He ran toward Alex at full speed, the ground jolting beneath his feet. With the slightest gesture of his head, Alex ordered Olivia forward. She barreled toward Silas at a full run. Although he was twice her size and were-wolves were stronger than shifters, he'd have to deal with her quickly if he was going to save Laina.

He tried to veer to the left and use her momentum to his advantage, but at the last second, she leaped into the air and caught him around the neck. Her legs wrapped around his hips, her force and weight knocking him to the ground where the two rolled across the packed dirt of the clearing. With a sound like a pop and a splash of something warm and thick, her body transformed into a snake that constricted around his neck, arms, and legs.

Alex raised the dagger.

No. No! Silas fought, pushing and biting at the boa constrictor Olivia had become, but to no avail.

Then, a miracle. A red fox sprang from ground to the altar, its teeth sinking into Alex's wrist. Meredith! Taken by surprise, Alex dropped the dagger. She didn't waste a moment. Meredith released Alex's wrist and caught the hilt of the blade between her teeth, her delicate black paws scrambling under his arm and off the stone slab.

And then Jason's face was above his own. "Damn, some women don't know how to let go."

He slammed a sharp rock against Olivia's reptilian head. She loosened her grip for a fraction of a second. It was long enough. Silas wedged a hand under her coils and lifted, sliding fluidly from her grip. Unfortunately, since Jason still held her head, the serpent coiled around him in a heartbeat.

A high-pitched cry turned Silas's attention to the altar. Alex had caught Meredith by the tail, her furry red body twisting masterfully to keep the dagger from his opposite hand. But she was in pain. She wouldn't be able to keep up the fight for long.

"Why isn't he using the amulet?" Jason asked as he wrestled the boa.

"Nickelova is dead. I don't think it works anymore."

"Then what are you waiting for?" Jason pinned Olivia's tail under his knee. "Go! Help Laina and Meredith." The boa snapped at his face as he squeezed her throat. "I've got this."

Silas took off toward the altar. Alex saw him coming and stopped reaching for the dagger. Instead, his hands landed on the fox's slim neck. He gave her slight body a hard shake. With a sickening crack Silas heard from yards away, Meredith's body went limp in Alex's grip, the dagger dropping from her teeth. He cast her aside as if she were garbage and scooped the blade from the dirt.

"You fucking bastard." Silas plowed into Alex, thrusting the dagger above his head.

They toppled to the ground, Silas on top. Alex managed to turn the dagger around, pointing it at Silas's face. With both hands clutching Alex's wrists, Silas could keep the sharp point from piercing his flesh, but just barely, and his mind was cognizant that if he was wrong about the amulet, one pulse could incinerate him. The ground shook harder, the sound of cracking earth coming from the vicinity of Panaal.

"Why can't you see, Silas? This life you're living is meaningless. It's an illusion. You call yourself alpha, but you have no real power. You are a pawn of the goddess. Panaal could make you a god."

Silas grunted, his muscles straining to keep the dagger at bay. "I don't want to be a god. All I want is to keep the people around me safe. And that can't happen while you're alive." He pushed harder on Alex's wrists, his arms growing fatigued from the effort.

A groan came from the direction of Meredith's limp body. Silas concentrated on keeping pressure on Alex even when the rogue wolf's eyes darted toward her. Out of the corner of his eye, Silas saw the movement of human flesh. She was alive, and she had shifted. With jerky, pained movements, she passed them and headed for the altar.

"No!" Alex yelled. "Don't be a fool."

Concentrate, Silas told himself. *Don't get distracted.* He kept his eyes on Alex even when his expression revealed extreme distress.

"You stupid girl," Alex spat out. "If you interrupt the spell, there's no telling the consequences."

A rush of elation lifted the corners of Silas's mouth. At that moment he was certain of three things. One: if Alex could have used the amulet, he would have by now.

Two: Meredith was attempting to destroy the spell and was clearly never the one who'd helped Alex. And three: he loved her. He still loved Meredith, his vice and his one true mate.

"Do it, Meredith! Do it!" Silas yelled. He risked a glance in her direction.

She'd fisted the top page of the open book and strained to tear it from its binding. A deep growl rumbled like thunder from the area of Panaal's chest, and a mighty wind blew through the clearing. Panaal bared his teeth, those black eyes fixed on Meredith.

"You fucking bitch," Alex yelled. "You'll doom us all!"

Leaning into the wind, her red hair whipping around her head, Meredith ripped the page in two. Carefully, she fed the pieces into the purple flames in front of the altar. The parchment caught fire at Panaal's feet even as the ground shook harder and the wind increased to hurricane proportions. Panaal's mouth opened in a brain-slicing scream, his teeth gnashing in Meredith's direction. But his bite passed right through her.

In obvious pain, Meredith lifted one side of the massive tome and slammed the book shut. Panaal's growls turned into howls as the god of the underworld descended slowly into the purple flames.

Alex gaped. A mixture of rage and disappointment strained his features. For a moment his muscles flinched. Silas used the opportunity to remove one hand from his wrists and punch Alex in the side of the head. With all his weight behind the blow, it was enough for Alex to loosen his grip. Wrestling the dagger away, Silas twirled the blade and centered it over Alex's heart, pinning his arms to his sides with his knees.

"You've won." Alex went limp under Silas's weight. "Take me in. Lock me up. Let the pack deal with me."

"I should. Maybe it's the right thing to do," he mumbled.

"Of course it is. What kind of alpha would you be, what kind of detective, if you didn't uphold the process of justice?"

"You have a point." Silas watched a smug grin crawl across Alex's face.

"You can't kill me, Alpha. It wouldn't be the right thing to do. Not when I'm surrendering. Unarmed. I'm giving myself up." The words held a well-practiced acerbity.

"I shouldn't. You're right about that. Only, I promised my brother vengeance. And I've recently learned that there is no substitute for family. I need them, Alex, and they'll never be safe as long as you're alive." He placed both hands on the hilt and looked directly into Alex's eyes. "This is for my mother, my father, my siblings, my pack, and for Soleil. Go to hell and take the horned god with you."

He thrust the dagger into Alex's heart.

Alex's mouth opened, but no sound came out. His pupils dilated with disbelief. Silas watched the light fade from his widening eyes until there was no more breath, no more fight left in his mortal enemy. And still he pushed the dagger deeper into Alex's chest, his hands shaking with the need to make certain he was dead.

He'd hated Alex for so long, dreamed about this day with such fervor, that he expected choirs of angels and a rush of elation. But as it became more and more obvious the man was gone, Silas merely felt hollow. Miserable that killing Alex was necessary, helpless that it was impossible to bring back all the people the man had killed, and thankful that it was over while remaining hyperaware that it was not.

A scream behind him seemed to bring him back into the present. He climbed from Alex's dead body and whirled to find Olivia in her human form, crouching over Jason.

"What have I done? What have I done?" Her hands were shaking. She backed away.

Silas ran to his brother's side. There was a red ring around Jason's neck, but otherwise his brother seemed undamaged.

Jason coughed into his hand. "I'm okay." He rubbed his neck and gave Olivia a sideways glance.

"Silas!" Meredith cried from the altar, Laina in her arms. "My legs won't work."

She was staring at the widening crater that crept toward her toes. Panaal was still trapped in the flames, sinking into the rumbling earth like it was quicksand. But it was the space around the horned god that was the problem. The ground was giving way, steaming black emptiness growing from the inside out.

Silas ran for her right as Panaal opened his flaming mouth. The beast laughed, a hissing charcoal bark that increased in its maniacal splendor. The earth swallowed the horned god, but it didn't stop collapsing. Meredith screamed as the creeping black hole claimed the altar and the book. Both tumbled into the abyss.

He was almost there. So close.

"Meredith!" Silas ran for her, swerving to avoid the widening crater.

She looked up, tears in her eyes. "I love you."

With a twist of her torso that made her scream from the pain, she threw Laina into his arms. Silas caught his sister.

And then Meredith dropped into the void.

TWENTY-NINE

"Meredith!" Silas transferred Laina into Jason's arms, thankful his brother was close behind him.

He ran to the edge of the crater, a foolish move considering the ground was still shaking. But what was love but a fool's errand? He peered over the side.

Panaal was gone, disappeared down the bottomless pit before him. The earth stilled. Thankfully the crater stopped expanding, its hunger seemingly appeased by being fed *The Book of Flesh and Bone*. Even the wind gave up its campaign against him. Charred rock steamed from the crater, a dozen small fires burning below, giving off the smell of sulfur and burning flesh.

He called her name into the bottomless expanse. "Meredith!"

"Silas?" Her voice was barely a whisper.

He searched the rocky edge. There—pale fingers gripping black stone.

"I can't hold on."

He didn't hesitate. Scaling the rough surface, he found a tiny ledge only half the width of his body near her fingers. He gripped the wall with one hand and lowered himself, stretching to reach her.

"My legs aren't working. He did something to me." Her voice was hoarse, her eyes brimming with tears.

"Reach for my hand." He could see her fingers slipping, her knuckles sickly white with the effort of hanging on.

"I can't."

"Goddess, help me," he prayed, then repositioned his anchored hand on a rock closer to her.

At this angle, he might be able to reach her, but he'd never have the leverage to pull her back up. Still, he had to try. Digging his fingers in, he stretched himself out—

—just as she lost her grip. She dropped, her arm brushing his fingertips until, by some miracle, his fist closed around her wrist. Her weight threatened the hold he had on the crater wall.

"You have to let me go and pull yourself up," she sobbed, tears flowing.

"I can't."

"You can. If you let me go, you'll be strong enough. You'll survive."

"I can't. I can't survive without you. I can't do it alone."

"Of course you can. You made it down here alone. You can climb up alone."

"Not this. Life. I can't do life alone. Not anymore. I need you, Meredith."

"Silas…"

"I love you. I refuse to let Alex take one more person from me. Not you. Not this time."

"Oh, Silas." She dangled helplessly from his hand and glanced at the eclipsed moon. In moments the full moon would be fully exposed again. He would shift back and lose his grip. "I'm not sure we have a choice."

"I'm not letting you go. We either both get out of this crater or we go down together."

"Ahem," Jason called from the edge above him. "No fucking way am I becoming alpha. Hang on, brother. Laina's awake and checking the truck for some rope."

"Hurry. This isn't as easy as it looks." A brown blur appeared behind Jason's head. "Jason, look out!"

Jason turned, but what now appeared to be a giant eagle did not attack. She coasted around his head and swooped down the rocky side of the abyss. Before Silas could react, she'd swept Meredith into her talons and carried her to safety. Silas breathed a sigh of relief to see Meredith on solid ground.

Fingers aching and limbs trembling, he heaved his weight upward, perching on the tiny lip of stone to rest. He could do this. He could climb the rest of the way. Digging his fingers in, he tried not to think too much about how easily he could fall. Hand, hand, foot, foot. Repeat.

Jason reached for him, lying on his belly at the edge. "Just a few more feet, Silas. You're almost there."

Laina appeared at his side, reaching down for him as well. "No rope, but I found this."

She dropped a hacked length of seat belt to him. Silas lifted himself another six inches and wrapped his hand in the black strap.

"I've got it!" Silas said.

Jason grabbed the strap and helped Laina pull. "Hang on, brother. We've got you."

"Fuck!" A searing pain lassoed Silas's leg. His gaze darted toward his lower extremities to see a tongue of fire originating from the pit below, wrapped around his ankle like a whip.

"Hang on, Silas!" Jason yelled. He and Laina strained to pull him up.

The tongue pulled harder, the burning, tugging pain threatening his hold on the strap and wall.

"I can't hold on," Silas said.

With a high-pitched cry, the eagle soared back into the crater, snapping at the fiery whip and slashing it with its talons. The burning thing slipped off Silas's bare ankle, receding into the pit below. Silas dug his toes into the side of the crater and, with everything he had left, climbed. Jason's hand landed on his shoulder, hoisting him over the lip of the crater.

And then he was in Jason's and Laina's arms. They huddled together in the kind of group hug only experienced in the most desperate of times, the type with tears and the blubbering of words that are forgotten the moment they are spoken because the feelings are too intense to be described in any language.

Silas was alpha. He'd saved his family. He'd saved his pack. And he wept openly like a child. And then, with an intense pain that bubbled along his spine, Silas gave himself over to his wolf, his brother and sister shifting beside him.

Silas became human again at the edge of the wood. He blinked into the sunrise, the night before coming back to him. Alex was dead. Nickelova was dead. And Meredith was both proven innocent and alive. He turned over to find Laina shifting back a few yards away.

"Are you okay?" he asked her when she was human again.

"Better. I think the shift helped. Alex did something to my head before. Everything was hazy, but I think I'm okay now. I'm just worried about the baby."

"We're going to get you help," he said. "Where are Jason and Meredith?"

"I'm here," Jason said from behind him.

Silas stood and searched the area, sniffing the air and following Meredith's scent. He found her near the crater, curled next to her mother.

"Silas?" she said, a worried expression on her face. "I can't move my legs. And there's something wrong with my mom."

"Too many times," Olivia murmured beside her.

Meredith stroked her mother's hair back from her face. "She needs a doctor." With her hand on her mother's forehead, she looked at Silas. "She's shifted too often, too close together. She's running a fever. If we don't get her help, she'll die."

Silas nudged Jason. "Take Olivia. I'll carry Meredith. We need to get them to the truck and get help."

His brother froze. "An hour ago she was trying to strangle me."

"Alex was controlling her," Meredith said. "She didn't know what she was doing!"

With a sigh, Jason scooped Olivia into his arms. "Yeah, it looked that way. But I'll trust her when I have proof. Everyone's a hero when they're trying to save their own scrawny necks."

Meredith cast him a pleading glance. "Please take care of her. Please."

"Give him time," Silas said as he gathered her into his arms.

Meredith leaned her head against his chest. "I don't know when Alex poisoned her, but I do know my mother wouldn't have helped him of her own free will."

"The pack will need answers, but she'll be treated fairly," Silas said. "I'll make sure of it." He watched Jason load Olivia into the back of the Suburban and hoped the woman would live long enough to receive a fair trial.

"Thank you for saving my life," she croaked, tears dribbling from the corners of her tawny eyes.

He lowered his forehead to hers. "And thank you for saving mine."

"Bingo!" Jason yelled from the Suburban. He held up

two cell phones. "Look what I found in the glove compartment."

"Any charge left?"

"Ten percent."

Silas helped Meredith into a seat, then dialed Polina.

"Silas? Are you all right? I've been doing locator spells nonstop." Polina's voice cracked with emotion.

"Alive and well, my friend."

"Where are you? I haven't been able to track you using magic."

"Then you'll have to settle for technology. I'm sending you my GPS location now. Phone's almost dead, but we need your help. And tell Gerty to call Bojingles. We're going to need medical attention. If she can provide transport, we'll take it."

"She's here with me. Logan and I will be there as soon as he can lock on to your location. Gerty too."

"Good."

Polina whispered something in the background. "How careful does Gerty need to be? Is Alex nearby?"

"He's dead. Nickelova too."

There was a pause as she took that in. "What happened to the book?"

"It's gone." He stared at the crater. "I think it's gone for good. You and Grateful are going to want to see this. By the way, how is Grateful?"

"She's fine. It's a girl. She named her Skyler. Sky for short."

"Tell her congratulations, and I forgive her for going

into labor while the world was ending. We stopped that from happening, by the way."

"I'll be there as soon as possible. Sounds like you have one hell of a story to tell."

He looked out over the steaming sinkhole that, for all intents and purposes, led directly to hell and chuckled. "You have no idea."

THIRTY

It was with some level of disappointment that Silas found himself again in Bojingles Fae Hospital. He'd spent so much time here in recent months, the staff addressed him by his first name. Thankfully, he wasn't here for his siblings this time. Jason and Laina had already completely healed from their ordeal. The doctors released Laina after confirming her pregnancy was proceeding normally with no signs that what she'd endured had affected the baby at all. Silas couldn't wait to welcome the new little pack member in the coming months. Jason was still sore but was home, recovering under the tender care of his mate, Selene.

He was happy for all of them, truly, but hated that the one person who was still in the damned place was Meredith. He needed her more than anyone right now. More than he ever expected to need anyone.

"The doctors say I may always walk with a limp," she said, her red hair bunching up on the pillow. "Alex broke a vertebra in my back, and it compressed my spine. It could have been worse. The fire lily juice has healed the bone and my nervous system, but because it happened when I was in fox form, they couldn't get the alignment quite right. One hip is slightly off."

"Will you need a cane?" Silas asked. "Because if you do, I want to get you one with a skull and flames."

"I won't need a cane." The hint of a grin broke through her annoyed facade.

"Well then, I guess you're not broken enough to replace. I'll keep you."

"How kind of you," she said flatly.

Silas folded his arms and leaned back in the chair next to the bed. "I talked to Manahan. Cleared everything up. You have your job back."

She gave him a warm, authentic smile. "I'm your partner again?"

"It seems so. You're not disappointed, are you? I could convince him to find you another assignment if you're sick of working with the likes of me."

"No. I'm good." She met his gaze, and this time her smile came at him at full force.

He cleared his throat. "I had a chance to talk to your mother."

"She's awake?"

Silas nodded. "She's having a procedure done this morning, but I'll take you to see her later if you want."

"Yes please. What did you find out?"

"She says she was tracking Alex. She wanted her revenge as much as we did. She'd been in a deep depression since your father was killed and felt like she needed to take matters into her own hands when Alex resurfaced. Unfortunately, Alex captured her and infected her with sulfralite. She admitted to stabbing Laina and posing as you to finish Soleil off when she was recovering from her gunshot wounds here in the hospital, although she says she only did so because she was under Alex's control."

"Did you ever figure out about Soleil and the heart?"

"Yes. Your mom posed as Grateful and gave Soleil the idea of obtaining the heart for me. Soleil must have figured out it wasn't the real Grateful. That's why she was trying to get the heart back. Only, Soleil didn't know about your mom. She must have assumed the shapeshifter who posed as Grateful was you."

"I shouldn't have shot her. That's what Alex wanted."

"You didn't know. And let's face it, if you'd hesitated, I'd be an extra-crispy corpse." Silas rubbed his chin. "Was it you I chased from your house after Soleil died or your mom?"

"Me. I figured out my mother was the one helping Alex when I saw the remnants of her shift on the floor of Soleil's chambers."

Silas rested his elbows on his knees. "There's only one thing I don't understand. Why did you run? Why didn't you tell me the truth the night Soleil died?"

"Once I put together that it was my mother, I knew that if I left right then I could follow her scent, catch up to her, and figure out what happened. If I stayed and explained everything, I'd never find her again. And I did,

Silas. I was able to follow her in my fox form to where Alex was keeping her. I hitched a ride in the back of Alex's truck and stayed a fox until I dug you out of his cage. That's how I was eventually able to make it to the ritual site and free you and Jason. But it also meant I left Carlson City with nothing but the skin on my back."

"You know she'll have to remain in custody until she can be tried. I believe Olivia will be cleared eventually, but the law is the law."

"I know. I feel lucky she's still alive. I still have a mother. That's something to be thankful for."

Silas could hear the tinge of empathy in her voice. He didn't have a mother or a father anymore. But he did have a family, and she was absolutely right. "Yes, it is."

"You'll be happy to know I saved the world without you," Silas said as he walked into Grateful's maternity room later that day.

His friend opened her eyes and adjusted herself in the bed. "Silas! Thank the goddess you're okay. I'm so sorry—"

"Oh please, Grateful. What could you have done? Even you can't magically stop a baby from coming... Wait, can you?"

"No. Believe me, I tried. I went into labor the moment I arrived at Polina's. It wasn't pretty. Rick had to bring me to Bojingles because I was coughing up bubbles with every contraction."

"Bubbles?" Silas laughed.

"Not funny. Then the lights kept going out. It was crazy."

"I guess the goddess wanted her born yesterday."

"Today. She arrived just after midnight. During the eclipse."

He handed her the gift bag he'd brought. "For Skyler."

Grateful reached inside and pulled out a floppy stuffed wolf. "Awww. Silas, this is adorable."

"Where is the little witch anyway?" Silas asked.

"She's sleeping in the bassinet." Grateful pointed toward a plastic box on wheels on the far side of her room. "Rick left a few minutes ago to pick up Lucas from my dad's. We were taking a nap."

Silas crossed to the bassinet and peeked over the edge. The babe, wrapped like a burrito in a pink blanket, blinked up at him with gigantic stormy blue eyes.

"She's awake, Grateful."

"Oh? Bring her here."

Silas scooped the baby into his arms, supporting her head and neck as he cradled her close. "You are a special little girl, aren't you?" he cooed to her. "Smart. See how smart she is, Grateful? She's already looking at everything."

"You're a natural with that baby," Grateful said with a laugh. "Have you thought about settling down? Having a few of your own?"

He handed Skyler to her mother. "Thought about it. Meredith is amazing. She's what I've been waiting for."

"But?"

"But we've known each other such a short time, and most of that time was under extreme circumstances. I want it to be right. I want to be absolutely sure that this is forever."

Grateful stroked her daughter's cheek and rubbed her nose against the baby's. "Is it possible to be absolutely sure about anything? I can tell you one thing—I wasn't sure birthing two magical children was the right thing to do. I'm still not sure there won't be unforeseen consequences. But I don't regret it. Not for a second. I think sometimes you've got to take a chance."

Silas kissed her on the forehead. "Congratulations, Grateful. And thanks for the advice. I'll think on it."

THIRTY-ONE

Three months later...

Under a canopy of stars, Silas joined hands with Meredith, the heat of the bonfire toasting the chill from the evening air. Sparks rose between the trees and blended with the stars above. It was a beautiful late-summer evening, every star visible in the clear night sky.

"I've never been to a celestial-fae funeral before," Meredith said.

"Neither have I." Silas lifted their coupled hands and kissed the back of hers. "It's a privilege to be invited. The celestials are secretive about their traditions."

"Isn't it strange how long they waited? It's been months since Soleil died."

"You didn't see what happened to her. There was

nothing left to bury. According to Grateful, the fae are heavily religious about astrology. Tonight is the perfect time for this ritual. Don't ask me to explain why. Something about the alignment of the stars. That part went over my head."

"Where is Grateful?"

"She's around. She's making sure the area is secure and nothing disturbs this ritual. She told me she felt like it was the least she could do."

"Don't look now, but there's someone coming our way, and her eyes are on you." Meredith gestured with her chin.

Dressed only in a cascade of filmy, glistening fabric, Astrial approached them, reaching for Silas. He took her trembling hands and greeted her warmly. She'd been crying, and Silas fought the urge to wipe her glistening tears away.

"Thank you for coming, Silas. I know for a fact that Soleil loved you deeply."

"I loved her too," he said. It was awkward to say the words in front of Meredith. The way he'd loved Soleil was different from the way he loved Meredith, but it wasn't the time or the place to explain that now. Still, he noticed Meredith's eyes dart toward the fire.

Astrial lightly touched her elbow. "Don't fret."

"Hmm?" Meredith forced a smile.

"Soleil wanted Silas to be happy. She was polyamorous and would never have kept him from you even if she were still alive."

"Oh, uh," she mumbled, "um, thank you."

Astrial bowed deeply. "I must go now. The ceremony is about to begin."

"That was weird," Meredith said once she was gone.

Silas snorted. "Different strokes for different folks."

"Just so we're clear, I'm the monogamous type. I definitely will not be okay with you, uh, stroking anyone else." She gave him a nervous grin.

He hooked a finger beneath her chin and pressed his lips to hers. "Good. I feel the same way."

They followed the crowd of guests to a long line of people surrounding the fire. Silas noticed a familiar face on the other side of the flames—Ryker, alone and despondent, his dark, upturned eyes reflecting the light. Or maybe that burn came from within. Behind the incubus, the vampire, Julius, stood on the brink of the woods, hands folded respectfully. The vampire looked less despairing. In fact, his lips held a whisper of a smile as if he was the keeper of a tightly held secret.

The celestial fae, all women, crowded around a carved wooden box. When they opened it, Silas's exhale shook with emotion. Inside was what was left of Soleil— a dense black orb cushioned on purple silk. The fae raised the box above their heads and began to sing.

The haunting tune was in a language Silas didn't know, but the melody brimmed with love and loss. The group of fae proceeded solemnly toward the fire.

A tall black woman, dressed in rings of purple crystals that reminded Silas of the planet Saturn, addressed the crowd. "We come here to celebrate this revolution of our sister Soleil. The universe is a vast and unfathomable place. We are drawn to each other by orbit, we hold to each other by gravity, and we stay in each other's galaxy by fate. Soleil was our sun, a bringer of light and warmth and pleasure. We bring her now to the fire of our ancestors, fire born of stardust from the far-off place of our origin. Be free, Soleil. May your light be renewed and shine for us always."

Astrial, crying beads of light that twinkled like tiny stars on her cheeks, accepted the box from the other fae and tossed it into the flames. A plume of purple embers sailed toward the stars. Silas squeezed Meredith's hand tighter as the fire consumed the box and the dark orb within. Soleil's remains unraveled like a tightly wrapped ball of rubber bands, a giant purple atom rotating deep within the pyre. Flames turned to sparks, which in turn transformed to hot embers. And then, abruptly, the fire burned itself out. All that was left was a heap of hot coals and charred logs.

"By the goddess," Meredith whispered. "Look!"

Silas narrowed his eyes on the spot where Meredith discretely pointed but couldn't see anything. Astrial stepped forward and removed one of the larger pieces of scorched wood. He gasped in disbelief. Under it was a small foot, the size of a human in the fourth or fifth year of life. Its skin was ash-colored but it was alive, kicking forward with a jerky movement.

The crowd closed in, the celestials clearing off more of the firewood.

"No way," he whispered.

"You didn't know?" Julius appeared beside him. "Celestial fae are made of stardust. Energy. They don't reproduce like shifters or humans. Not even like vampires."

A hand appeared in the ash, and then Astrial helped a little girl step out of the steaming wood, her bright blond hair seeming to glow in the darkness. Her knees wobbled as she stepped forward, delicate and naked, two gossamer wings unraveling from her back.

Another fae, this one with bright red skin and a dress that looked like white fog, approached the girl. "I name this child Luna and claim her as my own."

"Do any oppose this union?" the black woman asked.

No one said a word.

"Then I pronounce you mother and child. Take your daughter home."

"Th-that's her?" Silas asked Julius.

"Reincarnated." Julius rested his hands inside his pockets. "Someday she may remember you, if only as a distant dream."

"Wow," Meredith whispered.

"Indeed." Julius flashed her a little fang. "A vampire's end is far from as pretty or as functional. It's why we guard our lives above all else."

"That explains some things." Silas scratched behind his ear. "Why are you here, Julius?"

"To pay my respects."

"And?"

Julius's face turned hard and cold as marble. "I can see my attempts at civility are lost on you." He tipped his head toward Meredith. "It's been a sincere pleasure. Good night."

In the blink of an eye, he was gone.

"I probably could have handled that better," Silas said. "Not used to a vampire being cordial."

"You knew him?" Meredith asked.

"His name is Julius." Silas was about to explain how he knew Julius when Ryker appeared in front of him.

"Congratulations on ending the dragon fae and Alex. It's a strong man who can face Panaal and remain among the living," the demon said.

"Thanks, Ryker." The guy still made his skin crawl. "What became of the book?"

"It's gone for good. Swallowed into the depths of hell," Silas said. "Why? Are you hoping to dig it up?"

Ryker's eyes flashed red. "*The Book of Flesh and Bone* is one relic I'm pleased to hear was destroyed."

"You didn't want to add that one to your collection?" Silas asked.

"Actually, I was wondering if you could give Jason a message for me."

"Sure. What?"

"I'm closing Lost Things until I can find a place to relocate."

Silas frowned. "Business not what you thought it would be?"

"My reasons aren't financial. It's time for me to make a new start." The demon shifted uneasily in the light of the fire.

"I'll let Jason know."

Ryker bowed and disappeared into the woods. The fire had completely burned out, and a cool breeze coursed through the crowd. A line of people had formed to shake the new mother's hand. Others had drifted off to make their way home.

"Looks like everyone's disbanding," Meredith said.

"I know it's late, but there's somewhere I want to take you."

"Other than home and to bed?"

Silas grinned mischievously. "Oh, I'll get to that. But first I thought we could get something to eat."

"Perfect. I'm starving." She hooked her arm with his, and he led her to the car.

"RIVERGATE MANOR." MEREDITH EYED THE SPRAWLING FRONT of the estate, thinking it hadn't changed much since she'd last been there with her father. With its Italian marble floor and airy veranda, the mansion looked like it was plucked from a postcard of Venice. "I was expecting Valentine's. Does this manor even have a restaurant?"

Silas flashed a roguish grin. "Not usually, but I pulled in a special favor. Trust me."

"Special favors? In the middle of the night?"

"Well, I am special... and royal. Have I mentioned I'm the alpha?"

She laughed. "Maybe. I keep forgetting."

He took her arm and led her inside. "This visit is

about more than dinner. I thought it was time we discussed your apprehension regarding our shifting grounds. Now that we've been together for some time, I think it's important for you to be reintroduced to pack royalty, begin coming to pack functions again. What do you think? Or do you plan to move back to the Catskills after your mom is released?"

Her eyes flicked to the floor and back up to meet his. "I love you, Silas. I'm not going anywhere."

"Good." He reached out and briefly touched her face. "I love you too."

"So you don't mind having a partner long-term?" she asked, poking him in the side.

His eyes wrinkled slightly at the edges. "I think I can live with it. Come on."

He led her across the veranda and through the ball-room to a set of glass doors that opened onto the main garden. Red hibiscus the size of dinner plates welcomed them. Roses in a spectrum of cherry hues rivaled white hydrangeas for her attention, rioting below the twisted branches of blooming trees. There were more varieties of plants and flowers here than she could name.

"This is new!" The last time she was here with her father, the garden was a simple square of bushes and evergreens.

"Cameron planted this last year. Smell."

She inhaled deeply. "Gorgeous."

"So that our wolves always know which way is home."

She looked up at the stars just as Silas flipped a switch on the side of the building and strings of large white lights glowed to life overhead. A table for two was set and waiting at the center of the garden.

"What is this, Silas?" she asked.

A waiter in a black-and-white tuxedo stepped out of the north entrance to fill two champagne glasses.

"Dinner. I thought we established that."

"Fancy dinner. I feel underdressed." The jeans and dressy black sweater she'd worn to the outdoor funeral suddenly seemed inappropriate.

"You're dressed perfectly. Wait till you see what's on the menu." He approached the table and lifted the dome.

Meredith chuckled. "Chicken."

"Nothing says home like a whole roasted chicken." Silas winked.

"The same as our first dinner together. How sweet!" She laughed and accepted the tall crystal flute of bubbly he handed her.

"I want you to feel at home here."

"So that's what this about? The garden, the champagne. You want me to start participating in pack functions."

His face fell. "You caught me." He took a long swig and looked around the garden. "Do you think you could ever think of Rivergate as home? I mean, not that you'd ever have to live here. I don't. But my position in the pack means I have responsibilities."

She could tell this was important to him. Rivergate was an integral part of his life, a sanctuary for the pack, which would feel like home to an alpha. Understandably, he wanted to know that she accepted this part of his life. She wouldn't disappoint him.

"I can and I will. I know this place is significant to you, Silas. I'll start shifting here. I'll get to know the other members of the council. I'll attend all the society events if you want me to."

"Good. You have no idea how glad I am to hear that."

She nodded. "I think after all that's happened, we deserve something more. If you want to take this to the next level, I'm ready."

She gave a soft laugh and had to look away from the intensity of his gaze. She stared up at the crescent moon and thought about the lunar cycle, the push and pull of gravity. It wasn't unlike love, changing by the day yet remaining constant over the years. She couldn't expect to be with Silas forever. He was alpha after all, with all the expectations and responsibilities that came with the title. But she'd take what she could get.

"Meredith?"

She turned at his voice to find him on his knee next to the table. "What happened? What's wrong?"

He pulled a small box from his pocket and cracked it open. An obscenely large diamond shone from within.

"Damn, the shine off that thing could blind a small child," she rambled. Her brain flip-flopped in her skull, trying to digest what she was seeing. She looked at him and shook her head slightly. "I don't understand. What is this?"

He removed the ring from the box and took her hand.

"Meredith, you've been my partner at work. Now will you be my partner for life?"

She looked from his face to the ring and back again. Was he asking her what she thought he was asking her? Was he serious? "But... but I'm not a purebred werewolf. You're the alpha."

"An alpha who makes his own rules."

"B-but you're expected to propagate Fireborn Pack. You're *royalty*." She said the last in a stage whisper, as if she was letting him in on a secret.

"Are you against having children?" His bushy brows lowered. "It won't change how I feel about you, but I know Laina and Kyle would agree that it would be nice if my new niece or nephew had a cousin to play with someday."

"No!" she said. "I'd be honored to have your children."

"Then?" He positioned the ring near her finger.

"You want me to marry you and help you rule Fireborn Pack," she said dumbly.

"That's what this is, a proposal," he said, gesturing toward his knee. "Although I'm beginning to think there is more to the asking than meets the eye. It would be great if you could give me an answer. These stones aren't as comfortable as they look."

"Oh... oh dear." She tugged on his shoulders, but instead of helping him up, she somehow ended up on her knees in front of him.

He cupped her face in one hand. "Meredith, I can't do this alone anymore. When I became alpha, it wasn't by choice. I wasn't ready. Every day, I've tried to live up to the expectations of this role. But tonight is not about expectations. It's about joy. I've never laughed harder or smiled longer than I have since I met you. You helped me find my joy again. And it's about love. I love you, and leading this pack doesn't make sense anymore without you. As I see it, I need to merge two worlds. Either I bring you into this world as my queen, or I leave the pack for good. Because I can't live without you anymore. I need help. I need you. You're home to me now."

She placed her hands on his chest, searching his expression for any hint of hesitancy. There was none.

"Yes, Silas. Yes, I'll marry you. I'll be your partner, and I'll be the best damn alpha's wife this pack has ever had."

He slid the ring onto her finger and swept her from the stones, swinging her in circles in the center of the garden. Meredith looked at the stars above and the crescent moon that resembled her tattoo. She thought of her father. She'd come to Carlton City to avenge his death, and she'd thought she and Silas had attained their goal the moment he'd slain Alex. But maybe there was more to the story.

As Silas's mouth crashed down on hers to seal their engagement with a kiss, the stars above seemed to bless their impending union. And she knew to the depths of her soul this was her future. Silas was her forever mate. Their lives would go on. And they'd be happy. Insanely and unequivocally happy. They'd have love and friendship and family.

Perhaps that, she thought, was their ultimate vengeance.

THANK YOU FOR READING FOREVER MATED, THE THIRD AND final book in the Wolves of Fireborn Pack trilogy. If you enjoyed this novel, please leave a review wherever you buy books! Reviews are increasingly important to indie authors like me and help keep my costs, and your prices, down.

If you liked the Knight Games Series and The Wolves of Fireborn Pack, you'll love the Treasure of Paragon! Get the entire series for 50% off when you buy direct. https://shop.genevievejack.com/products/the-ultimate-dragon-book-bundle

Already read the Treasure of Paragon? Don't miss LEGACY OF FIRE, a novel of the Zodiac Dragon Brotherhood, available now!

https://geni.us/legacyoffire

MEET GENEVIEVE JACK

USA Today bestselling and multi-award winning author Genevieve Jack writes wild, witty, and wicked-hot paranormal romance and romantic fantasy. She believes there's magic in every breath we take and probably something supernatural living in most dark basements. You can summon her with coffee, wine, and books, but she sticks around for dogs and chocolate. Her novels feature badass heroines, fiercely loyal heroes, and fantasy elements that will fill you with wonder. Learn more at GenevieveJack.com.

Do you know Jack? Keep in touch to stay in the know about new releases, sales, and giveaways.

facebook.com/AuthorGenevieveJack

instagram.com/authorgenevievejack

bookbub.com/authors/genevieve-jack

tiktok.com/@Genevievejackbooks

More from Genevieve Jack!

His Dark Charms Duet

Lucky Me

Lucky Us

The Treasure of Paragon

The Dragon of New Orleans, Book 1

Windy City Dragon, Book 2,

Manhattan Dragon, Book 3

The Dragon of Sedona, Book 4

The Dragon of Cecil Court, Book 5

Highland Dragon, Book 6

Hidden Dragon, Book 7

The Dragons of Paragon, Book 8

The Last Dragon, Book 9

The Angel of Paragon, Book 10

The Three Sisters Trilogy

The Tanglewood Witches

Tanglewood Magic

Tanglewood Legacy

Knight Games

The Ghost and The Graveyard, Book 1

Kick the Candle, Book 2

Queen of the Hill, Book 3

Mother May I, Book 4

Logan (companion novel)

The Wolves of Fireborn Pack Trilogy

Fated Bonds

Feral Instincts

Forever Mated